The Rune of Ing

Kevin Andrew

THE RUNE OF ING

Garnet Press: Suffolk, England

Published by Garnet Press Ltd, Ipswich, Suffolk, England

ISBN 978-0-9564859-0-8

A catalogue record for this book is available from
The British Library

Typeset by Hope Services, Oxford, England
Printed in England by Lightning Source UK

For my wife and daughters

Author's Note

Bede tells us that King Radwald of the East Angles was a man of noble origins but ignoble actions. For the famous monk of Jarrow this meant essentially that Radwald had thrown up the Christian faith for his pagan roots; but Radwald, in these few short paragraphs which are, apart from a couple of mentions in other works, the only historical record of him, gives the impression of being either a complex man or a very simple one. According to Bede, this king was baptised in Kent not long after the Augustinian mission, but persuaded by his wife and a number of advisers he apostatised from the Christian faith. He then made an error that was an abomination to Bede but which may seem to us entirely understandable. He set up altars to both Christ and his other gods. We might make several guesses why he did this but we shall never know for sure. It seems reasonable to surmise that Radwald was not the only pagan king who might have come up with this solution.

Bede does not give us the queen's name, anymore than he will indulge us with details of Anglo-Saxon pagan rituals or the gods they may have worshipped, but we catch a glimpse of a woman who was influential. I have called her *Ealhhild*, a name that appears in the Anglo-Saxon poem *Widsith*, and her fictional character in this book is only a beginning. More than the novelist of classical or later times, the writer balancing on a timeline through Dark Age Europe enjoys freedom and suffers frustration in equal measure. *The Rune of Ing* is fictional in every episode but is built on the few bones thrown to us by Bede, on discoveries at Sutton Hoo, West Stow, and Ipswich (Gipeswic), and on critical studies of Old English literature.

The key political component of the novel at the time and place it is set is the expanding influence of Christian Europe, particularly that of the

Merovingian kings of Francia. This is the *Zeitgeist* to use a journalistic term, behind the fictional Kentish mission to the kingdom of the East Angles which informs the drama of *The Rune of Ing*. I have imagined this mission as taking place at some point after Radwald's apostasy in say the year 605 but before Athelbert of Kent's death in around 616. At this time the Kentish king was still overlord of the kingdoms closest to him but his hegemony over East Anglia seems to have been far from secure. These struggles between the various Anglo-Saxon kingdoms together with a later shared concern regarding the Viking invasions would eventually result more than two centuries later in the formation of England. The kings involved are often described as 'petty' which is an accurate but also loaded word. Few I'm sure would have the courage to describe Radwald as such if they were to meet him. The trappings of Sutton Hoo show clearly that by the time of his death at least, he was a man of considerable wealth and power. The marriage of Athelbert to the Frankish Bertha, who was already a Christian, and the subsequent Augustinian mission to Kent in the year 597 must be one of the most significant events in English history.

Principal Characters

The Royal House of the East Angles

King Radwald
The Lady Ealhhild, Queen of the East Angles
Lord Angletheow, brother of the Queen, Earl of Gipeswic and the
    Wulfingstow hundreds
Lord Aelfwine, brother of the Queen
Lord Eni, brother of the King
Lord Ragenhere, son of the King and the Lady Ealhhild

The thanes of Kent

Ambassador Uric, warrior, diplomat, representative of King Athelbert
    of Kent
Hengest, a warrior thane
Breca, a warrior thane
Godric, a warrior thane
Heoden, a poet
Father Julian, a Roman priest

The King's hall at Rendlesham

Leoba, a maid of the oxen
Daniel, an escaped slave
Nurse Gudrun, the Lady Ealhhild's special servant

The village of Wulfingstow

Imma, a boy of eleven winters
Leda, a girl of twelve winters
Mother Sheaving, a gifted healer, Imma's grandmother
Aldwulf, headman of the village
Eanfled, Frida, and Hilda, his daughters
Beadhild, mother of Leda
Urswine, father of Leda
Edwin, a woodwright
Frigyth, sister of Beadhild, wife of Edwin
Saethryth, a Saxon widow
Mother Eost, a village elder

Chapter

1

Leoba knew she did wrong but at the same time she did not know. It was exactly as Lord Uric had said. In some cruel way the King owed her a life. It was still impossible for her to think of her new lover as anything but a 'lord'. She could as easily call him 'Uric' as take to the skies with the meadowlark. Such familiarity might imply a feeling of warmth between them and she was aware that this was not the case. He was a wolfish man, this Kentish ambassador, and was she, a cattlemaid of the royal holdings, any less of a hunter?

Milking cows was something she did carelessly but expertly. After all she had been doing it for an age of summers. When the other maids spoke to her she barely answered. Her head rested against the strong flank of the cow and she felt its comfort against her cheek. The tallows on several upturned pails dotted about the shed flickered with a smoky light and provided scarcely enough for the milkmaids to see what they were doing. A child of less than seven winters with lively interested eyes kneeled next to her in the dirty straw. Where the child had come from Leoba had no idea. She knew only that she had been sent as a chattel to learn the milking. In twenty or thirty winters, if she survived everything the elves or evil might throw at her, she would still be here in exactly the same place. Unless she found a suitable man to marry her. She was a pretty child with cornflower eyes and nut-brown hair and so it was not hopeless. Leoba motioned for the child to grasp the udder which she did with uncertain twig-like fingers. The cow, which Leoba had chosen for its especially good and friendly nature, fidgeted a little as it sensed the inexperience of the child. But soon with Leoba's guidance the milk bounded under the small new hand into the wooden bucket.

'What is your name?'

'Leofrida,' the child answered. 'I keep missing the bucket.'

'Do not worry,' Leoba said gently; 'you have the idea. Strong but soft. Strong but soft. Like this.' She took over the milking and the cow turned its broad accepting head around to momentarily regard them both.

'Why do they chew and chew like that?' the child asked. 'They never finish breakfast.'

'Ha!' Leoba said. 'Are you hungry?'

The child nodded.

'Well when the cart takes the milk up to the kitchens we shall go with it.'

The child unexpectedly flung her arms around Leoba almost unsettling her on the stool.

'Do not waste your love on me,' Leoba said. 'I am not worth it.'

The child withdrew, seeming not to understand, and unhappily looked at her hands. Leoba knew what the child was feeling but for some reason she chose not to soothe her.

'Queen Ealhhild is an early riser and she likes her morning milk,' Leoba told the child.

'I can go with you?' Leofrida said hopefully.

'Not this morning. Perhaps next.'

'I want to see the Queen.'

Leoba raised her hand and the child, as if familiar with the signal, retreated into the corner. She watched as the child crawled through the straw and over to where another cattlemaid was milking. This other maid told Leoba there had been no need to frighten the child. 'She has done no wrong,' she chided.

'You look after her then.'

There were a few streaks of blood in the glow toward the sea like mottling in the yolk of an egg. Already the dew was leaving in wisps from the summer grass. The day would be hot again. Leoba lugged the wooden milking pail in the direction of the Queen's chamber. It was quite a step from the byres to the royal halls. This was one of her chores, as a familiar and trusted cattlemaid, to bring the Queen's morning milk. Of course it was not a chore it was an honour. Or at least Leoba had to pretend that it was so. She stopped to retie her hair for too many strands had come loose from the tail. She was a large-boned woman but not particularly tall. Her face, with its broken slope of nose and mild grey eyes starred about with lines, had obviously seen much of life. It was like a cloth used countless times to polish a table but it was not without a certain worn charm. She wiped her hands on her dress and took a handful of milk from the pail. It was neither warm nor cold; exactly as the Queen liked it. There was an iron brooch which held Leoba's dress at the shoulder and in its circle was the likeness of an owl. It was her protective spirit and the brooch had been a gift from her mother. She felt for it in a reassuring way and, thinking of her mother now, she was determined to finish what she had arranged.

She left the wooden bucket and came away from the path, picking up her dress over a knot of bramble, and in the twilight under the trees, unstrung the leather purse hanging from her belt. Inside the purse was a small glass vial which even in itself seemed to her exotic. The glass of it was sea green under a liverish sky. It had a ground glass stopper. She shook it and watched the tiny beads of powder, which looked greyish and suggestive of evil, dance around the inside. She felt a strong desire to put some on her tongue. There was more than enough to fell an ox. Or so Lord Uric had said. She did not understand why he wished to be rid of the Queen but accepted that the cunning world in which he moved was a world as far above her as the morning star shining weakly overhead. Her heart felt like a horse that was galloping away. There was something else in the purse. A large garnet with a subtle rosy water which seemed almost scented in its beauty. The kin called these gems 'blood berries' and the irony was not lost on the woman who held it in her clammy palm that this really was a blood stone. Her mouth was as dry as the ashes in a burial urn.

She took up the pail again and strode forward with a determined twist to her lip. The track led through a copse of trees and into the open and rising ground of the noble halls. Her heart, which still thundered away, she was unable to control, but her mind was set and free of guilt. The Queen was heavily pregnant but Leoba did not fret about this extra wrongdoing. She had asked the thane why she should not kill the King rather, but Uric had persuaded her that he hardly wanted the King dead and that if she should succeed in killing him how then should King Radwald feel the pain that she herself had felt? She would be relying on his ghost to feel it. A most tentative proposition.

In the porch of the Queen's wondrous hall she exchanged pleasant words with the ancient woman who attended most closely to the Lady Ealhhild. This woman seemed older than the hall itself which had been standing longer than living memory. Her bones, worn of all suppleness, appeared to grind rather than roll together and she used a crutch of ash to

3

aid her slow and painful movement. This particular morning Leoba had the milk ready in the wooden beaker that she used as a scoop and thankfully the nurse did not inquire why this was so as Leoba tipped it into the glass the old woman had fetched from the Queen's personal collection. Nurse Gudrun was a reader of the weather and Leoba asked her what the yellow bruising she observed in the sky to the east might mean.

'The sky is like the punched face of a woman, Leoba. Is it not?'

Leoba shrugged. 'Not really.'

The nurse looked at her as if irritated that her assessment of the sky should be disputed.

'It is the Lady of the Dawn is it not and does not her face look battered?'

'I suppose,' Leoba said, hesitantly. 'If you say so.'

'I do say so,' the nurse insisted. 'I do say so.'

'Well I must leave you,' Leoba said. 'Please wish the Lady Ealhhild well for me.'

She began to descend the steps of the porch with her pail of milk.

'There is a new god and the Lady says that he is a woman hater.'

'What new god?' Leoba enquired, turning for a moment to face the old crone.

'The god of these Kentish men.'

'Do not worry,' Leoba told her. 'Lord Ing fears no other god and the Goddess hardly needs protecting.'

'Why then is the Lady fretting?'

'She is close to her time,' Leoba said, smiling. 'It is natural she should fret.'

The nurse shook her head and then something unforeseen occurred which threatened what Leoba had accomplished. The old woman stumbled and the glass of milk slopped half its contents to the floor.

'You clumsy old fool!' Leoba cried, for she could not help herself, and flew up the steps to take the glass from the old woman's hand.

'What is happening?' an imperious voice demanded from within the chamber.

'It is no matter my lady,' Nurse Gudrun called. 'I have spilt the milk that is all.'

'Well fill the glass again,' the voice advised. 'Am I to die of thirst?'

'What are you doing?' Leoba almost screamed, because the nurse seemed about to tip the rest of the milk away. 'Half is good, nurse. The portion remaining is good, why throw it?'

The nurse allowed Leoba to add more to the glass from her pail.

As she left for the kitchens Leoba did not feel like eating breakfast but she must take the rest of the milk as she did every day and she would force herself to eat something. She felt as if she had swallowed a giant stone. She wondered if she should not have let Nurse Gudrun pour away the rest of the glass. That man was a demon and he was in her bed. He had possessed her and it was he who had done it. This, at least for the while, was how she thought of it, and it was a means of putting one step in front of the other. She now found herself wishing the Queen might survive. Yet only a short time before she had been set on the feudal rightness of her death.

The kitchen halls, of which there were two of impressive size, were busy feeding the working men and women of the estates, all of whom had been up at first light, attending to the first of an endless series of daily chores, as Leoba and her fellow maids of the oxen had risen to do the milking. The soldiery, billeted in the various warrior halls established only a field away, would throng to the kitchens later, and the thanes and lords collected about the King in the splendid gabled hall would rise still later with the expectation that breakfast would be already set before them. The Queen usually took her first meal with only Nurse Gudrun for company. She rarely appeared unless suitably attired and most of the morning she gave over to her religious preoccupations. A cloaked shadow might be seen moving between the trees behind the Queen's hall and people knew that a sacred grove of the Goddess was not far from there. This area of the woodland was out of bounds and it did not require a soldier to guard it. Fear of offending the Goddess or the Lady Ealhhild, and most ordinary folk found it difficult to distinguish the two, was more than sufficient to keep the ground holy.

The strip of gammon Leoba forced down with a beaker of milk wanted to strangle her. She made forced conversation with her fellow chattels. It was late summer and the talk was greatly of the harvest. A young servant girl of the King's hall was being teased about her, as yet unreturned, obsession with a handsome blade of the Rendlesham fyrd. Leoba, as an experienced woman of thirty winters, wanted to warn her that all men were trouble but she knew herself to be the worst follower of her own advice and so she kept silent. Lord Uric's voice was in her head. He told her the Queen was fatted as any sacrifice and that a bitter cattlemaid had dealt her more than enough death to bring her down.

Chapter

2

'Radwald!' Ealhhild screamed. 'Radwald!'

A huddle of kinsmen, their faces tortured in the sinking light, waited anxiously outside the chamber. None spoke, nor looked at another; all spent their gaze toward the shield wall of birch blackening against the eastern sky. They drew cloaks closely around shoulders that were not cold and turned their faces away from the sun. It seemed that even she were ill and that her blood drained fatally into a bath of liquid gold. At a respectful distance a crowd of commoners awaited the outcome.

'Let him go in,' the Kentish Ambassador suggested to the Earl Angletheow, Queen Ealhhild's brother, indicating with a gesture the Roman monk, Father Julian. 'The true God is a mighty warrior. What harm can it do?'

'I know he is mighty,' Angletheow answered. 'He will not let us alone.'

'It is not how the King felt,' Ambassador Uric said gently. 'He saw the Christ on a living tree.'

Angletheow said nothing.

The Ambassador smiled. 'I think Lord Radwald knows the right path.'

'The star of Athelbert wanes,' Angletheow warned him. 'I should take care. We look homeward to the east, not south to slavery.'

'Mutual advantage is hardly slavery, Earl Angletheow,' the Ambassador objected.

Angletheow curtly addressed Julian, the priest: 'Will your god be able to help my sister?'

'Not if he has decided to punish her.'

'Why should he have decided to do that?'

'I think we both know the answer,' the monk said unpleasantly.

'Would he be able to prevent this sword running through a beggar?'

'Perhaps not in time,' suggested Ambassador Uric, stepping quickly between them. He indicated for the priest to go into the sickroom. 'Let him go,' he said softly to Angletheow, respectfully touching the Earl's arm. 'What harm can it do?'

'Please try then,' the Earl said to Father Julian. 'I thank you for it.' He sighed deeply. 'The old woman and her *spell* are said to be potent. They have yet to prove it.'

Father Julian nodded. 'I will pray for her soul, that she be delivered from her sickness, so that she may...' He apparently decided against completing the sentence. 'Well it is in God's hands,' he added, as a last ray caught the halo of his tonsure and transfigured it into a cap of gold.

'Might his magic not succeed where ours has failed?' Aelfwine, the Earl's younger brother, offered. 'It has failed our sister; her fate is determined.'

'Then how shall it be overcome?' Angletheow answered angrily.

Once inside, Father Julian was confronted with the Queen who fixed him with the eye of the fallen and screamed for him to get out. '*Mother, save me!*' she cried, seemingly in a moment of lucidity, and grabbed at some old woman who was desperately attending her. She fell back onto the bolster, murmuring and muttering, her speech utterly incomprehensible.

Father Julian stared at the hideous crone who had been summoned from a nearby village and was said to be so talented and her familiar, an unspeakable urchin with dirty white hair and green eyes which in the shadow cast by the firelight glittered like those of a small unbroken animal. The look of the hag herself was so black it was hard to know if a soul resided there at all. A large wooden sandbox was aflame beneath a small cauldron suspended from a hook and chain. The smoke negotiated its way to the roof and out through the gaps of the end walls but also pungently overlaid the stench of illness. There was vomit in wooden bowls and blood-spattered sheets that filled three large willow baskets. Julian took in the rest of the room and noticed at the far end of the hall another woman who appeared quite as decrepit as any exhumed skeleton sitting on a chair by the hearth with her head in her hands. He knew this to be the fabled nurse who was the Queen's closest servant. He looked anxiously to the writhing and swollen woman he was to treat. Clearly the heathen priestess was possessed of some demon, inexorably drawn toward her state of defilement, and which finding there no light of God, had settled down in the dark as a companion to her lost soul.

Julian's nerve began to fail him; his faith or training was not that of an exorcist. He drew a perfumed handkerchief from his sleeve, a humble luxury he allowed himself, and a pragmatic talisman it had proved itself, enabling him to retain consciousness on several occasions since landing on the dark coasts. A small vial of holy water, netted in a little string bag, was suspended from his belt and this he now took and uncorked. He cared nothing for this barbarian queen, but was conscious of the advantage to be gained if he succeeded in releasing her.

He had scant knowledge of healing though there were several of his Benedictine order who were intimately acquainted with the plant lore. He did not agree with those who argued that such plants had been created for the healing of man. He saw sickness as licence, granted by God to the forces of evil, to smite a man with boils or other foulness; sometimes as a harsh test of devotion; sometimes as a balm for the soul; and sometimes for the transcendent purpose of his own mystery. There was pride in seeking to undermine the Creator's will. An obedient Julian accepted this and, stretched to the extreme by the rack of quaternary fever he had suffered several years ago in Rome, his voluptuary sins confessed, he refused all herbs and was comforted only by the prayers of his attendants and the knowledge that his soul was kneeling before Christ.

The fever had eventually subsided and he awoke one morning in heaven, the gentle tapping of a lemon tree at his casement, the room filled with the scent of citrus, and pale sunlight brushed across the whitewashed wall. The sheets had been changed and the linen was clean and smelled faintly of lavender. It was true there were brothers at that monastery who required little in the way of forgiveness, holy men with souls like fresh laundry, but Father Julian was aware that he was not one of them. He had suggested on his arrival that he lacked the faith not to mention the constitution for the mission he had been given. On the contrary, Augustine had answered, he had heard that not only was good Father Julian a man of unshakable faith, but that he also possessed certain secular skills which might be of considerable use in carrying out God's work. The light of Augustine that had so burned brightly must not be allowed to go out.

Father Julian made the sign of the cross and, continuing with his blessing, sprinkled drops of holy water into the corners of the room. A couple hit the fire with a sharp hiss. The priest was somewhat thrown awry by observing the heathens mimic the sign he made, nodding as if in some sort of religious conspiracy with him. He nearly gagged on the festering stench of the chamber, combined as it was with woodsmoke and a cloying sweetness, the source of which he was unable to ascertain. He detected a wisp of sandalwood in the choking miasma. The lavender-scented cloth rescued him. What would he advise any civilised man about to travel among the Germanic tribes? A perfumed handkerchief. A perfumed handkerchief and a good sharp knife.

He was relieved to see no devil appeared. The Queen had not recoiled from the touch of blessed water as if scalded and there was no sound that carried to him from the outside of squealing pigs or any other sign of demonic retreat. If Father Julian suspected that the evil had not been dislodged then in a moment this was confirmed by a wide-eyed Ealhhild, tearing at her bedding and once more yelling at him to quit her chamber.

'Your god is not our god!' she screamed, seemingly beside herself with frenzy. 'Get out, get out!' Again she made a grab for the arm of her aged kinswoman and fastened onto it tightly. 'Mother Sheaving, he means to poison me, he means to poison us all,' she then whispered loudly, her eyes wild and searching, as if she would flush phantoms out of hiding.

'Hush lady, hush lady,' the old crone soothed in a strange accent. 'He means no harm. There are many gods in the world. What matters is whether they be good or no.'

'What can you know of it?' Ealhhild shouted, her period of clarity evidently continuing. 'They leave the villages but come crawling to the halls. They are in league with the western kings, they are in league with Francia and Rome, they wish to absorb us and in so doing destroy us.' She fell back on the bolster, her soft wheaten hair dull and utterly lifeless, lank about her head. She appeared to have revived but her face was as white as any winter moon.

Father Julian retreated under another flurry of curses which brought the Earl running into the room. He offered to escort Julian from the chamber and the monk gratefully accepted.

'Brother,' Ealhhild said hoarsely, with open arms, as Angletheow returned.

'The priest's healing has worked.'

'I think it likely now he has gone I am feeling better.'

Nurse Gudrun had risen slowly from her chair and came to take her lady's hand.

'Has the worm gone?' the Earl inquired.

'It is difficult to know,' the healer said, shaking her head. 'If not then it surely sleeps.'

'It seems we galloped to the forest for nothing young leech.' Angletheow addressed the boy at Mother Sheaving's side and laughed, obviously relieved his sister seemed better. 'Still, you shall both feast in the mead hall tonight. It is a double celebration. The Queen revives, the King and his brother return from over the white sea. I have word from the coast that Radwald returns. He ships up river as we speak. The people throng the meadows.'

'He ships up river,' Ealhhild breathed. 'Nurse, I must get up ... I have so much to do. Hand me that looking glass. Oh a fat *ogress* he returns to!'

'You are weak, my lady,' Mother Sheaving advised. 'You have wrestled with a serpent. We cannot be sure it is over.'

'I do feel like a wrung-out cloth,' the Queen agreed; 'and my head aches fearfully; but my husband returns ... I must get *up*.' She tried to lift herself but collapsed in the attempt. 'Angle, help me,' she said weakly.

With her womb full to bursting she was a dead weight and the Earl struggled to lay her back with any kind of softness. 'My back breaks, Elly,' he complained. 'A block and tackle will be needed.'

'You speak of your elfin sister.' Ealhhild smiled faintly. 'Such a weakling for a brother.'

The Earl grinned. 'It is better, as Mother Sheaving suggests, to rest.'

'Perhaps it is better,' his sister admitted, closing her eyes. 'Angle you will have to advise the King I am unwell and ... beware the thanes of Kent ...' Her speech trailed off as sleep took full possession of her.

'She sleeps,' the Earl said, stating the obvious. At the threshold he said confidently: 'I leave her in your capable hands Mother Sheaving and those of your strange helper.'

'Imma, listen for the baby,' the wise-woman said when the noble had gone, pulling up the Queen's nightshirt and exposing an earth of belly, which the boy looked over with intelligent eyes. Nurse Gudrun smiled oddly as the boy known as Mother Sheaving's *Spell* put his ear shyly against the womb. Ealhhild's eyelids flickered momentarily. 'He kicks, can you feel him,' she whispered, placing a gentle hand on the boy's head. 'I know he lives.'

Mother Sheaving prepared a healing broth by simmering a stock of goose bones above the fire. The Queen, meantime, had slipped into sleep, her dry lips slightly parted, seemingly at peace again. 'I wish she would have taken some water first,' the old woman said with apparent regret as she busied about the fire, shredding a few choice herbs, dropping a few grains of barley into the stock, which she now thinned greatly with water. 'Imma,' she said, beckoning; 'come taste this.'

'It's too thin,' the boy told her.

'Too *thin*?' the wise-woman scolded. 'It's not for you, you foolish boy, it's for the Queen. You expect her to eat a horse?'

'Now she is sleeping I shall drink a little air,' Nurse Gudrun told them, turning slowly and leaning heavily on her stick. 'You are a favourite of the Goddess, Mother Sheaving, and your boy also it seems.'

'It is the Lady who is smiled on, at least for the moment,' Mother Sheaving answered.

Nurse Gudrun nodded and then, with the pace of a snail, tapped from the room, leaving only the famous healer and her young helper attending to Radwald's Queen. Imma watched the soup as it was gently stirred. 'She may choke on those bones.'

'Now you're being purposely silly Imma,' Mother Sheaving said crossly. 'You really don't have to try. Of course I mean to strain the soup.'

'Oh you mean to *strain* the soup.'

'Ha ha I'm sure,' the old lady said, sitting down with a sigh on a small wooden bench to one side of the bed. Tiny gems of sweat had broken from the noble brow but the patient seemed peaceful. Mother Sheaving leaned forward and brushed some damp strands away from the Queen's eyes. 'Such lovely hair,' she mused; 'very like young Leda's.'

'Leda's?' Imma had remained standing at the foot of the bed.

'Don't you think Leda's hair is like the Lady Ealhhild's?'

'Not really. Leda's is thicker, the Queen's is finer, like spun sunshine.'

The old woman laughed. 'If only the Lady had been awake to hear that.'

There was a pause during which the Queen's breathing became rather unsteady. Almost as quickly it settled and the furrow in Mother Sheaving's brow relaxed.

'You have noticed then?'

'Noticed what grandmother?'

'How thick our Leda's hair is.'

'Not really; it's you keep harping on about it.'

'I do not *harp* Imma.' Mother Sheaving grinned. 'I merely *observe*. She likes you.'

'She only likes boys who set a fire and then pee on it.'

'I think not,' the wise-woman suggested with a wry smile. 'I suspect nevertheless that her father has big plans. He is a brute but not dumb enough to be unaware of his daughter's price.'

'Do you think the little sackcloth's spelling worked?' Imma enquired, looking down at the Lady Ealhhild who had become restless and was now turning weightily from side to side.

'I don't think he would thank you for that likeness and I fear not,' Mother Sheaving answered as she closely observed her patient. The Queen had murmured for a covering, that she shivered, but had then kicked it off saying she was hot as a cinder. 'This is a strange *worm* we do battle with Imma. Attend to that soup … though it may not be needed tonight.'

Chapter

3

A bonfire of torches burned a red hole shipside in the dusk and men were in the shallows pulling at heavy ropes, laying rollers beneath the prow, beaching the bark that fate had carried safely over the wild cold in summer sea. The King had returned. Warriors vaulted over the side, smacked in mud, hugged close kin close, took torches, and squelched a line of honour for Radwald, as landing planks were laid up close to the resting ship. Here the river swayed into the land and cut through a shallow pastured valley. The heady scent of the Goddess was in the air and great feathery moths flew down toward the light fluttering around the burning torches. The gathering at the beach was silent until the King stepped ashore and then the evening erupted in wild and happy cries of homecoming.

It was a king in his late youth, trimmed beard, and fighting prime who hugged Angletheow and heartily welcomed the six visitors from Kent all of whom had come down to the river to first lay eyes on the object of their mission. The King was told of Ealhhild's attack and following recovery for which he was told he had the monk to thank. Father Julian simply bowed but when his eyes met Radwald's there was mutual searching in both. The priest was struck with a familiar sense of incorrigible godlessness in these Germanic eyes, an emptiness so it seemed to him, that was capable of wrongdoing without restraint; for how could restraint be applied without a concept of, without due acknowledgement of, sin? There was morality among them, it was not that, it was more that the morality was by necessity of their own making, it was not of God's, and as such was prone to mortal error. The lamp of Christ had been set carefully in the shelter of this man's head and yet some wild spindrift had blown it out.

The war gear and breathtaking tokens that Radwald and his brother

Eni had received from their extended kin among the northernmost Scylfings were now in the process of being unloaded. So much that the men put a large spread of fishing net and several ropes to good use. The King and his party had started up the long winding hill toward the hall but not before Ambassador Uric had noted with some discouragement the splendour of the gifts. The clattering gold was burnished in the torchlight and the night had formed a cave around it.

Uric and his thanes, Hengest, Breca, Godric, and the Kentish poet Heoden were collectively asked by the King why they had travelled overland from Canterbury instead of by the easier sea route. It was yet another occasion on which Father Julian, at least to his hosts, was cast in the role of fool since he had to admit to detesting sea travel or indeed boats of any kind. He omitted the fact that he had been taken ill on no less than three occasions during the short crossing from Francia. 'A man has legs not fins,' he insisted to them as the party made their way uphill. They had barely begun when a breathless messenger boy informed them that the Queen had taken a turn for the worse. All followed close as the King broke into a run. Julian was forced to pick up his skirts in a most undignified way or else be left entirely to his own devices.

The pregnant wife whom Radwald laid back on the bolster imparted a stain of sweat to the front of his dark blue tunic and the tearful kisses he had showered on her left a trace of the sea across his lips. 'She is dead … and the child too,' he murmured. There was disbelief on the surrounding faces.

'No!' Angletheow cried. 'It cannot be. She was spent but the fever left her, the *worm* left her, this Rome priest's god … is it not so?'

All eyes now turned to Mother Sheaving who, in deference to the King's arrival, had shrunk with her lucky spell into the shadows.

'Please,' Radwald said softly to her. 'Do we need to prepare offerings for a funeral?'

'Lord … I,' the old woman began. A bloom of hope appeared on the glass Mother Sheaving then laid over Ealhhild's ashen face. The healer put her ear to the fading mouth and perhaps she heard the spirit of the Queen whisper to her across the unknown spaces. 'She escapes the worm's coils by death … it stalks her … we must kill it Imma, kill it, or kill her in trying and perhaps save the child.' She turned to the King. 'Lord you must decide.'

Radwald looked at her in horror. He gestured that she should do what she must.

14

Imma watched his grandmother prepare the plants, which included the *adderwort* he had simpled from a hidden grove of the dense and sacred forest that lay at the gate of their village. In this secret place an unfavourable loam resisted all but grass and a few magical plants, among which was the adderwort, a herb that could be used as a bind of black around a serpent.

Mother Sheaving was readying for her journey. Protective thyme, feverfew and sweet fennel lay stewed in urine, which Imma had provided. Serpents of sickness could not abide these plants. There was a powerful tea Mother Sheaving had taken and this tea contained juice of deadly nightshade. She had not yet shown Imma the number of drops and she guarded the secret jealously; for it was dangerous practice. A starry sweat had appeared on her brow which was inflamed in the firelight. A short while later she was violently sick into a clay pot that Imma had ready. Then she lay down on a sheepskin at the foot of the Queen's bed. At this point Father Julian quit the chamber with a disgusted look but Uric remained in the shadow silently watching. The other Kentish lords lingered respectfully outside but Uric had begged to be of help. And once more he had pushed Father Julian forward but Radwald had waved him away. Around the bed the King and his closest thanes stood and waited. Imma began to tap quietly on a small deerskin drum. The noise caused Nurse Gudrun to look up with tear-stained eyes. He tapped slowly and softly but insistently and the sound filled out the chamber so that soon it seemed as if the sound itself had hands and pushed against the wooden walls to be let out. He stared at his grandmother with eyes of a different seeing and there on the rug she became the sleeping bear of her spirit guide which was both separate to and part of her in that it could possess her. Indeed it was the very picture of her ghost. Imma knew better than anybody how his grandmother's ruined frame was a false and mortal idea of her. With his drum he continued to call the bear.

He did not even glance when she uncurled and stood trembling with unspeakable tension at the bedside; he knew that she was looming over all of them; the troubled curtain which hid, but hardly completely, the world of ghost and demon from the world of men and women, was already trampled under her giant paws. Where she was only she could know but it seemed she did battle with something terrible because she began to shriek and stamp her foot on the wooden plank. On he drummed, louder now, because it was this that would call her safely back. Mother Sheaving threw herself about the room knocking her

15

bones against the posts and the men drew back in alarm; as well they might for if even the mighty Angletheow's neck be caught by her paw it would have been the end for him. The Lady Ealhhild began to writhe and murmur and Imma saw a flying worm rise from the basket of her ribs. His grandmother lashed everywhere in the most violent fitting Imma had ever seen. The thanes stepped forward bravely to hold her down but Imma cried for them to let her be; even at the King himself he cried; for what if she were held by a fine thread to this world and they were to break it; she might be lost between the worlds; and Imma could not allow it. And then it was like a stone from a slingshot. Mother Sheaving cracked her head against one of the carved posts and dropped to the floor. Her fingers which had been tightly holding the bind of viper weed let go and the drum fell silent.

Chapter

4

Leda woke to the splash of hail in the thatch and opened her eyes on a dark cave of room. A turning weight in the bunk above caused the board to creak. There was an early damp in the air and she moved her head on the furs and saw that the fire allowed to burn low through the night was completely out. It was nice and warm under the skins and there was nothing but the sound of hailstones plashing. At least to Leda it didn't sound like even heavy rain, which there had been more than enough of recently, the sound it made was different, and it was a pleasant companion to her thoughts which roamed far and wide beyond the narrow confines of her life. Her father started snoring and it seemed the very ground posts of the house shook with the noise.

When Leda drew the hanging aside a feeble grey light was struggling through the various cracks in the shutter, which also the weather had warped a little at the hinge, so that the shutter left a small gap at the top of the window frame. Through this an icy breeze blew making the girl shiver. She let the curtain fall back and hooked it onto the nails to secure it. Her mother was mumbling about the firebox and her sisters were now stirring.

Leda's mother, Beadhild, threw up her hands. 'This kindling's damp and this fire's as dead as that pike up there.'

Leda smiled at the prize catch hanging from its hook in the rafters.

'Shit, shit, shit,' Beadhild chanted over the flint she was striking, as if the fire would kindle at the magic words. She blew gently over the small pile of shavings and there was a wisp of smoke, a winding of tiny grey worms, but the fuel refused to catch. Leda brought some more kindling, which seemed to her more than dry enough, from the wooden tinderbox as her mother with a final exasperated curse threw down the flints.

Beadhild got up stiffly and then sank with a sigh onto the nearest chair. The house had a total of three but the most comfortable, situated by the window, was the humble throne of their particular petty king.

Something in her back had slipped during her last pregnancy and, despite being still fairly young, she was often forced to stagger around like a great-grandmother. In a year Beadhild had both arranged the pyre for her own father and given birth to a baby son who, now upon waking, demanded her breast with an ear-splitting cry. She gave suck to the infant while watching her eldest daughter who with the everyday patience required fired the curls of smoke into life. Soon fire-worms were snaking through the tinder. The pike turned in the hot air, along with a string of smaller catch and the smell of smoked fish wafted into the dark corners of the room. It was a welcome smell which meant a lovely richness to the soups at suppertime.

At the open door was a cold grey world with the seeds of winter falling into the mud. There was a lonely half-light about the village. Nothing. No sound except the relentless hail. The houses were hulked in shadow like thatched barrows. Leda shut the door quickly, put up the hood of her woollen cloak, and drew the pelt closely around her shoulders. She was a wolf stalking through the silent woods. She was starving; she was alert to the slightest sound; she had been separated from her mate and was doomed to wander. The winter grains hit her face, stinging her muzzle. She opened her jaws and felt the ice melt on her lolling tongue. The blinding hail made her blink. In her head she howled as she had heard the wolves howling in the forest the other night. Against the cold air, tight as a drum skin, the sound had rebounded overhead, causing doors to be more securely fastened, fires to be raked up, and comfort taken in the fact that the wolves would probably not venture out of the forest until later in the winter. There was no answer to her howl.

Under a dripping hawthorn Leda momentarily stood catching hailstones and then she was out past the willow fencing of the village toward the sodden meadow. There was a low fog and merging water sky but light enough to see an apparition appear at the edge of the *Motherwood*. A ghost horse and two black figures from out the mist. The girl pulled her hood closer around. Her face was almost the exact shape of an upside-down egg and she had a sprinkling still of summer freckles under her eyes and over the bridge of her nose. All harvest moon the boy and his grandmother had been away and now they were returning. She knew. Village gossip said they would be back by Yule. The sopping grass lapped at her hem. The spectre paused, seemingly hesitating, and then began moving away from her, tracing around a large area of waterlogged ground. The soaking grass slapped at her long woollen dress. A singular chestnut tree marked where they would meet. At that point the hail let up and the grey horse stopped, breath smouldering, like some ghostly dragon stoking up a fire. Earl Angletheow she recognised and bowed low in her hood. Imma, she would not let go of, until he set her somewhat formally aside with a degree of coldness not out of keeping with the weather. Now greatly embarrassed, she tucked her hair behind her ears, pulled her hood close about her, wiped away tears with a mitten, and followed sadly behind the plodding horse. Mother Sheaving, cocooned in woollens and pelts, lay unmoving on the wooden bier, which as the horse moved slowly forward left a flattened wake of grass behind it.

Chapter

5

The press of people at the door suffocated him but he had to simply put up with it. Folk were worried about his grandmother. They were also keen to ask her advice about a variety of ailments, having had to make do with the far poorer advice of another wise-woman from a nearby village, who, people said openly, was plainly stupid. Two young children, who might have been saved, had been lost to fever this harvest. It seemed unnecessary to Imma for it to be said. Firstly, they had stayed on in Rendlesham at the King's asking, secondly, his grandmother had been too ill to move following her struggle with the serpent, and thirdly, as his grandmother had whispered, it was truly the way things had happened for those children. Survival had not been their fate. Other children had also got sick and survived without the magic of the plant lore. They had got away with the *herb* kept in every house. That was their *weird*. The village was always under attack from evil. It liked to chip away at the youngest, the weakest and the oldest. That was the way of things. The family were lessened and then recovered in a new birth. Yet the higher force approving this was not evil; it was instead unknowable: a wall to bang your head against.

Imma stoked the firebox and waited for the hubbub to die down. He was being asked about the Queen's recovery and the birth of the new princess; all the news of the King's return; for detailed descriptions of the great hall, and anything else a head might think of. Imma continued to stoke at the firebox, answering only in single words, with his green eyes glittering toward the door where a blast did battle with the heat of the room. Eventually Aldwulf, the headman of the village, cleared away the well-wishers. Then there was only the crackle of the fire child, a slight creaking of the timber floor, and the sound of moving trees and seemingly distant voices.

'*Grandmother*,' Imma whispered. '*Grandmother* where are you?' He whimpered like an abandoned pup. He dabbed the sweat from her brow. She had insisted on returning home but it seemed to Imma like a mistake. Why had the Earl agreed to her wish? There was not a soul to help. Nothing but numbskulls for hundreds. He prayed to the Lady of the Earth, wildly promising her their entire harvest share if she would only move on his behalf. She could snuff out an elf with a water drop.

He dropped the poker with a clatter. His grandmother would certainly have stopped him had she been aware of what he now intended to do. He piled on the covers and skins so that his grandmother now resembled a woollen burial mound. Her wrinkled forehead, brown with age like a nut, left a bitter taste of death on his lips. His shoes had been cut by a half-wit they were so badly fitting and the leather lace of them refused to tighten under his trembling fingers. Wrapping up in the new winter cloak that had been given to him by the Lady Ealhhild he rushed out.

'Imma! Imma!' Leda called from her door. He saw that she was minding baby Alfred.

'Leave me alone,' he shouted as he broke into a run down the hill. Glancing briefly over his shoulder he observed her step back inside.

At the bottom of the slope he found his way barred by the twins Sigbert and Sabert who had turned from their wrestling game to watch. Their leggings and tunics were filthy with mud to the extent that it seemed the entire colour of them.

'Where are you off to now you stupid elf-nob?' Sigbert said threateningly.

'Look,' Imma pleaded. 'Let me go. My grandma may die.'

'My *grandma* may *die*,' Sigbert repeated in a high-pitched voice.

'Sod you,' Imma shouted. 'This stinking village would be all poxed over if it wasn't for her. You'll find out soon enough if you don't let me go.'

'Sod *you*!' Sigbert yelled, pushing Imma in the chest. 'She's a foul witch is all. And soon a dead witch. And you, you'll be a man-witch, you bitch's fanny ...' Imma grabbing him around the neck cut his sentence short.

'Punch him in the mouth Sig ...'

Imma tasted blood as a heavy fist crashed into his lip and the grey sky swung above. He managed to grab a handful of mud and tried his utmost to rub some into Sigbert's eyes as the older boy knelt down hard on his chest and began bashing him. A small ring of children had collected, their twisted pixie faces agog with the show.

21

'Give in elf-bitch!'

Imma spat his answer with a lump of blood and snot that hit Sigbert in the face. The pounding madly increased until red flowed in streams down Imma's neck. It seemed the beating would never stop. Then an unexpected fury pitched a clearly surprised Sigbert into the mud. Leda, screaming like a battle goddess, nearly pressed the boy's eyes out with her thumbs. Sabert managed to pull her off, after an entanglement of arms and legs that looked like a knot of eels in a muddy puddle. She left a bloody ring of tooth marks in his arm. Sabert yelled to the heavens and the sky swooned over Imma's head. And then it was over. They had been pulled apart by the strong arms of the headman.

It was probably only Aldwulf, the village ealdorman with the snow of winter in his hair and the cuts of worldly experience across his face, who could have calmed Leda using only words and a warning shake of the shoulders. A little she-wolf with blood on her tooth. Imma was sent back, along with the little she-wolf, to Leda's house where Beadhild cleaned them up, muttering and cursing the whole time. After all she was forced to heat a small cauldron of water and use a couple of rags from the freshly washed pile necessary for the endless cleaning of baby Alfred.

'Keep your head back can't you boy?' Leda's mother complained. 'You're dripping blood everywhere. I suppose you'd like me to get down on my hands and knees and scrub would you?'

'No, I ...'

'No what boy?'

'No, thank you,' Imma said quietly. 'I only came because the headman said.'

'Headman, headman,' Beadhild muttered; 'there's only one head I can think of that any man uses and it's not above his shoulders.'

Leda giggled and Imma looked quizzically at her. He tipped his head back pinching his nose.

'And you ... I don't know what's so funny?' Leda's mother had her hands on her hips. 'Aldwulf said you bit the boy and he's got his arm in a sling. What do you say when his mother comes over and asks what we intend doing about it?'

'They won't make much of it,' said Leda, defiantly. 'It was me, only a silly girl, who put his arm in a sling.'

'Yes well, the boys don't expect biting do they?'

'Then they should look out,' Leda answered, again defiantly. 'Hitting everybody all the time, pushing folk, kicking folk. I hate them. You should bite father, bite him in the throat!'

'Yes well ...' Her mother shrugged. Then: 'What's got into you all of a sudden? And what was all that ruckus about I'd like to know? No I don't want to know. I can't bite your father in the throat Leda, it's not noble, plus how would that help us? Who would bring home the harvest? Or that crazy fish swinging on the gallows up there? Eh? Who would bring home that crazy fish to swing about up there smelling the soup?'

Leda laughed and glancing up, pointed at the fish. Imma nodded. Since his head had been tilted back he had already observed the prize catch twirling slowly this way then that in the hot upper air of the room, a bag of ghostly silver, dead eye winking in the light of the fire.

Leda's mother accused her daughter: 'I can't trust you for five breaths. You just left your brother for the tree elves.'

'Where was he going to go? He's too lazy to even crawl.'

'That's not the point you stupid girl. Anything might have happened.'

'Yeah, anything.'

Her mother raised her hand and then brought it down again. Nobody said anything for a few moments. A pained look came over Beadhild's face. She pulled back the door with a clatter and stepped outside.

'Don't worry ... *I'll* look after Alfred!' Leda yelled sarcastically. 'Silly bitch!' She rubbed the back of her head where Sigbert had yanked desperately on her hair to keep her teeth away from his face. Her hair was long and Imma thought quite beautiful. It fell almost to the middle of her back and, when loose, it put Imma in mind of the mane of a white elvish horse. Usually though, as now, she wore it in a single tail banded by a strip of green cloth.

'You know I'm going to get teased even more?'

'I'm really worried about that right now Immy. You boys always stick on the important things. I mean how do you manage it?' She tipped her head to one side in an ironic manner. Her eyes were as blue as a cloudless summer sky.

'I need to do something for my grandmother.'

'Why don't you go and do it then?'

Imma took her hand and she didn't resist. For a short while they sat in silence and the snap of the fire seemed very loud. Then with a familiar grizzle Alfred was stirring in his swaddling. 'He needs mother,' Leda said sadly, as she gathered up the complaining bundle. 'I never saw a baby feed so much.'

Chapter

6

Imma had nothing to give her. His heart flipped as he beached his boat on the narrow foreshore. He had nothing to give her and the idea of upsetting her was too horrible. He flung himself to kiss the damp earth, reciting a prayer that his grandmother had taught him. With his mind almost gone, he pushed tentatively into the shrine, a tangle of tree maidens seemingly holding and then releasing him. He stood in a clearing and now it struck him that the Goddess was gone from her island. He had always assumed that throughout the winter moons this was where the Goddess went. He had expected flowers to be forever on the worshipped island. His mind had prepared him for a secret lovely place. He had been afraid he would be blinded by the blood month festival of her beauty; but death was at home. Lady Earth had dropped into the ground, dragging down the flowers and the leaves, her greenery fallen to the lowliest of grasses. Apart from a few defiant holly trees it was a dismal scene.

He was stepping further when a familiar grunting from somewhere behind panicked him. He turned in time to see an advancing angry boar. He hadn't expected to run into any boars on the island but this one emerged with unbridled fury, sending songbirds flocking to the bony canopy. Halfway across the clearing he sensed the animal at his heels and imagined the knife-like tusks slicing into him. He tripped. He lay face down and did not move. He heard the boar snorting. It hadn't as he had feared speared into him; instead it had stopped short, seemingly confounded. The boar rooted around him and appeared undecided as to whether to bite. Imma knew wild boar took meat if they could get it. He felt for his knife. This was it. The Lady had returned and she would have her sacrifice. Or was it Lord Ing! His mind raced. The boar was snuffling around his legs, the smell of it strong as a butter tub of musk, and then the pain was almost unbearable. The boar had bitten into his calf. Imma twisted around and plunged his father's knife into its back, the blade going deep between the ribs. There was an unearthly screaming as the boar withdrew and, plainly driven to a frenzy by the taste of blood, and by the unexplained pain along its back, prepared to charge. Now Imma saw it properly for the first time. He had no idea what to do when it charged. But then he was favoured: the boar sank to its knees. The Goddess, he was now thankfully sure, had guided the short blade to a vital target. He took his chance and, not waiting for the boar to struggle to its feet, stumbled quickly forward and plunged the knife in again and again, the warm blood spurting over his hand and arm. A few moments later the animal gave up its ghost. Imma collapsed beside the body.

It was not a fully grown pig, a youthful male, but Imma was unable to shift it; there was a heaviness about the large muscled body holding it to the ground. He had been lucky in the extreme. A wild boar hunt usually took at least three skilled hunters, the number necessary to carry back a successful kill. It had taken seven to capture and bring back the sacrificial boar for Yule which daily raged in its pen as if, like the family of the village, it sensed its helplessness before the rulers of the worlds. Imma rubbed some spit and salve into the bite, which thankfully was not too deep. All the same there was a gash and bloody wells from the long sharp teeth.

He made a bandage with bits of cloth he stripped from a patch of his undershirt. There did not seem to be a green plant to help; only the dead fern that crumbled in his hand. He had to blink against hot tears to see what he was doing. He wondered about the boar's ghost. Who or what had sent it against him? Did a sorcerer now lie dead somewhere? Nobody he knew, except his grandmother, had such a gift. Any fool could put on a pelt and leap around. There were so many fakers. Who did he know truly who could shift between natures? Nobody except his grandmother. Yet it seemed strange for an ordinary boar with an ordinary forest spirit to be on the island. It must have swum the river or been cast purposely from the undergrowth. The thought that it had been the shape of any god, known to him or otherwise, had been disproved. He was still alive. Unless another had taken his cause. Unless the Lady had taken his cause. He hesitated before removing his necklace. The blood which had spread over the boar's flank was now drying under an ashen sky. Imma draped the necklace with its four beads of amber, two of jet, and two of bone,

25

over the pig's back. It was, along with the knife, his most treasured thing. The necklace had belonged to his mother and now he gave it to the Lady of the Earth, begging her, the mother of them all, to force back the fingers of the black elf choking the life from his grandmother.

'*Mother Earth, Mother Earth, Mother Earth.*'

For the longest time he called on her saying no more than her name, kneeling in the sacred air, swaying in time with the rhythm of his chant. The Goddess would know what he asked for. He continued kneeling for a short while after, a tired child beneath a fish scale sky. The necklace would sink with these bones back into the soil. He imagined it around the neck of the Goddess and when he awoke it was dusk. The lonely shape of the boar reminded him with a start where he was. The moon, that strange death mask of the sun, was climbing the sky. How cold she looked behind her mask, her smoky skirts caught about her, a witness of unnatural things. Imma shivered and then a flush of fear got him limping back to his boat. A demon stirred in the bushes and the hair stood up on the nape of his neck. His skin was almost knowing, as sometimes in a fever, and tingled at the slightest brush of leaf or chill of air. His heart seemed caught between his ears, thumping, thumping, and the shadows rose and fell like a living breath. Unseen hands pushed him away from the shore and it seemed to him as though a giant owl came down with the night beneath its wings and carried off the tiny boat like a dying mouse toward the moon. And then nothing.

The twilight lapped around him. Behind the unbroken cloud neither sister of the sky seemed hiding there. The sound of a song thrush was confusing as at first he thought it was nightfall. Then, lying in the gently rocking boat, he thought he heard the rustle of a deer or something at the water's edge. Had he journeyed through the night to a land of ghosts? Were there black geese riding the waters at the end of the world? He thought he heard geese. Would they be able to give him news of his grandmother? He strained to listen. He was sure they were talking of his grandmother and yet he was unable to make out what they were saying.

A sickening throb in his lower leg. He sat up like a spelled corpse sending the deer stampeding. A large root of oak held the boat in a small pool out of the current and a break in the shoreline made a beach for animals to drink from. No force of will seemed able to stop his teeth from chattering or prevent knowledge of the pain in his leg. His hair was soaked with dew, his clothes wet and filthy, and his nose caked with blood. The breath plumed from his mouth. His flesh was numb as tripe.

He felt as though he had been buried in a barrow for years and been suddenly unearthed. He dipped a hand into the water and withdrew a mouthful. The effort no less than pulling water from a well. Yet it revived him.

He drove the humble bark onward, the crudely made oar like a candle burn in his hands, the river not wild but with a wintry firmness, and he was determined not to be dragged down and cast up wherever the river chose. He smashed the hands of the water folk away. Another night in the forest and he would be dead. He had no doubt. He tugged with strong hands on the thread that tied him until the Goddess welcomed him back to a familiar place. The village creek wound him in like an old woman winding wool around her elf-stabbed hands.

He trudged up the muddy hill dragging his injured leg and leaning heavily on a stick. It was after first light and yet he saw no one. The settlement at first seemed deserted, like the old village at the leaving of the kin, the abandoned wooden houses gloomy and rotting, empty spaces for the wind to play in; but then the sound of people drifted down to him, probably from the hall which at this angle was hidden from view. The village of Wulfingstow draped itself across three small hills which overlooked a tributary of the river that ran from the Island of the Earth to the market port of Gipeswic. The hills were like three green eggs in the palm of the Goddess. As Imma came closer the geese appeared agitated in the pens as if a fox had got in. The cattle in the byre turned to calmly regard a solitary limping figure and followed its progress up the hill, chewing a thoughtful cud from their winter hay.

Imma was surprised to see the door of their house propped open with a large stone. In place of the usual welcoming firebox brightness were a couple of flickering tallows. He grasped one and using its light dispelled the shadow that had fallen over his grandmother's face. It cast a tiny sun on her cheek and lit the land of her flesh like the Sun Goddess waking the world in time for breakfast. Hot fat dripped onto his trembling hand. He remained motionless studying her face intently. The fat cooled and clotted. Eventually he tossed the flame into the ashes of the firebox. A noose was around his neck. He looked beyond the framed grey light and saw the sky like a winding sheet above the village. The sound of wailing brought folk running to the door.

It was Mother Sheaving's ghost wailing like a banshee across the open ground between her house and the hall where everyone had gathered. It was the old woman singing to them from across the threshold of another

27

world. One idea was that Imma had run into the night tormented by the same black spirit.

Edwin insisted he had seen him only yesterday when he and his boys were mending the fencing but no one had seen him return. Leda had a bad feeling about where Imma had gone but she kept her thoughts to herself. Beadhild put in her opinion as to the boy's general health after she had patched him up. Whatever had happened the boy was now inconsolable and in no state to question as to his whereabouts. Eanfled, the eldest daughter of Aldwulf, had taken a thin soup to the old woman early in the evening and had sat holding her hand. The bowl remained untouched and it was painful to hear a loved one struggle for breath. Perhaps the boy had been unable to stand it and had gone out. Later that night the old bear had seemed to settle and Eanfled had stoked up the fire and returned to her father's house. At dawn she had found the fire out, the boy still missing, and Mother Sheaving dead.

The customary tallows had been lit in the house, which until the rites were performed belonged to death. Aldwulf had called a *meet* to discuss the practicalities and consider a search for the boy. People were concerned that the leech woman be attended to since she was sure to have a potent spirit. A few, even after examining the rapidly stiffening body, would not believe that she was dead; she would return they said, from this unseeing state, return when she had strangled the demon. Where would she return to, they insisted, if her body were burned? She would be like a man evicted. The village would pay for that in a terrible haunting. Aldwulf had decided that they would let the body lie for a night to see if her ghost returned. The door had been propped to let the wind carry away the foulness of the room.

It took both Edwin and Aldwulf to pull Imma away from the bedside and carry him kicking and screaming into the air. Outside they dropped the child on the cold ground and the whole village gathered in a wary circle around him. Here he lay, writhing in the mud like a wounded piglet, frothing seemingly under a strange witchcraft, until all at once he was still. There was fear and a feeling of panic. Leda gnawed on her hand. Imma had gone, nobody knew where, and this dark spirit of a stump had taken on his lifeless body.

It was left for Aldwulf to pick up the motionless orphan in his strong arms and carry him over to the oxen shelter where he laid him on a bed of straw. He shouted for furs and blankets and abandoned the child where he had laid him. The wounded leg he could barely look at. There

28

was an unwholesome smell coming from the gash which, reason as he might, he could not help attributing to the dark magic coming from the person of this strange child. Still, child it was, Imma, perhaps it still was, and he was prepared to keep it for the time being within the shelter of the settlement, and not cast it, as some were now calling for, out into the shadow of the forest.

Aldwulf had left him water and a hunk of bread and fat. The vivid smell of cow and dung was like a healing; it calmed him; the warmth of the tiny herd kept him alive when the stars were out and night swimming. The day had passed in a parade of frightening shapes and dreams. When he awoke again under the same starlight he thought he saw his grandmother lumbering above him in the heavens. The hundreds of Lord Ing seemed cold and unforgiving. They filled him with dread. His grandmother had told him once that the night was when Lord Ing turned his back on the world and the stars slid down the fan of his cloak; if he chose he would take a veil from the face of the moon; if not mortal men had to be content with the fire he had given them; this Lord Ing had done by plucking a single golden strand from the hair of the sun. Thinking of this story eased the boy slightly: it made the remote and kingly god seem more human, more concerned with the well being of kin, and less with his own unknowable reasons.

Imma could not understand the shape he saw in the stars; he was certain the Goddess would have welcomed his grandmother's spirit. A bear needed earth beneath her paws. All at once he was drowning in a marshland. The thought that the Lady Earth had been angered by his spoiling of her shrine had now occurred to him. It was more than possible that she had not accepted the boar and had taken his grandmother as a more fearful sacrifice. Now her unfavoured ghost had been cast into the lonely sky. He reached for his knife but found it gone. He curled up on the dirty straw like a frightened hedgehog struck with a stick. He was afraid to close his eyes for the visit of something wicked but then he saw figures tumbling among the shadows. He cried out again and again but nobody came.

Chapter

7

Aldwulf had ignored the pleas of his daughter to bring in the child. Eanfled insisted that the boy should be under a sound roof, that he would die if he were left there much longer, and further that they should approach the foreign village for help with the wound. Thus the calm good-headed sense that Aldwulf himself possessed had been gifted to his eldest daughter; but unlike Eanfled he also had a deep sense of the plentiful nature of evil; he had seen it; he had seen a man rip out another man's liver over a lost game of draughts; so much he had shielded her from. It seemed likely to him that the black killer of Mother Sheaving was now after the life of her grandson. The headman's duty was the safety of the village; but all the same he had been unable to cast out the child and Eanfled's arguments were slowly persuasive. It was true the boy appeared calmer and that the sweating he had was linked to the wound on his leg. Mother Sheaving had no such wound. So perhaps it was unrelated to her death. Indeed it seemed more like a battle cut simply festering, going bad with mischief which could be burned out. He had no real wish to approach the foreign village with its strange customs, ideas and magic; but there was a healer there. He had further ignored the more hysterical advice in his ear: to take the manikin out to the forest and let the black trees take him. A picture of Imma torn by timber wolves or worse made the old man shudder. He saw the eyes roll white in a savagery of hunger.

Truly, Aldwulf mused as he sat back creakily in his chair, the world of men was tangled inescapably with the world in which they found themselves. Men and women were the warp stretched in their generations by the weights of the loom and at every moment the strange weft of other nature crossed and made a mysterious pattern. So Aldwulf pictured the sheer oddity of crawling across the crust of the world. From his vantage by the open window he looked down the hill to the byre, which was as yet still hidden from him. The women of his house had responded sleepily to the sudden draught by disappearing under covers; three soft hillocks now rising, now gently falling in the gloom thrown by the single tallow that accompanied Aldwulf's lonely vigil. There was an ache in him where pain cleaved to the love he had for his wife. Mother Sheaving's passing had reawakened the sense of it. His arm rested on the sill and he felt the cold air take his hand. '*Leofruna?*' he whispered. The name rolled over his tongue and memory. The name also of his youngest daughter. Mother and little Leofruna had been cremated on the same pyre and mingled together in the same urn. He wondered, as he had so many times, about where they might be. He felt often a presence as a kind of caress that would raise the hairs on his brown arms like a soft wind ruffling through the rye. Leofruna watched him always; saw how he took care of the girls, debated with him in his head about this or that decision to be made. The responsibility of a tiny king weighed heavy on a simple and good man. He hoped with a kind of suffering that he might see her again when he died. Yet he did not quite believe it.

Sometimes he created a small farm in a golden light and Leofruna would be waiting at the door as death delivered him into her arms. He wondered whether a soul might shift permanently after death, whether it might run as a deer through the forest, spread the wings of a rook, or bring life to a mighty oak. Perhaps demons might become kin. Aldwulf wanted nothing of this. If Leofruna were gone he chose nothingness. The thought made him shiver. He took an odd kind of ease in the fact that it was not his choice. That much was certain. The golden dream had goodness however and it was wholesome food that he ate from. He had told it once to Mother Sheaving who had remained silent. She had merely nodded her friendly head as much as to say: 'Aldwulf that is a fine dream, you keep hold of it.' Now she was gone. Her ghost, he felt sure, would find itself sleeping in a hollow yew this winter, or be out hunting mice among the stubble. What use was that? He could hardly ask an owl for advice. He wept silently for his old friend. And then the clearest dawn sat up straight in Aldwulf's mind. He reached and pulled back the shutter.

The boy was an empty wineskin in his arms. The ragged cut wept from its dirty bandage. Away from the musk of the oxen, even in the open air, the stench of the sore was nasty. The boy would die if the poison

31

were not cast out of him. No healer was needed to tell him that. When he reached the threshold he was slightly breathless. He kicked open the door which shuddered loudly. 'Eanfled!' he cried. 'Frida! Hilda! Quick!' The young women stirred themselves, throwing back the covers, at the same time wishing to know the reason for all the noise.

Aldwulf buried the knife to its hilt in the hottest part of the fire. Taken out the blade took on the life of the fire. The stinking bandage was unwrapped and thrown squeamishly into the flames. It caused a filthy smoke, which Frida attempted to flap toward the open door. The glowing knife was like a branding; but Imma had been pinned on his belly. Aldwulf held down his shoulders, Eanfled and Hilda pushed down his legs, while Frida who had clearly discovered a strong stomach set to burning out the poison. 'It is a bite, a *dog* bite or something,' she muttered. The scream of a murdered child ripped through the early air and gathered an audience. The first to put their heads in at the door were Edwin the carpenter and Leda's father, a somewhat sickly-looking Urswine. 'What in the night is that accursed *imp* doing in your home?' Urswine shouted. 'You'll bring evil here. Get it out! Get it out of your house!'

'It's my decision,' Aldwulf cried. 'My house, my decision!' His broad face was contorted both in the agony he felt for the child and with the effort of holding him down. The hot blade sank through the noisome flesh and the wound sizzled as if a demon writhed. Imma bit clean through a chip of firewood. Aldwulf was forced to let him sit up to spit out the splinters or he would have choked to death.

'It is a *child*, it is Imma, can't you *see?*' Eanfled yelled angrily at Urswine who stayed like a smouldering lump at the door. 'Get gone yourself and have a drink to straighten out your eyes!' Urswine took a step into the room.

'Strike her and I insist your arm is left as remedy,' Aldwulf warned. His eyes burned with a blue fire and the pupil narrowed as at a hated thing. The square chin was firm in its intention. The shovel of his hand pushed away the whitening hair that had fallen into his eyes. Urswine might have known he could take the old man but he dare not. Instead he went out cursing the whole world and Aldwulf in particular, pushing rudely through the others at the door. Edwin the woodwright also turned and left. He had said nothing but like the majority seemed torn between feelings of fellowship and an instinct for self-survival. Recent years had been good to them but a curse like this could wipe them off the face of the earth.

The banishing had been accomplished. There was some clear weeping from the cooled flesh but that was all. Aldwulf and his daughters all wished for the same thing now: that any demon present had been driven out of doors and was no longer free to foul the wound with its unnatural spit. As if to further play this out and make all clean Frida took up a besom and swept furiously at the floor, making a pile of dust and chippings, which together with any dark remains, was hopefully sent from the house. The knife was left buried among the reddest embers to free it of the work it had done.

Chapter
8

The lateness of the year had slowed the onset of rotting. Six days Mother Sheaving had lain, the reek of illness having left her unassuming home, and each new morning a fresh bloom of frost appeared on the inside planks of the house. It was believed the unusual freshness of the air was evidence that her ghost might yet return and so the funeral had been delayed. It was a tense time for the settlement. It threw gloom upon the preparations for Yule and gave the necessary rites a solemn aspect. The feeling was not the usual one of heady celebration. The touchable fright that Mother Sheaving's spirit could come back grew daily. Villagers who had feared her in life suggested there was evil at the bottom of all spiritual meddling whatever the good cause that hid it. These kin now had the satisfaction of being proved right. Yet the clean condition of the body entranced the people as how best to deal with it. The clever eyes that had been closed tenderly by Eanfled were reported to have sprung open to reveal a glassy stare. No warm being would return to see out from such eyes. Then there was a change in weather and the frost that was white along the timber in the early morn became a soaking dew and the sun bled warmly though the escaping mist of the meadow. There was a feeling of the *rising* around midday and people saw it as endearing restlessness in the sleep of the earth. Shadows were immediately lifted and laughter was once again heard from the workshops and houses. The Goddess was telling them that she had not abandoned them. It was as obvious as the cool clear sunlight.

It was Wuffinga passing with a spade over his shoulder. He had intended to turn over a patch of softened ground as a preparation for vegetables but his discovery made him set down his spade and go running to report what he had detected. It was the ninth day and the corpse was rotting. Such a stink can hardly be deceiving. Bodies were not normally allowed to lie. Winter or summer they were always dealt with quickly. Mother Sheaving though was a special case. She had been left to lie but now her eyes were closed again and they remained so.

She was laid out by three women who held the key-chains of their houses including Beadhild who wore a comical peg on her nose. Frigyth, the wife of Edwin the carpenter, and a widow from the third hill called Saethryth wrapped a length of mantle against the smell in more customary fashion. There was now no doubt that this particular set of clothing had been abandoned by its ghost and was beyond mending. The yellowing body was stripped and pastes applied paying particular attention to the face. Mother Sheaving's grey hair was unpinned and combed with her own comb of deer bone and arranged about her shoulders in a younger style. She was then dressed in a green tubular gown. Her face shone with the whiteness of the ointment. Two amber tags were placed on the closed lids of her eyes. Her hands were folded across her stomach and her leech necklace of beads and charms appropriately arranged. Her small tan bag of dried healing herbs was attached to the belt of her dress. The cuffs of her inner gown were bands of a pretty woven pattern. Beadhild, rooting around in the old woman's paltry belongings, found a tiny precious jar of madderwort dye and smeared some on the lips of the corpse. Mother Sheaving's small and large toothed combs together with other personal womanly things were placed in a leather sack at her feet. A buckled purse of mysterious amulets, which had been removed from the thick belt of hemp the wise-woman had always used, was refastened to the new cord belt. The hempen rope was coiled and set beside her head. Small tokens of respect that had been left at the propped door, and which included a fine stone of beryl, were fetched in and placed. So the former healer of the village was made ready. How it was that these bodily necessities and small luxuries of a mortal life would assist her on her voyage when the passing of the flesh had already begun and the ghost fled was not something that was asked. It was a mystery and as such could not be understood. It was a magic process and as such could not be understood.

There was a snap in the air and a smell of woodsmoke. The living sounds of the day were blanketed in a silent dusk. The torches appeared as a line of fireflies moving over the meadows. At the front Aldwulf strode: it was his honour to carry the sacred flame. Directly behind, four men bore the rigid stretcher of death, two each to a pole. The women who had dressed the corpse and certain other women such as the daughters of Aldwulf carried the objects to be placed on the pyre. And then the whole of the larger settlement, the men, the women and children, and at the back a strange sight: the feverish young Imma carried on the broad back of Wuffinga, the amiable giant who had volunteered for the task. Imma's trouser leg remained rolled to the knee; the boy could not bear even the thinnest wafer of cloth to touch it. An evening breeze had arisen and it caused the torches some stutter so that on the backcloth of the field they appeared as smudged and tender stars. Imma toyed further with the edges of those stars by crushing them in his tear-filled eyes. He could squash them out like batter on a heated skillet.

'*Hey*,' the low voice of Wuffinga rumbled and the boy felt a huge apple roll under his wrist; 'don't choke me ... hold onto the shoulders not my poor neck.'

Imma nuzzled into Wuffinga's back. This rock was good: it was dependable land.

'*Hey*,' Wuffinga again complained; 'you'd better not be wiping your nose on the back of my cloak.' The women directly in front turned around disapprovingly.

'Now see what you've done,' Wuffinga muttered; 'got me in trouble; got me a haunting from your late grandma I shouldn't wonder.'

'She wouldn't haunt you Wuffinga,' Imma whispered in his ear. 'She liked you.'

'Hmm,' Wuffinga said uncertainly.

A clear night crackled above them, the stars fizzed in the heavens, the moon witnessed with half a face. The night was ablaze for his grandmother. Lord Ing looked as though he was readying to accept her. The sky was to be her final dwelling after all. It did not seem nearly so bad to him now. Not on this night. Not with the pyres of the ancestors seemingly rekindling on the field where a thousand or more made answer to the flares of heaven. To Imma's broken heart it was magical. A handful of sparks was thrown like dice along the edge of the world. Lord Ing was gaming with his wife, the Lady Earth. It was good fortune and the people were a witness to it. All the hidden folk of wood and meadow stood to watch. The kin felt them strongly in the shadows and feeling them believed that they saw them.

The pyre had been made of the best kindling for a pure burn. Supported by split logs from below and then built up crosswise to the height of a man's chest it was broad at the base and then narrowed to a platform for the body. Tinder with no staying trace of green was piled high around and stuffed with straw ready for the torch. A clever fire-starter was created by cramming a wide space between the logs near the ground with the same highly burnable stuffing. Mother Sheaving was lifted and placed as easily as a pile of dry leaves. Her things and small tokens were then arranged exactly as the women had rehearsed. A basket of apples and bread there was too and a smoked joint of ham from the blood month slaughter. For a few moments her face shone lunar-like at the sky. Then Aldwulf plunged his torch into the starter. A moment later Edwin thrust a second torch into the branches at her feet. The resulting blast dried the tears on Imma's cheek. He clung tightly to the rock which now, in common with everybody else, took a step back. Mother Sheaving was embarking on a ship of fire. Imma's initial wonder shrivelled to a silent grief. There seemed something nasty now in the violent snapping of the fire. It would not stop until it had burned them all. The fumes from flesh and hair, the blister of bones unglued, sinews loosed, and guts unstrung; the fat sizzling, dripping the way molten lard drips down a tallow; these were the sights and sounds and smells of a burning. And above it, most noticeable of all, the roaring hunger of the fire. The breeze threw flaming brands at them and the smoke was bitter to taste. Still the village looked on, eyes watering, as the skeleton threw off its flesh. A stiffer wind and the sail blazed and the heat cracked at the bones until they were light as owl feathers. The people turned and left the fire to its final work. The last shore was of less importance than a successful journey. Tomorrow they would bury fragments of Mother Sheaving in the ground so that the Goddess would remember her. Today they buried her in their hearts so that they would remember her. If the wind took some of her so be it. If the rain took some of her so be it. She was sheltered in the shared memory of her family.

About a week later the Earl Angletheow on his fine dappled horse returned to see the woman who had saved the life of his sister. He was visibly moved to learn of her death. He gave Imma a warm bearskin cloak as a token and told the boy that if ever he were in need to come straight to the hall at Gipeswic. He would find the Earl most generous.

Chapter

9

Radwald's protector had triumphed over the demon that drove him. Queen Ealhhild's counsel had been to listen to it carefully or she had warned, it may abandon him. The sun was dying in her days and it was nearly festival. The King sat, wrapped in a fine warrior's jacket, on a seat of stone to the side of the great gabled hall. This beautifully carved palace was built on a rising of land so that from his seat he was able to see down and across a dip of skeleton trees to the river. From their barrows on the hill a short sail downstream his father and grandfather had a similar view. All three kings looked riverward and in this respect all three looked out to sea.

The King clutched in his manly fist a wooden beaker of apple beer which the serving girl had brought him. She had the blackest eyes he had ever seen; so black that they appeared to consist only of pupil. Not many people really had black eyes, except in stories. These though, belonging to this comely girl, were a rook's eyes. Her hair was a rook's wing. He desired to shake her in his jaws and palpate her between his sharp teeth before tasting her. She was not a chattel without worth. She wore her hair tied in a horse's tail with the cord ends dropping down her back. Her dress, which was of a thick weave and not of peplos fashion, and the cloak fastened above her breast by a single brooch were both the colour of a storm cloud. A flat yellow belt zigzagged her bodice. She was a favoured servant. Radwald almost wished for some of that early licence when warrior bands had returned in glory to the homelands having slaughtered and raped all before them. It was a happy routine. A woman's body or that of a man if one so preferred was part of the plunder. Such things were still done of course. The kin had lost many of their own women to past desolation. Terrors such as these though, had

38

become long before he was born, not acceptable either to the settlers of his own kin or practical to the winning over of a mixed population.

He sometimes desired to smash the few native villages he had in his grasp. He did not smash them however. They had accepted him as king, as they had accepted his father and grandfather, paid onerous tribute with what they had, and sent representatives to the local meets to petition for fairness. Eventually, it seemed to Radwald, the courage of sons fighting for his banner, would entitle them to it. He could not accept though that they were the same. He could not accept his brother-in-law's argument that blood spilled together in battle became one blood. Yet his own ancestors were not pure Angles; a claim that the Queen and her brothers could quite legitimately make. He furrowed his brow. A flock of birds had lifted from the trees. He watched them settle on the green like runes.

His own ancestors though were friends of Ing, like his beautiful lady. There was the one blood. Through the complexity of his kingdom this shined like a chain of beacons to the past. The Angle kin were true to it. All the coastal northern kin were true to it. If the Saxons and others sometimes fought under a warrior god that was strange to him they still recognised the Lord of the World, the way he was forced to accept the influence of Athelbert; but now that ruler had taken a new god: the hero of the Franks. The Franks. Radwald did not trust them. They too had once known the god of all and had abandoned him for a foreign god the way they had cut out and sold their own tongue for profit. The beacons to a glorious past were snuffed out and smouldered sadly on the peaks.

The power of the new hero could not be denied. He was cunning. He hid behind veils of weakness, wielded power the way a woman might wield it, and persuaded others to do the warrior work for him. This was shown in the womanly priests he sent from the southern sea with their sandals and shabby dresses. Radwald had recognised Father Julian again; the same monk sent with him for counsel after his own baptism; the same pinched face, the same weak wrists that could no more handle a sword than a spoon, the same haunted aspect, and the same pathetic figure who had been driven with rotting vegetables from the few villages in which he had attempted to preach. A report of a particularly vehement attack from a native village was both surprising and intriguing. After all the symbol of Christ was seen around many a foreign neck. The King wondered about the apparent contradiction. Ignored like a stray dog this Julian had requested passage back to Canterbury. The priest's susceptibility to seasickness had become a standing joke. People did impressions of him retching over the side of a boat. This was why Radwald had asked him about his overland mode of travel. He knew perfectly well. Now the monk was back and in good company this time. Radwald liked the Kentish Ambassador; he respected him as a man of valour, as the representative of Athelbert and as a man of wit and practicality. This Uric talked persuasively and appeared honourable. No one had been more concerned as to the Queen's condition. The Ambassador's past was mysterious. He had not been present at the court of Athelbert when Radwald had visited at the time of his baptism. But then Radwald had not been seen in Kent since.

The King drained his beaker. The cider taste was sharp. His mind ranged seaward over the river. The servant girl had got him thinking. He examined the workmanship of his purse, the golden figure work, the wolves with garnet heads, the tiny totem of his god. He felt this power between his own legs. It was an ancient creative power; it was both dark and light; but it was incomplete and made whole by an opposite bountiful female power. He had not felt this power under the water. He had expected to feel a surge of some previously unknown force but he had not. It had not happened to him and he suspected strongly that it had not happened to Athelbert. The Kentish gold-giver had to pretend for the sake of his Frankish wife, who braided her hair in Mediterranean style and wore hoops of silver from her ears, whereas his lovely Ealhhild was a woman of the tribes of Ing. She had warned him against this new god and he had listened. The servant girl came to take his cup. She lingered a moment awaiting further instructions. The King looked searchingly at this glittering crow causing her to blush and flick awkwardly at some strands of her hair. He continued to probe and colour flushed into her like red wine into water. She had a small mark above her lip, which a tiny nervous tongue darted out to touch. Radwald did not particularly relish her discomfort but he did not hurry to ease it either. He was used to such subtle displays from his subjects and he preferred it to fawning, which he could not abide and dare not trust. The discomfort the girl showed was genuine and because to Radwald his kingly power and begetting power were one it hardly mattered which caused her greater awe.

'What is your name?' he asked her softly, absorbed by the shape of her closed mouth which was rounded at one corner and sharper at the other so that her lips resembled a fern leaf dipped in a red dye. Her face was soft as bleached muslin. The King put his hand to his own face and felt the weather-beaten roughness. He was not old, he was in his prime, and he still wore his parted hair to the nape of his neck in a young warrior style, but the northern sea had done its work well; the skin felt like rind to the touch. He ran a finger over his thin blond moustache. '*Rhiana,*' he repeated, smiling. 'Well Rhiana, you will be married soon?'

The girl nodded. 'My father has been approached,' she began and then hesitated.

'Yes,' the King said, nodding. 'And how old are you Rhiana?'

'Eighteen summers, that is I am eighteen summers next summer.' She appeared momentarily confused. 'He has been asked for my hand by an Angle warrior my lord. His family are of the land like my own family but now he is a soldier,' she concluded proudly.

Her family had obviously sent her to Rendlesham with this purpose in mind and now it had been realised. Stirred by the glamour of a fighting man the girl was too young to see that it meant solitude and not knowing whether he lived or died. These were peaceful times but Radwald knew that a tempest was gathering; the clouds rolled from north, south and west; only to the east, the direction in which he now looked somewhat wistfully, was the sun sailing her ship high into the sky with all good portent. His trip to the homeland had stirred his heart deeply. Things were simpler there and purer. The kin knew exactly who they were. Yet there was a stronger part of him that was deeply buried in this new soil. The roots were shallower than this slave's perhaps but this land was a journey's end for his kin. If it had not been so it would not have come about. In this Radwald accepted no other argument.

'Your father is right to be proud of you. What is your man's name?'

'Saward, lord.'

The King frowned. 'You might delay the rite beyond Eostre. The sickness of my daughter is not auspicious.' He waved the girl away and she was gone.

Now in his imagination he was ploughing out to sea, clinging to the coasts, and wary of the lee in the unexpected wind. The rain beat into a reefed sail, dripped from the cross-stick, cut into the heart of a man, and then dropping the sail altogether the ship was oared to windward by its crew, and the muscle of a man's arm was set against the cruelty that wished to push the boat aground. The shore was an enemy at such times, wanting to make ribbons of the ship, and the only hope was in achieving the greyness of the sea. This knowledge remained after land became a friend again. In his youth Radwald had delighted in the adventure of lonely seamanship. Breaking free from the rivers and inlets of his father's kingdom he ventured far and wide around the coasts. In a summer calm he would lie on his back and listen to the gentle breathing of his boat. So it was that the fields of ocean summoned him away from the green land that was his inheritance.

'*Ambassador,*' he said gruffly.

Uric bowed. 'Lord.'

'Sleep well?'

'Lord I always sleep well.'

'Is Father Julian coming?'

'No, lord, the boat you see ...'

'I insist that he come. It is hard to be taken seriously when you will not move yourself from the fire. He has been given a good fur cloak hasn't he?'

'He complains of a musty smell.'

'The fire of the year is almost out,' Radwald said, gesturing at the watery sun; 'but we shall be there by mid-morn and she will give us light enough to return I'm sure.'

'I will tell him to stir himself from the fire my lord.'

'Tell him Uric of Kent. Tell him if he does not I may put him in it.'

Radwald stood and for the moment turned his back on the river. He was stalking again in his mind the sleek feathers of the serving girl.

Chapter
10

Across the water flocks of razor-billed birds attacked the mud with determined appetite. The reach bristled with boats of all sizes. A quickening tide and favourable breeze helped the ship make short work of the channel. A towering tree of a man planted firmly at the stern held the rudder. The young Earl Ragenhere sat proudly between his father the King and his uncle, the Lord Eni. Opposite sat Father Julian, Ambassador Uric, and the Kentish singer Heoden. The singer, much to the irritation of Father Julian, but delight of his other companions, had taken out a small bone piccolo which he played skilfully as the banks slipped by. At each and every note the monk cringed behind a mask of pleasure. A tiny piping songbird had settled inside his head. The King seemed to regard him closely as they passed beneath the imposing burial mounds which overlooked the river at this point. The monk glanced across at them, up the steep slope that was entirely cleared to where the three tombs declared their sovereignty. The sun poured a silvery light on them and they rose out of the morning fog like a clutch of islands.

Julian shuddered and, quickly pretending it was simply the cold, pulled his sheepskin cloak about him. He had allowed himself some cloth wrappings for his sandal-shod feet and wore red woollen leggings and a tunic under the faded brown of his habit. The humble garb of a monk was unsuitable, unless that monk was a ferocious ascetic, for northern winters, without considerable modification. It seemed no accident to Julian that the heathen hill they passed beneath cast a deep shadow across the bow. Three trees reached thinly skyward out of one of the mounds and even these were drawn on the water by the white sun. They encapsulated the dread but not the hope in Calvary. The sun was perfectly corpse-like, a cold grim halo behind the crucifixion. The monk crossed himself and glanced over his shoulder at the meadows which were still banded in mist behind the shipyards. When his gaze returned to the burials the spindly trees now occurred to him as three giant hairs sprouting from some obscene belly.

Now the ship was flowing fast and was birthed into open water. The crew hauled around once they were a safe distance from the estuary but the currents drew them out and it was work to maintain direction. The wind was livelier out of the shelter of the banks and the sea had a mind to buck the boat. What remnant of colour there was in the long-suffering face of Father Julian completely left it. His countenance became as grey as the eastern offing. A sharp crosswind caused the boat to pitch unexpectedly. The sail was immediately taken up and a stabilising oar utilised on the lee as the vessel tacked briefly to windward. A ship of lesser length passed making for the estuary and for a moment drifted as the men stood up and briefly bowed to the King. The wind ruffled through their bobbed hair and pointed beards. Radwald acknowledged them with a nod. A fine rain began to fall, soaking into cloaks and furs, and for Father Julian making a miserable trip complete.

All his willpower was needed to suppress the vomit that welled in his throat. His godless companions were readying themselves to get out of the way and he was determined not to give them satisfaction. Uric handed him a square of cloth which the monk took with a mannered dignity. He endured a row of grins as the puke puffed out his cheeks. Somehow he swallowed it down. The burning nausea this created made his stomach turn violently. Again, calling on all the angels in heaven, he fought it back. His knuckles were white against the edge of the seat. He clenched his buttocks in desperate agitation and the sweat broke out across his brow.

'It seems we have a dead man with us,' Lord Eni said.

Heoden the poet smiled. 'Do not worry Father we will give you a Christian burial.'

Julian was comforted on the dismal sea by the presence of the Cross above him. It had been there all the time. The Lord had seeded it here, in the middle of this rotten plank of boat, the Cross, as plain as the tears in his eyes. Through these tears he saw God hanging on the mast. He blinked against the needling rain with gratitude knocking at the door of his heart. Though Julian could not quite believe the revelation of what he witnessed the Lamb remained plainly in front of his eyes. The monk threw himself to the boards and his cloak was wet with blood. He washed himself clean in it. He fervently kissed the wooden cross he wore around his neck. 'Lord Jesus have mercy on my soul!' He said the words again and again. When he recovered he found his fellow travellers staring at him with a mixture of awe and horror on their faces. Radwald in particular eyed the mast uneasily. 'What do you see there priest?' he demanded.

At first Julian did not answer. He had crossed a boundary and not yet returned.

'What do you see there priest?' Radwald said again. 'Pick him up.' He gestured to Uric and the Kentish poet.

The ship had rounded the coast and was now oared back to the land. This river was much wider, a yawning maw of commerce, and a couple of vessels loaded with goods heaved up river with them to the fledgling port of Gipeswic. Father Julian sat upright in his seat, looking over the cleared and fallow fields, ranging his eye over the tops of the trees, seeing God's work in everything. He had known it must be so, but had not until now believed it, that this strange and isolated part of the world was also a part of God's fielding. It too, these meadows, these trees, all were blessed in like manner. He did not quite feel that he travelled through the Holy Land but his nausea was cured and even the rain, like a tiny thorn, had been removed from his side.

Downstream the osier beds waved wearily toward the sea. At the woven quayside a few men were salvaging nets and a step from the withies a workshop was busy turning piles of stripped willow into baskets of every size. From open timber doors smoke emerged, straggling up the hill like the wooden huts and shabby yards. A flock of noisy geese waddled across the muddy track. A large pig rooting in the mud next to one of the houses glanced up to watch them pass. Father Julian looked into one of the shacks and was greeted by the grimy face of a cooper struggling to band a barrel. In a second, craftsmen were at work carving imported antler into combs and handles, needles, toggles and weaving hooks. The dying fall of a hammer was heard.

It was here further up the hill on the muddy road leading to the local field of ancestors that the rock was situated. The King had also agreed to the building of a humble chapel. All who wished to offer sacrifice would be allowed to do so. It was a breakthrough. The baleful influence of Lady Ealhhild, the heathen priestess, had been fortunately restricted by her illness. She had been too unwell to partake fully in the various debates. Despite this she still murmured things against Francia and Kent from her sickbed and every day her protestations grew louder. Julian had to admit, although he crossed himself as the thought came into his mind, that Uric was probably right. Her death might have been serendipitous. She had survived and only God knew why.

Father Julian was pleased with the choice of Gipeswic. The place had a slightly cosmopolitan flavour. It was no more than a collection of hovels clinging to a muddy bank of course, but the occasional ship brought with it something different to the uncivilised majority; a sense of otherness, and, more importantly, a sense of not being barbarian. A few plucky merchants, Julian understood, those who could afford exorbitant taxes, plied their trade from the Frankish coasts. The quality of wool from the flocks fattened on Radwald's rain-soaked pastures made the inherent difficulties worthwhile. Therefore, to Father Julian, the place was like a pinprick in a piece of parchment through which a ray of sunshine might be caught.

The modest cross stood up from its block like a bodily resurrection. The lower part of this stone carving, which in its entirety was considerably higher than a grown man, was still roughly hewn so that it resembled a heap of crystalline earth from which the cross grew with uncanny life. A Gaulish mason had been tasked to create it. The stone itself had been carted from the crumbling Roman town that lay to the west. The priest had no doubt. It was the green shoot for which he had been waiting. In the middle of this desert a scarlet poppy bloomed. He looked at his feet; the wrappings he had around them were caked with blood; he looked at his hands; a dirty bloody stream flowed from them. He was an unworthy man for such a sight. For the second time that morning he fell to his knees. A small crowd gathered at a distance their eyes full of wonder.

Radwald stepped forward and touched the stone. It was cold as winter ground and instinctively he disliked it. A cross of wood seemed more fitting. Hadn't the Christ died on a stake? Yet stone was lasting. This rock would stay here unless he took pains to destroy it and even then perhaps it would remain. Something new had been carved from something very old and from that antiquity it drew strength. Radwald was at once in awe and hate of it. He wished to harness its power but distrusted it. He was drawn and at the same time shunned it.

'Well priest?'

'Thank you sire,' Julian answered. 'It is beautiful. I hadn't expected it to be so ...' He hesitated. '*Complete.*'

Radwald frowned. 'But it is not finished Father Julian. Surely it is only half-done. Where is its maker?' Murmurings from the nearby gathering suggested that if the foreign craftsman had an excuse it would be a poor one. 'No matter,' the King said. 'It seems he knows the work well. What do you say to it brother Eni?'

'It has a sullen beauty like our sea.' The younger man nodded. 'It appears worthy of a god, solid like a god, unyielding in purpose like a god, but is it wise to have it here lord?'

'It is wise brother,' Radwald said uncertainly; 'think of it as a millstone to smooth certain edges. Is that not right Ambassador Uric?'

'It is perhaps an odd comb to take the ruffle out of kingly feathers.'

The rag-tag collection of spectators had pressed closer. An urchin with a withered leg swung forward on a crutch of ash and poked Father Julian. Her curiosity had evidently driven her to prod the kneeling priest in his lower back with her stick. It was as though an outrageous person had stepped on his spine. Julian spun round with a hand clutching to the point of audacity. Seeing the child his anger evaporated. The child stared back with corn poppy eyes as wide as saucers.

'Child,' Father Julian said softly, '*touch this cross*, not me its poor and inconstant servant.' The only Germanic word he had used was 'child'. The rest had been in his particular dialect of Latin. Unsurprisingly perhaps the girl looked blank.

Ambassador Uric translated for the girl: 'He suggests that you touch the rock.' He also waved for her to do so. Despite the translation the girl again prodded Julian with the ash. 'It appears it is not only her leg that is withered,' Uric remarked.

'Let us see what compassion there is in such a monument Father,' Heoden then said. He showed the girl what she must do by placing his own palm upon it.

Father Julian was deep in prayer. The appearance of the crippled girl was not a coincidence. His heart gushed like a split wineskin. Here on this filthy patch he was able to reach out and grasp again the feet of the Lord. He smothered them in thankful kisses. The drops of blood were sweet as the honey must be in heaven. This lowly teller of second-hand miracles was about to witness the divine energy of love. He looked up and the sky was folded in seraphic wings that caressed the rowan reaching from the higher ground.

The girl stretched out and brushed her hand against the rock. In doing so the crutch of ash slipped and she collapsed feebly onto her chest. Her cheekbone struck the base of the cross as her face hit the earth. No one moved. The girl groaned and rolled onto her back exhibiting the graze the stone had made across the bone below the eye-socket. Still no one moved. Her leg was plain for all to see. The stump was unchanged: accursed the very same.

'I bless this rock in the name of Simon called Peter, the chosen rock of Our Lord,' Father Julian said numbly. He could not take his eyes from the crippled child. Several had stepped up to help and two men carried her as the gathering broke apart and drifted down the hill.

'Come Father,' Heoden said kindly; 'the gods are stranger than we can fathom. Perhaps in time the evil will be driven off.'

'Yes, yes,' the monk agreed, nodding. 'Perhaps in time; it was foolish of me to ...' He broke off murmuring to himself in his own language. He seemed to be holding up the weight of the stone with his own chest. A great change had taken place in Father Julian. He did not need to place his hand in the Lamb's side again. He knew the blood smeared across that Fleece existed. This humble stone was not to be sanctified by a miracle. No matter. The monk had been filled with a commensurate joy only once before: when he had been recovered from a mortal fever. He had been bathed in the uncreated light of God. He had been written down a second time when the Lord had appeared above him in the ship. He had turned steadfastly away from the things of this world and he had been again rewarded. He would find that poor girl and give her the benefit of the beatitudes. He would bless her and she would be made whole as she was already in heaven.

'Tell the mason not to return,' Julian whispered. 'The stone is complete.' He felt battered by an angel. He stood and was hamstrung in the mud. He was helped to his feet by Uric who gripped his arm so tightly that it hurt. Julian protested and received a look of undisguised contempt.

'Shall we depart Father Julian?' suggested Radwald. 'It is cold and there is hot mead and roast mutton waiting for us.' He did not wait for an answer but turned on his heel. His son and younger brother followed. Some way off the King glanced over his shoulder. 'Come Kentish thanes,' he called. 'You have got what you wanted. The wood of your shrine will follow.'

Chapter

11

Ingelda, the wife of Gipping the merchant, carried round a splendid drinking horn to toast the magnanimity of Radwald in accepting their hospitality. The merchant himself looked as if the source of his blood flowed from out of the Scylfing Sea and his wife was as fair as Onela's queen. He had settled in this loom hook of river where he exhibited a talent for working with the merchants of the Frankish coast. Success may have lain in the contradiction between his fearsome appearance and the gentleness with which he bartered. His hall was comfortable with embossed shields and embroidered hangings but not ostentatious. It bowed before the magnificent gabled hall of Rendlesham. It was filled with the smell of roasting, and meat was brought on flat plates of bread. Glazed bowls were filled with apples and roasted chestnuts. The hungry men ripped at the food with glistening fingers. Cider warmed with nutmeg and cinnamon was slung down thirsty throats. Father Julian requested from Ingelda, another northern goddess from whom he averted his eyes, nothing but water, which was immediately brought to him. The water had the same earthy taste to which he had become accustomed but it was clean and refreshing.

'Be healthy!' Radwald cried, lifting the drinking horn high. Each man then took his turn to wish good health to the party.

'Come Father,' the King yelled when Ingelda offered Julian the cider. 'Wish us good health.'

The monk stood and sipped at the sweet beer. He looked like a brown moth uncurling its proboscis. 'Be healthy,' he said unconvincingly. 'I thank the King for his generosity in providing me with a permanent home.'

'Well said Father.' Uric applauded.

The King laughed. 'You are welcome Father.' There was a pause and then: 'Do you not see my good thane, Uric, that the port of Gipping flourishes. We have no need of other *alliances*. What do you say Ealdorman Gipping? Is trade not good?'

'It is good,' Gipping answered, nodding. 'It could always be better.'

'Things can be better but *blood* is thicker than water would you not say Ambassador?'

'It is an undeniable truism lord.' Uric sliced a piece from the apple he held and for a moment kept it on the blade. 'Are we not your cousins in Kent?'

'We are of one bone Earl Uric. One blood it is true, but our minds follow different stars. Ours hangs where it has always hung: over the northern sea. I am surprised you can still follow yours blinded as you are by the sun.'

The Ambassador smiled and dipped the apple piece into his beer. He looked thoughtful as he pushed the slice into his mouth. After reaching into his purse he spilled a large handful of coins onto the wooden table. They clattered like hail on a platter. It was a theatrical gesture but secured the attention of the mead bench. 'Are these not better than beads or poultry?' Uric shouted. 'Lord, I give them as a gift.'

The King beckoned and the coins were gathered and set down in a pile at his elbow. He nodded, waiting for the Ambassador to continue.

'The head is imperial is it not?' Uric said. 'It is like that of *Caesar*; but it is not Caesar's.'

'I do not want a home in Rome's image,' growled Radwald. 'Have I not made it plain?'

'The stamp will be in your image lord. Your head, your authority throughout the land.'

'What pray would our Lord Athelbert say to that?' Radwald inquired. 'Has he not already pressed his head to the new likeness of the Emperor?'

The Ambassador looked puzzled.

'I mean this Counsellor Uric,' said Radwald, presenting a minted cross between his thumb and index finger, 'that we take what we need from their example and reject what we do not. In short time we will acquire the knowledge of the stamps and I will see to it that the mirror is that of a wolf. Indeed was not the founder of Rome suckled by a she-wolf? Our fathers have a wolf's claws for fingernails. What does this tell you Ambassador?'

'That you have nothing to fear from an alliance of convenience.'

'No, that we have the same *authority* my Lord Uric. The milk of the wolf is the founding spring of our destiny. The walls of Rome collapsed on rottenness when our ancestors pushed them over. A great hall is being built once more around the death of a barefoot Caesar but the same stench comes from within. Tell me, can Kent not smell it across the short sea to Francia?'

'We cannot smell it my lord.'

'I understand; a whore's perfume must be pungent.'

A chord from Heoden's lyre drew Uric's hand away from the hilt of his sword and settled the Lord Eni. The King's ship was steadied and becalmed. Heoden played on, strumming a plangent tune from the air, and the language was that of the gods and ancestors themselves. It seemed better that the men of the day said nothing.

'Come Father Julian,' Ambassador Uric said, somewhat stiffly, when the harmonics of the last notes had died away. 'If the King grant it, I should like to assist you in your search for the crippled child. I believe you wished to give her a blessing.'

When the two of them were outside, Uric said: 'Tell me Father … is it true that pieces of the tree of sacrifice have been discovered?'

'You mean fragments of the True Cross?' Julian answered.

'Yes, that is what I mean.'

The priest's ankle gave way in a frozen muddy rut and he was forced to hop in a silly fashion.

'I believe I have twisted it Lord Uric.'

'Can you walk?'

'I can stumble if you give me some assistance.'

The Ambassador offered his shoulder and the priest hung from his neck like a shapeless satchel. Together they made some progress of the downward slope.

'Pieces of the sacred Cross,' Uric persisted. 'Do they exist?'

'Of course they exist. Unearthed from the very hill outside Jerusalem.'

'Where do they reside now Father?'

'They are scattered: a piece in Antioch, in Constantinople, in Rome; they are supreme objects of veneration and pilgrimage as I am sure you understand.'

'Would you not say Father that all pieces of wood were in some way 'true' seeing as the Cross was in fact of wood?'

'In some way, perhaps, any piece of wood is representative.'

'Representative, yes, yes, that is what I mean, *representative*.' The Ambassador paused with a thoughtful look and then resumed: 'There is a tale I have heard the islanders tell that Joseph of Arimathea came here after the Resurrection.'

'I have not heard that tale and so I ...'

'Might he not have brought something with him when he came?'

'*Something*, Lord Uric?'

'A splinter, a rivet, a strip of cloth?'

'It is impossible to say.'

'Impossible, yes. How might the *authenticity* of such an item, such a relic be proven?'

'I can hardly say, except that God himself should authorise it.'

'He might do that by a marvel perhaps?'

'A miracle, yes,' Father Julian said breathlessly. 'A relic such as that, if it were to exist, must surely be underwritten by miracle; but Ambassador Uric let us remember the caution of our most holy Father Gregory that in this day we should not *expect* miracles.'

The priest hobbled to a halt. The sinuous path they had taken appeared deserted; every door was shut against them. Then there was shouting from a nearby house. A scrofulous dog that lay in the yard of a seemingly empty workshop woke and began barking in answer. A man Uric said he recognised from the motley gathering who had followed the nobles to the stone that morning then ran across the muddy lane in front of them. Uric called out to him but the man did not look back. 'I might ask him the whereabouts of the child,' Uric said. He left Julian against a suitable wall and set off in pursuit of the stranger.

The monk sank wearily down the planks until he felt the cold ground. The stick and parchment dog lay in a ditch and was quiet. Man and dog regarded one another and momentarily Julian had the unpleasant sensation that he viewed his own reflection. In order to disturb this discomforting mirror he threw a stone which hit the animal on its protruding hipbone. With a yelp of protest the dog sprang to its feet but stood its quarter. A lift of Julian's arm was enough to send it slinking from sight. The priest shook his head. He felt like a letter from the Pope that had gone astray. The seal had broken, unfolding him open before the elements, and here he was an unwanted jumble of words in a shit-strewn lane. 'Here I am Lord,' he murmured. 'Your good and faithful servant; dispose of my life as you wish.' He was relieved when Uric appeared at the corner.

'Father,' Uric said, running up to him, 'I have discovered something.'

'The child?'

'Yes the child, but first we must fetch the King.'

'Why?' Julian enquired as he was whisked away on the Ambassador's arm, limping quickly as if a wolf pursued them. 'I only wished to give the child my blessing ... please Lord Uric slow *down*, I am in trouble.' He glanced back over his shoulder and saw a man at the turn in the lane apparently watching their progress.

'Yes I have discovered something,' the Ambassador said excitedly.

'Pray tell me then Lord Uric.'

A door opened and a woman with hair in which a blackbird might nest grinned at them. The sentiment behind the smile appeared friendly. The lantern jaws made her monstrous. Her dress might have been rubbed specially in the mud for the purpose of a first impression. Father Julian returned her nod as they passed. Where did these old crones come from? They were always on the verge of materialising: from under stones, from behind trees, of a sudden into the light over a darkened threshold. It was a land of exceedingly ugly witches; but a voice at his ear told him to beware rather the beautiful ones; the ugly ones could take care of themselves.

'What have you *discovered* Lord Uric? Is it the child?'

'The child yes, but something else.'

'*What?*' Father Julian insisted, putting down a temporary root in the mud.

The Ambassador took hold of Julian's shoulders and looked him straight with a searching eye.

'What is it child?' the priest murmured. There was an innocent quality in the dilation of the soul he was confronted with and it had caused him to slip into a confessional mode.

'Call it a feeling, Father,' the Ambassador said.

'A feeling?'

'Yes, that something marvellous may happen.'

'Something marvellous,' the priest almost whispered, sounding the three syllables of the word slowly and feeling the last of them kiss against his palate; it was tenderness to his emotional susceptibility. 'Something marvellous,' he repeated. 'A miracle! A miracle has taken place!'

'The marvel at this moment resides in me,' Uric suggested; 'but ...' A cloud came over his eye as his thoughts appeared enveloped by a mystery. Julian searched an impenetrable glass in vain. He looked out a sign, perhaps for doves to alight along the thatch of his imagination, but the sky was a spotless veil. He believed that something momentous had taken place. He did not know why he believed that but his faith in it was as unblemished as the firmament above.

'My Lord Radwald!' Julian cried as he ascended the steps of the merchant's hall. 'My Lord Radwald!' There was lightness in his step which carried the bruised ankle on a cushion of air. Under the lintel however he tripped and fell into the room with a dull thump. His nose hit the hard oak and was blooded. He stood with what dignity remained. Not for the first time that day the Ambassador offered Father Julian a handkerchief; but the priest was already dabbing at his nose with his own scented cloth.

'You seem determined to ape the holy fool, Father,' Radwald observed dryly, standing up and coming round from the end of the table. The whole of the mead bench was also standing. Ingelda had paused in her rounds and was like sculpture; serving folk too were motionless.

'My apologies Lord Radwald, my apologies, but we have rushed to return.'

'From where?'

'From where my lord?' It then occurred to Julian that he had no idea. He turned to the Ambassador who was apparently lost in thought.

'You look *troubled* Lord Uric,' the King remarked. 'What have you found?' The entire room stared from the King to the Ambassador and back again. 'Well?' Radwald said patiently.

'It is difficult to explain,' Uric answered. 'I found the child, you remember the stricken child by the stone?'

The King said nothing, waiting for the Ambassador to continue.

'What ... she is healed?' Heoden said with wonder.

'No ... but I feel she shall be,' Uric replied with certainty.

'You *feel* this Uric of Kent,' Radwald said with sardonic emphasis; 'you are the wrong sex for prophecy. Are you taken by a female spirit?'

'I know not Lord Radwald. I know only that the child has been enchanted.'

'Again Ambassador Uric such things I would have thought beyond your knowledge.'

'She is held enraptured by a spell my lord. The seas wash against the lids of her eyes.'

'You mean she cries?'

'That is not what I mean lord.'

'Then speak plainly. What is this mischief?'

54

'By your leave I ask you to accompany me. I ask all of you to accompany me,' Uric cried, addressing first the King and then the mead bench in general. There was silence. A few restless embers crawled in the nest of the hearth; a watching chattel stoked them and they fed like incandescent maggots. There was the sound of the wind playing around the rafters. It seemed to be alive. Everybody waited for the King's decision.

'Where is the child?' Radwald demanded when they reached the house of miracle. A crowd funnelled behind the noble party like ale under the stopper of a drinking horn. It was a source of wonder to Julian that only a short while before the place had been deserted. Now it seemed that every soul in Gipeswic sought them out.

'Stand back you fools!' Lord Eni shouted.

'Stand back!' the young Lord Ragenhere cried also, obviously anxious to assist even though he was of age merely nine winters.

Only King Radwald, the Kentish Ambassador, and Father Julian entered the house, which was a typical family dwelling of thatch and low roof with beds built into the corners. Firelight hunted shadows around the walls. Faded colours were in the hangings but blackness clung to the timber. There was a large wooden trunk to one side under the window, more than big enough to store a body, and on it were piled a great many blankets and furs. A pregnant woman seated on a three-legged stool was turning a spitted joint above the firebox. Her face lifted up to them like a snowdrop in the dusk. She stood and, wiping her hands on her dress, bowed awkwardly before the King. The man of the house, having dropped the bar behind the door, remained where he was, watching. The gossip of the waiting crowd must have been spirited away because inside the room there was only the hush of expectancy.

'Come forward child,' Radwald whispered. Clearing his throat he repeated the command more loudly. There was a rustling in the corner and a shadow moved in the cave created by the upper bunk frame. 'Come forward!' the King said again; this time in a peremptory tone and the shadow slipped from under the frame and in the firelight became flesh. It was the same ragged gilded child who had fallen by the unfinished cross. There was the graze on her cheek from where it had struck the stone. These were the same bleached eyes but now they held splinters of amber. The same flaxen tangled mane, the same coarse dress of acorn-coloured wool, the same stick that supported the withered useless leg. She looked up at the King as one bewildered before a god. Her parents too melted back into the dark awed as they were and unworthy. The light of kingship made a miserable candle of the firebox. The woman moved heavily forward to respectfully shift the joint away from the heat. She clutched unexpectedly at her side and was forced to sit down on the nearest bed. It was almost as if her perceptive infant bowed in the womb before Radwald.

'I see nothing different,' the King said irritably. He glanced over his shoulder at Uric who merely shrugged and withdrew into the shadows.

Father Julian stepped closer with two fat tears welling from his eyes. He saw the urchin in a beatific vision: she had the face of the Christ-child. He saw this because he had been suddenly and apocalyptically filled with love for her. He fell to his knees and was about to bend forward to kiss the instep of her foot when a hand on his shoulder took a grip of his garment and pulled him to his feet. 'Father,' the King muttered; 'this is *most* unseemly. I fear I shall never understand either *you* or your god.'

'Forgive me sire, for a moment it was as though I looked on the face of God.'

'Your god is *here*? Where is he? Should we fear him?'

'There is nothing to fear sire. God is good. God is love.'

Radwald raised a sceptical eyebrow. 'God cannot be all good Father; if as you insist he is the source of *everything*, then must he not be evil as well as good?'

'We have discussed this Lord Radwald. Evil is the work of the fallen angel, tripped by pride into the abyss.'

'This *angel* as you call him, is he not in fact a god?'

'No, sire. He is a supernatural creature.'

'Like a god?'

'Like a god but not God. There is only one true God.'

'But Christ? Is he not a god?'

'He is God.'

'The same God?'

'The same.'

'And this spirit, this *comforter*, you talk of is she also God?'

'He is God, sire, stepping from the Father.'

'They are three but one then?'

'It is a mystery sire.'

'That it is, Father, that it is.' Radwald nodded wryly. 'In that it makes no sense … but I understand that it need not; that much I understand.'

'*In nomine Patris et Filii et Spiritus Sancti,*' Julian enunciated loudly, making the sign of the cross and then with a thumb retracing the sign on the girl's forehead. 'I bless thee child, even though thou art lost, even though in innocence thou art lost ...' He trailed off in wonderment. Under the pale heaven of her iris, the dark pool of the girl's pupil mirrored back a vision of her imminent baptism. His own eye blazed in the sun of a desert and beheld the crumbling banks of a red-clay river. He saw the bluebird of the blessing he had given dive through the vault of her iris. Plunging through her pupil it descended the endless depths of love. The world was created for the priest once more as a parable. It had become clear to him that the life of the gospels was vividly repeated; that is he was following footsteps; the only thing needed was that he remove the beam from his eye to see it. It was not vicarious experience, it *was* experience.

The girl started and glanced over her shoulder as if she saw the reflection of a goblin in the monk's eye. Julian touched her on the arm to re-engage her attention. 'Do you think, Lord Radwald, that the parents of this child would agree to her baptism?'

'They might if it would cure her. Is this what you are suggesting?'

'Holy baptism is not a *charm*, sire.'

'It is a sort of magic is it not?' the Ambassador said, stepping into the firelight.

'It is not the right way to see it,' Julian insisted.

'What is a blessing? Is it not given on behalf of God?'

'It is.'

'You say there is no magic in it?'

'Not exactly Counsellor Uric.'

'So there is magic in it?'

'Of a sort if you will,' Father Julian said exasperatedly; 'but not *heathen* magic.'

'Magic is magic I should say,' Uric suggested with a smile. 'Would you not agree lord?'

Radwald shrugged. 'Magic is always magic.'

There was a rapping at the door. The child's father answered and it was the Earl Eni asking after the King. The heads of Gipping, Heoden, and Ragenhere were glimpsed as they nosed in the doorway and then Ragenhere turned away shouting again at the determined crowd.

'In short time we shall be with you brother,' Radwald answered, indicating with a gesture that the man should close the door.

'Would you say that *baptism* was a blessing Father?' Uric continued.

'It is not the same as a blessing; it is a far more sober undertaking.'

'It is then a more powerful magic?'

'In answering I risk trotting back to your wrongheaded opinion.'

'Forgive me, Father, but as you know we have a great liking for wordplay and riddles.'

'Yes well, speaking as one from a more …' He was about to say 'cultured civilisation' but managed to prevent himself. 'Speaking for myself,' he said, 'I find them extremely tiresome.'

'I should like to see you succeed in curing the child,' Radwald said thoughtfully.

'I am following what my heart is telling me,' Julian insisted. 'The rest is up to God.'

'My own baptism,' Radwald said, and then hesitated. He put a palm to his temple. 'My own baptism felt like an offering, an offering of myself, to what I know not.' He sighed. 'I feel it was not accepted Father.'

The monk touched the King's arm. 'It was you who rejected Christ. He has not rejected you. You are still a *Christian* sire. Still a Christian.'

'In past days Father Julian our people believed that the king was a god. Some still do, that is to say our festivals are not dramas but *are*.'

'You sire, what do you believe? This is the only matter of importance.'

'If you mean do I feel a fist around my heart squeezing bloody tribute and giving life to my legs and my loins then yes I feel the old gods. I fear them too. They will lay waste to this land if they are not respected.'

'They are idols my Lord Imperator, blocking out the holy light,' the priest insisted, 'destroy them; these feelings you talk of, they are real, they come from God, life comes from God.'

'What about *here* Father?' Radwald said grimly, making a codpiece of his hand.

'Even there lord … but beware concupiscence. Enjoy your wife in the sanctity of marriage.'

'We are not married according to your Christian law.'

'You are not, sire.'

'Is Christ not loving enough for other beliefs, other ways of thinking?'

'Christ is love, sire.'

'Yet he would throw us into the fire you speak of … my beautiful Ealhhild, whom I know to be absolutely betrothed to me according to our ways.'

'I cannot answer for Christ, for who can know what he will say to us face to face? This life is a fog before our eyes, we cannot, much as we

58

should like, see past it; but the Word that was left us and the teachings of the Holy Church are clear enough. The teachings are clear enough for me to say fear for your soul my lord; fear for your wife's soul.' The priest paused, declining to look directly at the King when he said this. Instead he gave the appearance of seeing through him as if Radwald were merely a ghost. 'Your wife sets herself against God. No good can come of it.'

There was a loud creak as the pregnant woman shifted her position on the bed. The other occupants of the house glanced at her; even the bewildered child whose eyes seemed to implore her mother to rescue her. The father stared dumbly at the fire; the mother looked nervously to the Ambassador; and the child was like a sentient lamb: she had begun to shake in fear.

'Yourself my lord, are you absolutely betrothed according to your ways?'

'For myself I cannot say as much,' the King answered candidly. 'Lord Ing leads men ploughing into other fields and it has always been so.'

'Perhaps then,' the Ambassador ventured, 'Lady Ealhhild has less to fear from her death.'

'Perhaps,' the King readily agreed, 'I know only that she will follow me wherever I go if it is at all within her power. It is a kind of loyalty my fine Kentish thane that the Angles still honour ... but we stray. We have become distracted. Shall I ask her father, *Father*?' He turned to Julian.

'I have seen such things this morning that I ...'

'What things Father?'

'No matter,' answered the priest; 'please ask the girl's father.'

The King explained slowly to the man at the door what exactly would be required of his daughter. He couched it in terms of understandable reference. The charm, having been royally delineated, caused beads of consternation to break out along the man's forehead. He looked worriedly at the Ambassador who nodded in encouragement. The man, who was a lumbering bearded giant with his head bowed by the rafters, then mumbled something barely audible.

'Look up from the floor man,' Radwald demanded. 'You have nothing to fear. This is not a kingly request. The decision is yours.'

The man's countenance became one of agitated puzzlement.

'I myself have been through the ritual,' Radwald then declared. 'See here. Take my hand. Am I not flesh and blood?'

In answer the giant strode over to his daughter and picked her up. The child did not protest but her mother wailed in fear and had to be calmed.

The emergence of the King through the door caused a great deal of excitement in the crowd gathered outside. Once again the Earls Eni and Ragenhere forced back the overly curious with threatening gestures and made the way possible for the King and the rest of the baptismal party, which did not include the mother who had expressed her wish most strongly to remain. They left her with a stricken pall across her face and with her hand spread over her belly as if she feared this strange magic might affect her unborn baby and she wished to protect it.

There was a point in the Gipping, a little beyond the port, where the river ran shallow over an ancient ford. It was a locus of exchange between the halves of Radwald's kingdom, and it was here that folk assembled to bare witness to an extraordinary scene, lining both banks of the river, some even venturing up to their thighs in the water to watch.

The girl's father had carried her on his back to the destination of what he obviously saw as her sacrifice. Father Julian had been so overcome on realising that this man was prepared to offer his daughter, for his king, for the hope of a cure, to propitiate an unknown god, to elicit some kind of benevolence, that tears had sprung into his eyes making a rheum which had obscured his sight. As he left the house the monk had struck his shoulder against a protruding nail. Had the cloth of his habit not protected him he might have been impaled. But his momentary loss of vision had yielded a higher form of seeing. Julian viewed the ultimate giving of this humble man as the working of Grace. What else should it have been? He had regarded the souls of these barbarians as the abode only of devils, shut off from the light of Christ; but the sun was bleeding through a fog of blindness and it had formed a halo around this clownish working man and thrown the shape of Abraham on the ground.

The air was filled with the chatter of curiosity but this gradually fell into an expectant hush until only the sylphs of air that caressed the dead gently nodding heads of the reeds were talking. There was the drop of a wading bird into the lap of the river. It fluttered skyward again, a living toy of the gods. Radwald and his thanes followed by the father carrying his child had waded into the water. A spectral sister had appeared in the sky, her cheek pale as milk under the fold of her hood, and she began to smudge the afternoon in wetted ashes. Father Julian gesticulated for the giant to dunk the frightened child. King Radwald also motioned for the man to dip her.

The child had buried her face in her father's chest. All that could be seen was a dirty trembling rag of hair. His neck was the obvious branch to which she clung above a drowning. In a single movement he immersed her. For a timeless instant they weltered like a whale and its newborn calf. The water cascading from them was a hallowed quicksilver. Or rather this was how Father Julian thought of it when later he ran the sacrament over in his mind. Something miraculous had occurred. He was certain. Yet the club of flesh that did for the child's lower leg had been unchanged. He had scared the girl half to death but she had been saved. She had shaken the bars as if to claim the sanctuary of her father's heart. She had reluctantly turned a deathly face and with silent blue lips had allowed Julian to trace the *chrism* across her forehead. But only the King himself had prevented her from rubbing it off. It was no matter as for an angel that might now admit her it was indelible. Julian had looked into the sky and, seeing there a thousand doves, in gratitude had sung a joyful hosanna. The crowd had understood not one word. At least this was Julian's impression. They thought of him still as some kind of sorcerer.

Chapter
12

Swaddling wrapped the sky in grey, its spheres in cloaking fogs, and the sun bent her back under a crookedness of age: this was her end. There had been a heavy fall of snow in the night and the virginal meadow ran unspotted from the children's feet to the black trunks that lifted high into the roof of the forest. Shapes were moving over the meadow, the children felt them, and knew that elves did not leave footprints. They followed them airily across the silent ground pretending for a time that they also left unmarked the journey of their mortality and then they played at wolf and bear again, each of them trying on a nature, each of them in the other's skin as Leda had suggested. The she-bear stopped and made claw prints; the smaller grey wolf that was her companion did likewise measuring out a stride with knuckles. They had for a time escaped the morning ritual and were busily engaged in making their own. The water had been fetched, the hens fed, and firewood collected from the shed. It was festival and the children were allowed a generous leeway. Most were content to shadow the excitement of the adults, playing at snow games, safe in the lee of the osier fencing, and not looking to the vast mantled world beyond where an eerie lifelessness lay below an ember of sun.

The celebrations of the men and women were at first separate. The men packed into the Yule hall awaiting vows on the sacrificial pig which had become strangely docile in its pen of lights. Darkness had descended and been dispelled promptly from under every shelter by an almost uncountable number of torches and tallows. Candles flamed before the reddened eyes of the boar and appeared to enchant it. People passing by the pen stopped in awe: there was an air of acceptance about the animal, which displayed an interested mind still in the snuffling of its nose and in the occasional sweep of its short bristling tail.

The women's hall was a timber and thatch blaze of inner fire which the bringing of the oaken log had added to. Singing of an ancient song accompanied it. Beadhild in the fullness of pregnancy had been brought with much rejoicing to the chair of highest honour. She was weary as after harvest with swollen ankles and a pod of whales in her womb but she was happy that the Goddess of Life had chosen her. Other women of the village were with child but only she was in readiness.

A stumpy carved totem of the Lady Earth, dressed in holly and mistletoe, looked across the flames of the firebox to the Great Mother's Chair and the room attained the heat of a bread oven as the women began a dance of victory. Beadhild, sitting in the palm of the Great Goddess, beat the time slowly on a large shallow drum of doe hide, softly, gently to begin, and the women stepped crabwise in rhythm with the ancient work song. If this song were to stop then so also human beings. The eldest, of which Leda's grandmother was one, stooped with difficulty into the dance, forcing unwilling bones to bend, almost in an expression of memory; the youngest sprang into it, feeling with bare feet the soil beneath the rug-covered planking. Stumbling toddlers were pulled away from the fire. Leda carried the near yearling Alfred on her back, strapped and enveloped in a deerskin pouch, the only male presence, a little imp of Ing, watching with glittering sapphire eyes, the secret rites of the women, and tolerated only because he would not remember. As soon as he was able to walk with a degree of confidence his place would be with the men whether his father could be trusted to take care of him or not.

In the shimmering pen blood fell from the throat of the chosen animal. A clay basin caught most and the rest spattered to the ground and over the clothes of the men next to Aldwulf whose own tunic received the greatest share. Wolves howled across the bitter air and the night was cold and death to the men huddled at the sacrifice. They glanced to where the women were and looked forward to the feasting. Under the soaring cries of the wolves was the incessant drumbeat from the *Mothers'* hall, which grew steadily louder, punctuated with yells and shrieks, and then an awful crying out as if the wolves had got in.

Imma was called to the bowl. The warm blood steamed in the frozen air. On his tongue it was a tingle of sweetness. Only yesterday Sigbert had suggested he took his rightful place among the women. 'You are like the moon,' he had told him. The moon was a brother who had fallen in love with unmanly magic and become a sister. 'You are a man-witch,'

Sigbert had told him. The howling was closer now and a couple of men took torches out toward the paling.

The Yule boar was being flayed. The skin would be saved and stretched on the stake that guarded the village. Each Yule the old skin was taken down, burned, and then replaced with that of the sacrifice. As the fire was kindled for the offering it drove still more of the darkness into hiding. The rhythmic pain of the women's song echoed around the walls of the night. Imma listened to the women. It was as though they were calling to his grandmother. The loin of the boar had now been carved as the choice cut. Fear clutched at Imma's heart as the chosen boys readied themselves for the task. They must cross the unknown and lay their offering at the feet of Lord Ing.

Shouldering torches, flaming the snow, the men went ploughing over the field with the voices of the Mothers ringing across the glassy air. At the highest point behind the houses there was a broad mound from which the sweep of hill down to the willow fences and beyond could be watched by the Lord of the World. In this mound the ashes of the burned skins were sown like seed. The soil was black, a dark treacle that was almost living, in which the shanks of the god were buried. The stake itself, which was a seasoned log of oak, was written from top to bottom in a single rune. Each individual rune represented a man and when a boy had passed through another was added. All were therefore *Ing-wine*; that is a friend of the god.

The mound was blanketed with snow and gold dripped over it from the torchlight. The stake, which most called simply the *Rune*, had a shadowy blackness to it like a crow's beak. How old the Rune was had passed from memory. Aldwulf remembered it as a boy; it had always been here. A few said it had come from Angeln with the first of the kin and there was a ready number to believe it. The bloody skin was draped and the mound received its first drops, like dark crushed berries on the muslin snow, and now the sign regarded the assembled men with its limp and gory head. A flame cast light through the eyeholes and the boar was alive to them. There was a gasp from the boys. Imma's heart pounded like a cudgel against a barrel and it was quicker and seemingly more desperate than the steady persistent beats that came still from the women's hall. Under a sky of black ice the boys stripped to the waist while their kinsmen looked on in woollens and furs. Each man took his turn to take a fistful of blood from the basin. This they smeared on the Rune in a celebration of brotherhood. A song of Ing in exile was taken up, telling of the god's wandering over the ocean east of Angeln, and of his homecoming in the wagon of his ship. The song was more of a chant, restricted in its melody, and rhythmic like the riding of a prow over the waves. Ing was returning the men were sure of it. Wuffinga drew the special ale which held a wicked barley spirit, and the boys, who had fasted all day, took plenty. They drank to the gills but Wuffinga made them drink again. This they did with skin rumpling in the cold and with minds already swinging from the fast. Imma washed his face in the snow and even ate it but eventually he too was ready.

There was a warm humming in Imma's head and it grew louder as he held out his naked arm. He concentrated his effort on keeping it still. Both Sigbert and his brother had already passed through and stood proudly shivering to one side with wolf skins around their bloodstained torsos. Now it was Imma's turn. Aldwulf grabbed the boy's wrist and readied the knife. Imma hardly felt the blade open his flesh. His arm was numbed by the cold. He saw the blood well along the line and it was black in the torchlight. The world became fuzzy and the humming in his head took on the music of the homecoming. He felt his legs dissolve. Yet they held him up. Now he felt the pain, for a moment it was still far from him, but then it arrived sharply. The Rune of Ing was carved in four straight cuts along his forearm and blood flowed from the marks. He held out the other arm, clenching his fist against the pain, which sang strangely in his head, and then he felt a freezing wetness to his dangled arm: it was like a club of iron. The bowl was held out and into it he punched both fists smearing the blood of the fighting boar into the blood running down his arms. He must fight Lord Ing as the others had done. He stepped up to the stake and was in awe of it; the ghoulish boar glowered over him, waiting. Slowly he began to swing his arms feeling the bones shudder as they struck against the Rune and they were like slender branches whipping against a trunk. He smashed harder, faster into the wood, the wounds on his arms opening and shouting as he ground them against the grain. At times he fell or hit his head only to struggle to his feet and begin again. 'When must I stop?' the boy had asked before beginning. 'You will know,' Aldwulf had answered.

He did not see the god. It was always the same immovable tree. There was one very odd moment when he saw himself from a distance. A boy of eleven Yules trying to punch down a house. He gave up in despair, sinking to his knees in the blood-spattered snow, and his head felt like winter sunlight. His chest rose and fell, a choking sea of effort, and then the warmth of a fur placed around his shoulders. His uncle helped him to his feet and with an arm supporting him Imma stumbled down the mound to where his kinsmen were waiting. Cloths were tied tightly around his forearms. And then he was sick.

When the men strode downhill they appeared not to notice that the women's song had stopped and yet it was something most unusual. As they approached the hall it seemed as if the women were very unsettled by something. The men looked anxiously at each other and were clearly unsure as to what to do. It was not seemly for them to look in at such a time. The Goddess might be angered, not to mention their own womenfolk; but something about the voices rising into the air caused the men to pause outside the hall, their breath ghosting about them and the blood of the boar caked on their palms and knuckles. The taste of it was still on their lips and the scent of butchery hung about them in the cold virginal air. There was a whisper also of roasting which floated from the feasting hall but the men, if they registered it at all, for the moment ignored it. There was a small hole in the nearest shutter through which a single stalk of light spangled showing where a curious eye might peer through; but not a man dared to do it.

In front of the circle of astonished men the hall door was abruptly thrown back with a tremendous clatter and firelight leaped like a lion into the night. With it came an excited Leda who stopped short before the huddle of men seemingly surprised to see them there. A few men peered past her through the open doorway, sheer nosiness overcoming their fears, but all that could be seen was inexplicable chaos amid the smoke and fire of the room. Leda's father and Edwin started to stumble up the rising stretch of snow, the one questioning the strange and sudden appearance of his daughter and the other seemingly bewitched by what was taboo.

'Girl!' Urswine cried. 'What is it?'

Leda, without answering, turned on her heel and rushed back inside. The hall door was shut with a mighty rattle in their faces causing a small drift to slip from the roof and fall on their heads. There was a moment of hilarity as the men brushed the flakes from their hair and beards. Presumably everything was as it should be. The women surely would have called to them had something been fatally amiss. The song had finished earlier than usual that was all. The women were enjoying themselves. Let them enjoy themselves was the general feeling expressed. All the same they stood as if spellbound where they had halted someway down the slope. Light escaped from every crack of the wooden hall and the heat was slowly melting the snow, which dripped steadily from the overhanging thatch. To the men gathered on the dark cold hill the hall might have been like a planking around something precious, something golden that could not be contained, and it was as though they had been given a glimpse of it.

The blood had dried in the cloths and a freezing claw of wind took Imma by the arm. He had become a man and Leda would see it when he showed her the marks. He felt sick and strange. He looked with the other men to the light breaking from the Mothers' hall; the wind blew the heady smoke of the libations over their heads, and Imma stretched his nose wolf-wise to catch the scent. He thought of the festival butter melted and poured on the fire, the herbal mead sprinkled until the fire child choked, and rancid beautiful smoke like a lungful of heaven. He saw a pair of giant paws breaking open the women's hall, like the splitting of an exotic fruit he had never seen, nor even heard tell of, and the pulp of it was a wonderful red ochre and the seeds were black as apple pips. His head swam and he leaned on Aldwulf who smiled down at him. Aldwulf's teeth were the colour of yellow cream, although one or two were browner. He drew back the sleeve of his tunic to reveal his own scar; then placed a weighty hand on Imma's head.

The men had turned away and were trudging over to the feasting hall when their attention was arrested again by the clattering of the women's door. Leda galloped toward them like an equine goddess. The men parted as if expecting her to run straight through and on down the hill. Instead she came to a halt in front of them, her cheeks flushed with the heat of the sacrifice and her own agitation, her flaxen hair loose about her shoulders, her dress a dried spray of blood, the hem of it soaked by the snow, her hands and face painted with the ritual marks of the Goddess, in blue and in yellow tints, her lips smeared with red ochre, and her eyes glittering with fire and purpose. She wore a thin brown belt of leather that pulled in her dress at the waist and from which depended all the usual womanly things such as keys and hooks and small bags of charms and beads. Several men gasped at this vision of the girl. Her father opened his mouth to speak but fell silent. Others resembled him in opening and closing their mouths like a catch laid along a riverbank. Leda's searching gaze fell on Imma. He was pleased she immediately noticed the wraps of the Rune and for a moment she appeared distracted but then she spoke:

'Imma!' she shouted breathlessly, 'the women want Imma!'

'What is this young Leda?' Aldwulf spoke for all the amazed men.

'Imma!' the girl repeated. She seemed almost possessed. Perhaps it was the Goddess who spoke to them in her shape. Several men took a step back as from the scorch of a flame. 'The women want him; they say he has an inheritance.'

'Leda, my cousin's daughter,' Aldwulf said patiently, 'what is the meaning of this?'

'Mother is in her time. She is ready. A sea came from her womb and soaked the Chair of Life.' At this several men turned away as if there was something further down the slope that had engaged their interest.

'The waters broke over the Chair of the *Goddess?*' Aldwulf appeared stunned.

'They say the bark of the baby is here uncle.' Leda shivered and stamped her feet in the snow. The aspect of awe she had evoked had diminished and the men now evidently saw her again as the beautiful but obvious farming girl they all knew. Her womanhood was almost on her at twelve Yules that much was clear but the flame which might have been the Goddess had died to a human flicker. Imma could not stop staring at her. It had barely registered that it was he who was the object of her mission. This night had the form of strange and wonderful dreams.

'The women must deal with it as always,' Aldwulf decided. 'Why do they want the boy?'

'They say he has Mother Sheaving's *touch*; that she will come to mother through him.'

'But the Goddess at this time ...' Aldwulf hesitated. 'No it cannot be. No man has ever ...'

'We are amazed, uncle, and in fear. If we feel it is right the Lady leads us to it. She is here uncle; she is at our feast.'

Imma stepped forward and, much to the amusement of several men, placed his bear pelt around her shoulders. She smiled at him because now he instead of she began to shiver.

'Eanfled!' Aldwulf called loudly. 'I must speak to Eanfled!'

A shape stepped from the silhouettes clustered at the doorway and came down to them. The shape resolved quickly into Aldwulf's eldest daughter. Her dress was a living sheaf of corn, a lovely faded weld, and she wore an inner gown of blue. Her necklaces were a treasure of multicoloured gems and beads, spells and agates, ready to catch at a touch of torchlight. In the centre of her bosom a circular brooch which had belonged to her mother pinned her light linen cloak. It was a humble splendour of bronze and amber. She was a tall, proud and resourceful woman, but her face, which now was decorated with the ritual paints of the Goddess, had an angular plainness that made it seem as though she might chop a man in half with her nose.

'Father.' She smiled. 'Soon we will be ready to come to you in the feasting hall.'

'What is this about Beadhild?'

'She is in the throes of her work. We are in wonderment, it is ...' She seemed unable to find the words.

'And Mother Sheaving's boy?'

'Who has become a man at only eleven I see,' Eanfled said. 'What marvels this Yule has shown us Imma.' She offered to take him by the hand. She had cared for him since the night in the cattle byre and he had no wish to disappoint her. In short time she had become a mother to him, a young mother such as he had not known, a mother who after the chores were done, might indulge him in a game of hoops, laughing and clapping at her throws, chiding him if he was a bad loser, which was often, or she might run with him down to the meadow shouting for him to slow down in case he tripped and smashed his nose on a stone. He liked running races with her because the disadvantage of her long skirts meant that he won easily. Sometimes he felt guilty that in enjoying Eanfled's company so much he had forgotten his grandmother.

'Might it not be dangerous for him?' Aldwulf now asked his daughter. Her hair flowed loosely behind her and the cold wind caught at it.

'Father, the women have invited him; he is welcome.'

Aldwulf shook his head. 'This is a singular night indeed.' He was clearly unwilling to give the boy to the women whatever the reason.

Eanfled repeated her assertion that he had been invited.

Imma took her hand but was still unsure both of whether it was right that he should go with her and more importantly exactly what the women expected of him. His grandmother had trained him only in the most desultory way since she had always been intent on his learning the metal craft. The craft of his father. Indeed that thought had often been like a solitary bee in the hive of her head. Imma was not afraid of Beadhild's labour; he had been present at many arrivals but he did not wish to lose face with the men.

Then there was the discordant music of a woman in labour, seemingly at first from a middle distance, from under the earth almost, but then

69

unmistakable and immediate. Certain of the men had already drifted away and gone up to the feasting hall. These female concerns were not theirs to share. Nor apparently did they wish to share in them. They had completed their sacrifice and now they must celebrate. Let the women complete and come to join them when they were ready. Beadhild's husband seemed the least troubled. Children shook from his wife like grain from an ear of wheat. He had said as much many a time. The onset may have been auspicious, Urswine may well have granted, but it was a womanly mystery. Let Beadhild come show him his wonder child when she was ready. Let the women bring his wife and child to the feast and he would raise a toast to them. This was plainly her husband's attitude.

Imma felt caught between two worlds; but he allowed Eanfled to lead him over the threshold of hers. Inside the womb-like hall there was shadow and a blaze. He was bathed in a river of scents, some of which were cloying and some acridly bitter. The smoke of the room took elusive shapes which formed and unformed all about him. The women turned as one and he hid himself behind Eanfled's skirt. The door banged shut with a rattle. Out of the corner of his eye he was aware of the Earth Goddess in her winter green but he dare not look at her. These were the women and girls of his own village but they appeared different. Leda was different. All were arrayed in a rainbow of fabrics with the patterns of the Goddess on their hands and faces.

Across the roaring of the Yuletide fire Beadhild was slumped on the Great Chair like a fallen queen. The quick movement of her breast was accompanied by a laboured breathing. Her eyes were closed and, as she was not yet crouching, it was clear that the time of real effort was still to come. Beadhild's sister, Frigyth, the wife of Edwin the woodwright, and another woman called Eormenhild, attended her to right and left, holding her hands in sympathy. They withdrew as Imma, nudged ever closer by Eanfled, reluctantly approached. Beadhild's gown was hitched so that she was able to spread her knees for a degree of comfort. She had kicked off her soft leather shoes and her splayed feet were the colour of dirty pastry. Her eyelids flickered as he touched her arm and then she winced as a huge wave came in and broke at the entrance to her womb. 'Ah my daughter's favourite,' she said weakly.

Imma glanced round at Eanfled. He was not sure Beadhild spoke either to him or about him.

'She said you would come. You are still small enough to wear around my neck. I would wear you as a necklace young Imma.' There was a pause and a grimace against another wave. Her hair was damp and the tints of the Goddess were smudged on her face. She took his hand and ran a boulder of pain over it. 'Put your arms around my neck,' she whispered; 'something wonderful is happening but the *blood* Mother Sheaving, the blood.' Her head dropped as if she had passed out. He had seen how she sat in it, how her dress was stained by it, how it dripped from the Chair of Honour, and how the women were entranced by it; they seemed not to know if it were witchcraft or sacrifice. It was like linking arms around a burning log. Her neck was slimy and the stench of her body was strong.

'I have seen you resist evil, Imma,' she whispered in his ear, 'I have seen it, the elves always shot at you, they tried often to kill you, but your grandmother would not let them, you would not let them, you fought them off, always you fought them off.' She frowned so hard it was as if she wished to crush ghosts of pain under the weight of her brows. 'I must get *up*,' she cried, releasing Imma's grip around her neck. Her sister and Eormenhild came to assist her. She was getting up from the Chair of Honour.

The faces of the assembled women were struck by wonder but the expression on Leda's face seemed to speak more of dread. The midwives helped Beadhild out of her green gown which was stained darkly in large patches. The dress was then draped onto the empty Chair and it looked as though an invisible Beadhild still sat there.

The women were now divided into those who continued to stare at the Chair and those who stared at the crouching Beadhild. The midwives held her hands. Imma stood to one side. He wanted to run away and hide. The women should not have brought him here; but then Beadhild looked up at him and a faint smile played across her cracked lips. She was a suffering lump, her soiled inner gown clinging to her waist, and yet her life shone out of her. It reached out to him from the desperate blue of her eyes. He wanted her to keep it in, to save it for herself. The baby seemed to tear from her and the sheepskin was soaked in bright poppies of blood. Frigyth wiped the labouring woman's face with a damp cool cloth. Beadhild was beckoning him to come near. 'Stand where I can see you Imma,' she gasped. He stood agitatedly in front of her, wincing in sympathy but he could never understand. The woman though appeared not to care about this. 'I nursed you Imma,' Beadhild said to him breathlessly; 'do you remember?'

He answered with a puzzled look.

'No of course you don't,' Beadhild moaned, 'what am I saying, I don't know what I'm saying, of course you wouldn't remember …'

Imma found it hard to concentrate on the words that came from her; they were hard to make out, like additional and mysterious sounds of pain.

'When your mother died, I nursed you for your grandmother, until you were able to take some mush and goat's milk, do you remember Imma?'

Why did she keep asking him if he remembered something he clearly would not be able to remember? The toiling woman was in a fever, not making any sense. He turned, as if to ask for an explanation, but the women around him were like living sculpture. Even in Leda's eyes and those of her sisters, Gelda and tiny Eady, there seemed less familiarity and more wonder, less dread and more worshipping fear. Only baby Alfred seemed to sense the realness of his mother for he now began to wail for her. Imma saw him handed to Leda who started to jog him up and down until he was happy.

There was a bellow from Beadhild like a hind brought down by a pack of wolves. The baby had crowned, another bellow, and an awful tearing and its head was dragged out by the pack. Then with a display of balance and strength that might have felled the Rune of Ing, Beadhild, keeping her spine as straight as a post, reached down and with bloody hands twisted the baby so that the shoulder came free. The child slithered in a wash of blood, slipped from her grasp, and beached with a soft plop on the sheepskin. There was a frozen moment during which the witnesses of this event stared as one at the messy object lying there. With a cry Beadhild picked up her baby, which was still anchored to her, and attempted to unwind the cord that had coiled itself like a snake around its neck.

The infant was an unnatural blue. Death had kissed the boy before he could even open his eyes to see a world; before he could, with little rowing fists and sky-treading feet, catch playfully at the sylphs of the air. Before he was even able to feel the warmth of his mother's breast he had been shipped back to a dark unknowingness. It was a poor blessing for Beadhild.

The midwives cut the rope that should have launched the child into his earthly life, tying it off initially with a thread of wool, and were now concerned for Beadhild who, passing out, had collapsed onto her back. There was concern because it did not seem to the midwives that the

72

anchor had come completely free. It seemed a portion of it remained deep inside. The midwives, with red fingers, cleared the way as best they could, and they had a drawing paste. They spoke a womanly charm over and over as they applied it. The paste needed strong magic and Imma was asked to join hands with them as they sang. He had heard it often. His grandmother sang over this paste whenever a woman needed to be cleared. It was the same charm, the same paste as when a baby came much too early, before it had properly formed itself, when it was expelled from the woman in a breakage of blood. Imma had seen one the size of a piglet's kidney, a pointless pebble of flesh cast over the sea by the gods. Who cast the pebble that it should be flung so uselessly into the world? A small sacrifice to the Goddess was usually enough to ensure a more lucky delivery. There was a problem, however, surrounding such a trouble, and the problem was that hags were drawn to the scent of this blood. They were envious of the living woman from whom it issued. The drawing paste had to be powerful if it was to deceive them long enough for a woman to be completely cleared and healthy once again.

The women now flocked all around, making Beadhild comfortable, holding her almost lifeless hand, patting her cheeks. A sour cider was brought and held to her nose. She came to long enough to whisper that she hated the smell of sour cider before her head sank back onto the pillow of blankets placed there. The women smiled and nodded and the vinegar was held to her nose again and this time brought her round.

'My baby?' she whispered in a parched tone and the dead child was brought and laid on her breast. She brought up a big fleshy palm to cradle its head. 'A boy,' she croaked, feeling a moment between his legs. 'He would have grown up to make some girl very happy.' She smiled, tears glistening along the lids of her eyes. 'Or miserable,' she added, and the women laughed with relief.

Leda gave Alfred to her and laid him alongside his brother at the other breast. The boisterous infant greedily found the nipple over the low cut of his mother's slip and began to feed, one of his small hands coming up to possessively cup the breast. 'There, take your brother's share,' Beadhild whispered, and then she asked for a drink of water which was immediately brought. After taking a sip with an exhausted and grateful expression she sank back onto the pile of blankets that propped her, gazing up at the smoke-filled rafters. For a while she floated there on sacred wisps that nosed about the thatch and looked down on the wounded woman who had survived and who lay there on a blood-soaked blanket and glanced fearfully at the raven on the roof beam and the dog curled in the corner regarding her with a yellow eye. There was an infant at each of her breasts, a big one yet alive and a tiny one dead, and which was the cause of greater suffering for the woman? For the one now dead was beyond the nightmares of this world and the one alive was vulnerable at any moment to them. If there were other nightmares the dead child went to then it was better not to think of them. Beadhild felt personally that the baby went to the arms of the Goddess and never woke up; for this was Beadhild's dream, an oblivious and peaceful sleep free from the endless pains that, like a hot wire, seared her everyday flesh, free from the petty difficulties that, like a dog licking out the marrow of a bone, gnawed endlessly on her; and as each separate night, sleep would come and release her from prison so death would come and free her for ever. But the Lady Earth forbid she be barren like that woman on the third hill. Nothing Mother Sheaving had done could induce a child to journey in her. The woman, whose name was Saethryth, harboured desert wastes of sea, fields of stony waves that resisted all broadcasting of her husband's seed. So it was that Beadhild got to thinking of her living children.

The midwives were shifting her hips, pulling the soaked skin from under her and changing it, and she felt a thick cloth pressed between her legs. She was aware vaguely of some chatter over whether they should move her now or later but she still floated in the rafters with the smoke. Leda was a good girl mostly, Leda helped her, and Gelda had learned the washing of clothes in the stream, and even poor Eady fetched in a few sticks of kindling, and how was she to do without Alfred who had the appetite to leave nothing but a flap of skin for her breast. She silently begged Lord Ing to make Alfred a proper man and this meant utterly different from his father. 'Leda,' she called weakly. 'Here mother,' she heard as if she was under water and her hand was taken. 'You are a good girl Leda,' she said, pressing the girl's hand with fingers that felt strangely weak; it was hard to squeeze her girl's hand but she felt the movement immediately and more strongly given back to her; 'in four winters you will be a suitable woman and I know you wish to marry the *Spell* of Mother Sheaving.' 'Mother!' she heard and there was reproach and insistence in the voice. 'You are like the Sun Goddess, Leda, I cannot imagine how you are mine.' 'Hush mother, hush,' she heard again as if she had been ducked in the river. 'You must rest.' But Beadhild, for some reason, wanted to persist, digging for words that seemed hidden from her like clams under a beach, and each time she unearthed one from its bed of sand, she found that it could be cracked open and the pulp eaten for its meaning. 'I will help you Leda,' she began, saying each word carefully, not so much that her daughter might understand but to catch the sense of it herself and intending to go on with what she wanted to say. At the same time, however, she was lifted up and borne away. She felt soft wool enfold her as her legs came together and her shoulders were hunched, her babies had gone and her daughter's hand slipped from her. In a dream she passed from light into dark, from warmth into cold, and it seemed that the night sky came into her head and sang to her.

Chapter
13

The unwholesome stench from Beadhild had drenched the air and soaked like a stagnant fog into the beams and timbers of the house. Kindled juniper had been powerless against it. The truth was simply this: three hags had come stumbling but quickly over the meadow, freed by the *dead-time*, by the sleepwalking earth, by the newly born but as yet still feeble Lord Ing, and they had come stumbling in the darkness through the withies and up the hill to Beadhild's house. It was true the door had been flung open and Imma had seen nothing except a chasm of black and heard nothing except for the wind in the trees and it was precisely then that he had fallen, tripped and pushed by the hags, and both Leda and Frigyth had helped him to his feet and shut the door but too late. The hags had then laid ugly hands on Beadhild. The ragged piece that abided in her was changed to a fetid evil. Three there had been and three was the usual number. Witnesses came forward to suggest they had seen the fearful shapes hurrying down the hill, because dark as the night had been, devoid of stars or any of the Mothers of Light, the shapes had been darker still against the shadow of the snow-covered hill.

Folk were busy after the building of the need fires. Too eager the men had been to finish the sacrifice and get to the ale. This was what the women suggested. Lord Ing had not returned to them. The boar skin was a useless flapping rag on the stake; it had not graced the shoulders of Lord Ing. The women had finished their singing too soon, distracted from the Great Mother by the onset of Beadhild's labour and they had mistaken the sign of it. This much was obvious the men grumbled. The unfortunate baby was a sign. Now look what had happened: Beadhild dead and hags seen about the village. Nightmares hungering for flesh frightened people but with oaken spines the villagers set to doing what they could. Fire was life and the feast this year was ended by intense and necessary work.

The wood stores were almost emptied and men sent to the coppice to cut and fetch more. The cutting of it was hard and the ringing ran up the bones of a man's arm until he warmed himself into it, standing knee-deep in the snow and swinging the axe under a motionless sky.

Livestock gave up some feed as tinder and a grey day blazed with the fuel of Beadhild's body. The dead child too was food for the fire. The tears had scalded Leda's eyes, leaving them raw and bloodshot, and had Imma ever quite believed what folk said of him that he was a spell against the evil that had hacked the life out of his family he now began to feel that it was he who was the casting stone from whom disaster rippled. Death was a villager, it sat down to supper, but Imma felt leaden that it always took the hand of those close to him and refused his own. What if it were to take Leda from him? Her father had been too drunk to help with the pyre. What would become of her? He picked up a branch which had fallen among the bracken and it came apart in his hands, entirely rotten within, and this was what his feeling was like, a useless powdery rottenness which blew away on the wind.

There was something else: an uneasy sense that he had done something that was now being paid for. The law of justice, the inner sense a body had of this justice said that a wrong done must be repaid in some way. It was a reality which like the snake had its tail in its mouth. He had been present at the saving of Queen Ealhhild and at the favoured birth of baby Alfred. Whatever luck had sat inside him was now padding among the stars with his grandmother. Why had his grandmother ruffled his hair when silly folk said untrue things about him? His grandmother should have told him he was no *spell*. He exposed the scabbing of his arm. He felt a tiny trickle of pride in seeing the scar. The new skin on his leg was the colour of boiled ham. Sometimes he imagined and truly seemed to feel again the bite of the mad boar. It happened now and he checked carefully to see whether the wound was not still alive.

When the next day the village gathered on the field of ancestors, Leda insisted on digging the hole for the urn, but eventually she agreed, because of the tough ground, to help from Imma and her great uncle, Aldwulf. The diggers sweated in their thick clothes and Imma's throat hurt with the continual rasp of cold air. The remains of the pyre had the likeness of a pupil in a white and lifeless eye. Imma crumbled a small piece of charring which left a black smudge on his fingers. The pyre smelled not much different from a dead firebox. Kneeling at the side of the ashes Leda, seemingly in a trance, began shifting and rearranging the shards of bone as if she would complete a puzzle of her mother's head. 'Come girl,' Aldwulf said tenderly, 'have you your mother's precious things?'

Leda nodded and gathered up the ashes and fragments. The clay dun-coloured urn was spelt around with runes in a repeating spiral and, although a bit lop-sided, was a decorous work which had sat in a corner of Beadhild's house. Leda used some snow to wash the ashes from her hands and let the drops fall into the urn like an offering. She unstrung four beads from her own necklace, dropped one into the mystery that this homely pot now roomed, and gave one each to her younger sisters, motioning that they do likewise.

Leda's Aunt Frigyth, who had taken responsibility for Alfred, attempted to coax the baby into dropping the remaining bead into the urn as his sisters had done. Firstly he tried to put the bead into his mouth but his aunt was ready for that; secondly she found she was unable to shake the bead from his grasp as she held his tiny arm over the mouth of the urn; thirdly, Alfred, with small regard for ceremony, flung the bead away from him into the snow. Leda laughed and rescuing the bead put it to her brother's palm and dropped it in on his behalf. Glancing over her shoulder she saw her father coming. Before he reached her, he crumpled in the snow, and to the amazement of his daughter, let out a wail such that it was like a great rock splitting under the hammer of a storm god. 'The feeling is for show,' the girl thought bitterly, 'it is only for himself.' All the same there was an uncanny timbre to it that made her go to him and take his arm. Yule was a time of chill silhouettes and dark shadows and so after the urn was buried, sprigs of holly were tossed onto the deathly patch, for colour and for hope, each neighbour in turn paying a last respect.

'My poor Beadhild,' Urswine said over and over until it became a source of irritation to his eldest daughter. 'My poor Beadhild.'

Leda took the hands of her sisters and turned away. The village began stepping over the fields, putting distance between themselves and the ancestors, picking up again the tools of this world. Leda looked back and saw something at once she half expected to see and yet would never have imagined to see, which was the sight of her father, still bowed in the snow by the pyre, seemingly broken for love of her mother.

That same day a hare had been seen loping over the meadow and it had been seen by the men going to the coppicing at the edge of the Motherwood. The hare was large, about the length of a one-year-old child, and its ears had been very noticeable standing out as black as charring compared to the tan of its rump. Edwin had thrown a stone at it and the hare had bounded away over the snow. The men talked about maybe setting a snare but then to their clear astonishment the hare loped back and even approached the edge of the coppice. Its whiskers were straight and taut as lyre gut and its eyes, so Edwin later recounted, were a ghoulish yellow gashed only by darkness. These eyes like septic boils were enough to freeze the sweat on a woodman's brow. Wulf ran at the animal swinging his axe and was almost on it when some hidden root or clump under the snow had caught at his foot and tripped him. The falling axe bit deeply into the youth's shin as he tumbled and it was a wonder it had not felled the bone of his leg. The hare was away with long and powerful stretches and the men running to Wulf's aid swore it had disappeared into thin air. It was evident that Wulf had contended with witchcraft.

Saethryth, a Saxon widow who lived on the third hill, was at her darning when she heard the noisy fuss outside her door. She was an exhausted woman whose ribs had begun to show but her long thick hair was dark as a rich soil and it shined dully still the way a fallen light plays on the skin of gathered horse chestnuts and her wide accepting eyes were those of a startled deer. The firebox was warm and bright and she was enjoying the cosiness of her house. How small she felt when she would look from her window toward the cold vaults of heaven and, closing the shutter against them, return gratefully to her evening chores. That afternoon had been grey and brisk and she was happy to be at her patches, threading the wool yarn with a bone needle through the skirt of her favourite dress. The dress, of a homely natural ash, except where it was patched with various colours, was like an old friend to the widow. She had been married in it, dressing it up with bright bands of colour around her girdle, but she had not thrown it in a dusty trunk after the ritual, as many a woman might, either to keep it safe as a treasure or perhaps in an attempt to forget what it represented, but ever practical had worn it whenever she felt like as a token toward the working part of a marriage.

Her family had set out from the shores of the great river at Lundenwic and left behind the small trading port which was situated up river of the old Roman town. These giant stone walls loomed through the morning fog of her happy childhood. Her father, a tanner by trade, sick of plunging his aching hands in the bark-steeped troughs, had one timeless drowsy summer paid heed to the spirit of adventure that resided in his breast, and lit out with his small family to the outer reaches of Sabert's kingdom. He sailed a tiny skiff which had been crafted with his own hands. He exchanged tips from the boat builders at Lundenwic for modest leather gifts such as an amulet bag of kid yellow that would serve a craftsman's wife well and be a pretty adornment for her belt. That summer, with its scent of river thatch and mud, and the feeling when the dawn wind woke them to a brackish light, had made a groundswell in the widow. It provided energy under her keel and sailed her through the difficulties of her life.

The family had eventually followed a ribbon of river into Angle lands. They built a farmstead on a foundation of lonely but workable soil about a half-day's walk from the hall of a warrior earl who accepted a small leather token as a sign of good faith for the land and a promise of skilled labour for full payment in time. The earl, whose name was Angletheow, had impressed Saethryth's father with his fearless bearing and fair dealing and in turn this earl had himself been impressed by the adventurous soul of the tradesman who had wanted to feel a sense of home again in non-Christian lands. Much good farming acreage remained uncared for; a man of determination was to be encouraged when he requested to plough a piece of it. The Saxon man whose family had lived by the river with the foreign name of Thames for at least three generations thus found himself settled in the locality of Wulfingstow. It was a common enough occurrence. One day when he came up to the village to see if his knowledge of tanning might serve him as a trade for a few sheep he took his daughter Saethryth with him. He had not intended it but that day had proved not that his skills were worthless but that his daughter of eighteen summers was the more valuable to a certain Ricbert of the family on the third hill.

It was the time of Lord Ing's courting of the earth. The middle of the month of Milkings. What better time to exchange a daughter for a few fine sheep? The sheep had returned with her father to a hag-free life by that ribbon of river where they grew fat and woolly on the sweet grass that was rich enough for cattle cudding. And that was how Saethryth the widow came to be in her house when folk came crying up the hill to lay hands on her and accuse her of witchcraft.

Some of the Angle kin did not like this Saxon girl. Saethryth did not

80

help matters, for she was different in her manner and in her speech, and further had a whimsical listlessness that could be misinterpreted, especially by those keen to misinterpret, for a charmed soul. Saethryth was clearly different but the most important reason for her difference was not that she was Saxon but that she was different. Her mind led her into magical modes of thinking. Her husband put it down to the quest she had undertaken with her family when she was seventeen summers old. In some way, Ricbert had reasoned, his wife had undertaken two journeys and the accompanying one had been into the enchanted land that formed the fields and hills of her mind. It was peculiar because Ricbert tasted only butter from the shallow bowl of Saethryth's hips but certain villagers hinted that she had enticed him with what was in truth rancid. She had an obvious hunger for the strong body of her husband but this appetite never beckoned a child to set out across the sea of her womb. It was unnatural how she continued to enjoy her husband but was forever barren.

Sometimes the law meet found the many-headed complications of a quarrel led back to a single cause or more than likely to a single person. Such an inquiry might have found the undermining of Saethryth to have sprung from a well of jealousy that was sunk deep in the emotional soil of Ricbert's second cousin, Eormenhild. Who was this Saxon slut who had come and bewitched the object of her unreturned desire? But Eormenhild was dissembling and made much play of welcoming Saethryth to the village. It was easy to blow on the embers of prejudice by drawing attention to Saethryth's disarming differences; to notice in a gossipy weaving house, how the Saxon girl would pronounce certain words strangely and to mention how endearing it was, or to suggest that how Saethryth would pin her hair, was something quite remarkable.

Saethryth, one summer, in her wistful way, had been carried along on her own path, and been discovered in a drowsy glade, enjoying the sun like a forbidden lover. So lustful had the shifting of her hips seemed that Edwin had been compelled to step from behind the tree that hid him and cast a cape of shadow over her. Tiny flies were dipping in the shafts of sun between the elder trees. The sweat of her was as sticky as honey. When he awoke from an almost hemlock sleep Saethryth had gone.

He found her sitting on a low stool outside her door plaiting the hair of her niece by marriage. She nodded to him and asked him in a friendly way, as the wife of a good neighbour might, what brought him to her door, across the way from the headman's hill. It was clear to Edwin, through the fug of his mind, that an elf-girl had taken the shape of Saethryth to trap him. The elf-witch had known that he, Edwin, lusted after the Saxon girl, that he had lost interest in his wife, and thought her plain in the same drab clothes. Saethryth continued to talk naturally to him as if nothing had happened, except for a hint of something in her eyes that belied her. But he could not be sure of it. She was playing him like a fool. This fallow girl had taken his seed; he felt she had stolen it. And then a pulsing again at his temple, like a swollen stream under the skin, and then the blood breaking over and into his face.

'Were you in the farther wood today Saethryth?'

The girl shook her head. 'Why?' she asked.

'Are you sure you were not in the farther wood today Saethryth?' Edwin repeated. His head felt like a bladder full of ale. His mind was swinging in the sun. 'It's mighty hot today Saethryth,' he gasped, putting his hands to his face a moment. 'Is it not mighty hot?'

'It is Cousin Edwin,' the girl replied. 'Hot enough to bake bread.' She continued to plait little Etheldritha's hair. The child regarded Edwin inquisitively and then hesitantly asked him if he might make her a small sheep as a toy.

'Wouldn't you like a horse, or a wild bear maybe?' Edwin answered, laughing, and looking at Saethryth with smiling eyes. It had been an elf or a dream or both. Yet he felt he knew this young woman's body intimately as she moved inside her loose shift; but did he truly *know* it, or was it only his imagining? For he had often imagined her naked.

'I like sheep Uncle Edwin,' tiny Etheldritha said. 'And I would like one of wood.'

'Uncle Edwin is too busy to carve you a silly sheep,' Saethryth told her niece.

'Of course I will carve her one.' Edwin smiled. 'Is it to be a ram with horns Etheldritha?'

'It doesn't have to have no horns,' the child answered, 'but it must be a sheep.'

The adults laughed at the singularity of the child.

'I like sheep,' Etheldritha said again, seemingly uncertain as to whether the grown-ups had fully understood her request.

'A sheep it is, little Etheldritha, a sheep it is.' Edwin nodded.

Saethryth stood up and gazing down the hill shielded her eyes from the sun. 'Here comes Ricbert from the field now.'

Edwin turned to look.

'He will be thirsty,' Saethryth said. 'We have a jug of cool water under the boards, with a cap of flax to keep off the bugs.' She smiled, for some reason rubbing her hands against her hips. 'Would you like some Cousin Edwin?'

'I think you have saved my life.' Edwin sighed and soon enough he felt the slap of Ricbert's hand on his shoulder. 'I saw you duck away on some fool's errand,' Ricbert said to him. 'Where did you go?'

'Over to the coppicing,' Edwin lied, looking at Saethryth, whose conscience seemed as clear as if they had only arm-wrestled. 'I am to carve Etheldritha a sheep.'

The shuttered house was hot, dark, and unmanageable. In the morning it kept cool like a cave but over the course of the day the sun had baked steadily into the thatch and now the air inside was stifling.

'This must be what breathing is like for a dragon,' Ricbert said, laughing; 'for love of Lady Earth, Saethryth, let in some air would you?'

'What air?' his wife challenged. 'You mean the smith's bellows outside?'

Ricbert grinned. 'Just fetch the water, wife,' he said.

'I'll fetch it over your head,' Saethryth answered.

'Fetch the water, wench, and be quick about it,' her husband said jocularly. 'I am after all,' he said nodding at Edwin, 'the man of the house.'

And then Saethryth said something she did not probably mean, to the effect that if he were such a man how was it that her womb remained as empty as a firkin after Yule.

'What about your cup of water?' Saethryth yelled to Edwin from the door.

The truth was elusive as a wisp among the willow bones. Saethryth with a handful of lighted hay span him around the trees until he was dizzy and he fell heavily to his knees. The stream that fed through the wood was sluggish but cool in the late dead summer afternoon and buzzed with the mysterious courtships of the dragons and damsels which skimmed this way and that across the water. A gnat whined in his ear and he brushed it away only for another to return as a continual annoyance so that he became like the horses in the scorching paddock whipping up their tails against the flies that plagued them. Several living specks were struggling in the sweat of his body and Edwin, throwing off his shirt, plunged into the stream and lay face down like a drunk drowned in waist-high water.

It hardly seemed possible but not long after this, moon by moon, the belly of Ricbert's wife grew fatter. The couple made pilgrimage to a glade in the Motherwood to give thanks. Edwin had made them a fine plaited basket for the flowers and plenty. It was almost harvest and people trembled with gratitude. It was a bounteous month of golden days and hallowed rainfall. It was the month of maternity for the earth herself. It was the month when noble or commoner would stoop to kiss the very clay.

The boy was a shaving of his mother and had been but seven days on the nipple when he fell ill. The coughs were severe, like little rib snaps, and the baby drew breath with a sound like Edwin's lathe when he was turning out a bowl of oak. In the night the rattling in the baby's chest struck against the starlight and the villagers came out of doors to listen and shake their heads. Saethryth struggled to comfort the infant and her breasts became sore as she did endless battle to give him nourishment. She cursed the elf that shot at her child. She broke her head against the wooden wall. Ricbert sat on the step of the house with his head in his hands. The salve that Ricbert's mother, who had some knowledge of the lore, had rubbed into the infant's chest had been as useless as cuckoo spit. It was a time shortly before Mother Sheaving had come to the village. Ricbert himself seemed a milksop in the face of illness. He picked up a handful of soil and ground it through his fingers. He stared uselessly into the dark. He stood up and, grabbing a mattock which leant against the woodpile at his elbow, went forward into the night swinging it against the elves that plainly he saw.

All through the falling and sacrifice Edwin had ached for her. Pent up in the wood shop under a dying sun he had looked across the hill and been arrested by the twists of smoke rising from the thatch of her house. Now, in the still short days after Yule he felt forced to go to her. The Yuletide that year was black and sodden and the well-trodden paths of the settlement had turned as boggy as any river flat. The pigs had made a muddy bath of their fenced woodland patch and seemingly rolled and rooted with abandon. Edwin dropped a platter he was working on and told his son Wulf he had something to attend to and would soon return. Setting out for Saethryth's house he took a circular route around the outer fencing as a press of cloud squeezed a fine spray of rain and by the time he arrived at her door his woollen cloak was wet through and he was muddy to the shins. It was no surprise that Ricbert was absent for Edwin knew him to be lending a hand with the mending of a roof over on the far side of the hill. It was unfit weather for roof fixing but at the same time the weather made the fixing all the more urgent. At that lost afternoon time all the doors and shutters near to Saethryth's house were closed as tight as clams. The door was unlatched and when Saethryth glanced up from where she was kneeling by a clothes box under the window it was the elf-girl who looked at him.

That had been a long time ago. Her child was dead and she had miscarried another. Soon after, Ricbert had fallen badly from the roof of the house. He had been thatching. It was not far to fall and Ricbert was a strong man but he had hit his head on a tree stump. It was the same stump that Saethryth had often nagged him about. The distraught woman had attacked it with an axe and not much later the men of the village dug it out together and burned it. Saethryth started at the furious rapping and the hairs stood straight as pins on the nape of her neck. Yet she had no idea what the noise outside was for. She could pick out few words except shouts of 'hare' and 'come out' and 'elf-witch' among various curses. The dress fell limply in her lap as the widow gripped the arms of her chair. She scanned the room with platter-wide eyes, like a fearful child, looking for some place to hide. But her modest house was not a palace.

The door crashed on its rotting hinges and her neighbours, who had clearly shifted their shape from family to a monster with many heads, seized her roughly, tearing her out of the chair and throwing her outside to where the rest with guttering torches were waiting. The neck of her gown was ripped and her hair pulled so murderously that Eormenhild was left with a handful between her fingers. With a shout she dropped the curls and Urswine killed them with a flame. A faintly sweet smell of burning hair arose. As Saethryth fell to the ground she caught sight of Edwin's face, which seemed knotted by some unnameable suffering. She hardly believed it was he who kicked her so hard that her ribs felt as though they had collapsed against her backbone. All breath and hope were driven from her. She was pulled to her feet by Urswine and by Edwin who squeezed her upper arm as though he would crush the bone to powder. There was then a flurry of heated accusations that the widow tried her best to make sense of and answer.

'You put a curse on Beadhild and the child,' Eormenhild jeered. 'You hexed her in her work. We all saw it.'

'The only thing that grows in your womb is jealousy!' another added. Saethryth looked up at the woman who had said this and saw it was Beadhild's sister. The widow licked at a trickle of blood she felt at the corner of her mouth. 'I'm sorry for your loss sister,' she said pathetically, 'but I ...'

'You called those hag-shrieks to kill her!' Frigyth cried. 'Look away from me, look away or I will put out your eyes.'

Saethryth dropped her head and looked only at her feet. She turned her head slightly sideways. 'Edwin,' she whispered, 'you have known me.' The grip on her arm tightened until it was an agony. She knew the power in Edwin's grip. She had felt it once before around her neck like a hanging. There was spittle on his beard as though he were some mad dog. 'You are an elf-witch,' he hissed, 'I see you by the coppice in the shape of a hare this dying afternoon same time as Eormenhild says you were nowhere to be seen among the women. Admit it. Admit you were the hare. Admit you put a spell on the axe that bit my son.'

'I was at my mending all afternoon,' Saethryth answered. 'I was at my mending *all afternoon*,' she repeated helplessly.

'Let go of her!' a commanding voice shouted gruffly from the back. 'Give way and let me pass.' Aldwulf shoved aggressively through the throng. 'Let a man be an owl rather than a crow!' he shouted, looking directly at Edwin, who yet refused to release the woman. Aldwulf tapped the cudgel he was carrying against the carpenter's thigh. 'Tell me Edwin,' he inquired, 'have you ever seen the marrow that leaks from a cracked skull?'

Saethryth sank to her knees and her head hung low; but still Edwin held on to her arm.

'Beware her eyes uncle,' Frigyth warned, 'they are a dragon's eyes.'

'I see a frightened woman's eyes,' Aldwulf said. 'Have you been at magic, woman?'

Saethryth shook her head. 'I have not,' she said, almost beyond hearing.

'Speak up,' Aldwulf demanded.

Saethryth cleared her throat. 'I have not uncle,' she replied, a little louder.

There was immediate protest from the gathering and Aldwulf was supplied with many details of her magic. He asked what the search of her house had produced.

'She is a sorceress,' insisted Edwin, 'she does not need herbs or the making of a potion ... she does not need nails or the doll of a woman to kill her; darkness does her bidding.'

There was general agreement about this. 'Tell him Edwin,' a man's voice said. It belonged to the bereaved husband. 'I say fire her now and be done with it!' Urswine shouted. 'Aye fire her now!' The cry was severally repeated.

'No,' Aldwulf stated, 'she must have her right. She must have her *right*,' he bellowed, shaking the cudgel in his grip with the force of his charisma; however the force plainly spent itself against the unforgiving wall of fear. A strongly smelling torch announced the verdict of the majority; an unmistakable scent of elder like a piercing through the nose. A hawthorn wreath was brought and forced spitefully onto the widow's head.

They were pushing the widow down the hill toward the bonfires. The air was damp and chill and the snow everywhere was like a pegged-out ghost. But they did not burn Saethryth alive. A rope was brought and she was strung up over a grim branch of oak that was not a part of the Motherwood. It was the weight of Edwin that formed the major counter to her swinging. She was not like the silent dolls they had burnt because she whimpered and pleaded for her life and then there was screaming like a terrified hare before its neck is snapped.

'Let her be, let her be!' Imma yelled suddenly, beside himself, managing to pull himself free from the grip of Sigbert who had been holding him with a fiendish delight. 'Don't you see it was me? It was *me* who made it happen. I upset the Goddess. I upset the Goddess when I went to her island. It was me. *Leda*, your mother is dead because of *me*,' he cried, sobbing at the same time and looking hopelessly at the astonished girl.

A hush came down over the hanging and there was only the eerie sound of the creaking branch and the desperate kicking of the widow and then a muffled thud as her body crumpled into the snow. The woman coughed and heaved as if she had been rescued from drowning and put her hands defensively to her throat. There was a large red wheal where the hemp had strangled her. The hawthorn had gouged deep. She gasped as bleeding she pulled it from her. A cold wind blew across the open ground. Sheepishly, people called for Aldwulf to be brought. His staff had been knocked from his hand in the frenzy and his eldest daughter smacked to the ground. The headman would know what to do, the people muttered and nodded.

The scent of elder was still strong as Aldwulf was allowed to speak:

'I am thankful the Lady has put the sense of love back into you!' he thundered. 'Love also is an instinct, why trust it less than fear?'

His staff was given to him and the rod of authority once more in his grasp was like a mending.

'Now young puck explain to us the meaning of this?'

And the same cold wind, the same damp chillness, rustled through the oak they stood beneath.

'Let us leave this place,' Aldwulf said finally.

The light made the crowded hall cheery. The stench of tallow smoke was so strong it was like swimming through mutton soup but in no part of the room was darkness allowed to remain unchallenged. Large shadows shrunk back against the hefty planks and pressed themselves blackly into the roof space. The inhabitants had gathered and things which only a short time before, in the largeness of the looming night, had made sense, were cast, by the indoor firelight, as shameful. A kind of madness had overtaken them; but even the madness may have been bad witchcraft, as several were now suggesting it was.

Imma was seated on a stool at one end of the room and between him and the rest of the attending villagers sat Aldwulf, Ricbert the Elder, who only a candle before had been calling for the burning of his daughter-in-law, and a woman of numberless years called Eost, who was called on to fill the space left by Mother Sheaving but who lacked her gifts and who, folk said, had both the nose and irritability of a Motherwood shrew. Despite her lack of deeper wisdom she displayed a natural canniness which was the result of her intelligence and long experience.

'What was the hope of your insolence boy?' Eost inquired.

Imma shifted uncomfortably. His shoes made a restless scraping on the wooden floor.

'Look at us boy, not at your feet,' Eost demanded.

Imma glanced up but catching sight of Leda his eyes once more fell to the floor.

'What is in that mind of yours boy?' Eost asked him. 'I know you have a brain for how could the Spell of Mother Sheaving not have one?'

'Mother Eost, with respect,' Imma cried, raising his face with a glint of defiance, 'I have passed through this Yule and have the marks to prove it.'

'Such tomfoolery,' answered the old woman.

'I think we are drifting,' Ricbert the Elder then said; 'the point is *why* did you go to the sacred island and what did you hope to gain by doing it?'

He was a tall man, of winters only three or four younger than Aldwulf, and his height, being in the body, made him appear, seated as he was, extremely imposing. Unlike the majority of men who wore their hair to the shoulder or jawline, some still, even as age made it fall from the crown, Ricbert the Elder favoured a shaving close to the head and took considerable pains over it. Time more profitably spent sharpening sickles, axes, and chisels was spent sharpening the shaving knife he used, stropping its elfin blade over whetstone and leather, so that it should be up to the task. He spent more afternoons over it, people said, than Mother Sheaving did over her leech knife. His daughter, Athelthryth, married with children and brimful of chores, was much taxed over the matter of her father's head. At each nick she would be bawled out and it was a wonder she hadn't shaved off his nose. Athelthryth suggested his childless daughter-in-law Saethryth might perform the task but Ricbert the Elder refused. 'I'm not having that witch cut me up,' he had stated flatly. He was therefore a strange inquisitor.

'I was frightened for my grandmother,' Imma answered. 'I would have done anything.'

'Even to spitting in the face of your doe-eyed Mother,' Ricbert suggested, nodding vigorously. The veins were crawling like knotted worms under the skin of his head.

'I never knew my mother.'

Ricbert passed his hand over his head as if to flatten his non-existent hair. 'I mean our Mother the Earth!' he flashed. He had the brows but not the beak of a bald sparrowhawk and he continued to nod so excitedly that it seemed he might throw down in a fit.

'I want a human mother,' Imma answered, 'what use is the earth to me?'

'Imma!' Eanfled gasped, for it appeared she could not help herself. Several of the women had put their hands over their mouths and there were a couple of cries from the men at the back.

'She feeds us all Imma,' scolded Aldwulf, 'as well you know; she may decide this rising not to; what do you think of that?'

Imma shrugged and looked down. There was a beetle crawling across the boards under his feet but then it fell sideways through a crack. A moment later it reappeared with its little horns waving and its front legs scrabbling to hold on to the edge.

Aldwulf frowned. 'What would your grandma have said to hear you say that?'

'She would have put my head in the soup.'

'There are folk calling for you to be disowned or worse.'

'I know it. They hate me. They have always hated me. Just like they hated grandmother.'

'They *respected* your grandmother.'

'They were *frightened* of grandmother.'

Aldwulf shook his white and shaggy head. The great shovels of his hands rested on his knees. There was a pause as Eanfled stepped up and tossed a bundle of faggots onto the fire. Once again the scent of elder seemed a comfort to the closer family huddled there. There was a cry from the back that the boy should be sent out of the village. Aldwulf raised his eyebrows. Imma noticed the bristle-like hairs that curled out of Aldwulf's big broad nose. They were white but not the same white as the honourable hair of his head.

'When I was in the shrine a boar was sent to kill me,' Imma began grimly. At the same time he pulled up the leg of his trouser to remind them of the scar. 'All I wanted was for her to save my grandmother and she sent a boar to kill me.'

The showing of the scar had generally widened eyes. Aldwulf merely nodded, Ricbert the Elder passed his hand for the hundredth time over his scalp, and Mother Eost stared Imma down with twinkling eyes which were like a pecking blackbird's. 'You are still angry at the Goddess,' she noted; 'I think maybe her boar is following you still. What do you think of that?'

'Why didn't she help me?' Imma cried. 'All I wanted was for her to help me.'

'You are feuding with the Goddess,' Eost observed, for some reason fiddling with something on her belt, 'how can it not bring bad luck?'

'The only person I had in the world and she let it happen,' Imma said bitterly.

'This is pitiable,' Ricbert the Elder put in, 'the boy must make peace with the Goddess or it will be the worse for all of us.'

'Imma you must go back to the shrine and make an offering,' Aldwulf decided; 'the women will help you prepare the right thing.'

'My *mother* died because of your feud,' Leda burst out. 'You think only of yourself. I hate you Imma, I hate you.' At this she turned and forced her way out of the room. The remaining villagers closed behind her like the sea behind a ploughing ship.

Imma looked shamefully at the floor. The beetle was still clinging to the edge but all at once it lost its footing and slipped through the crack, gone into the darkness under the house.

'Am I to blame, uncle, for all this madness?' A stone was pressing in the pit of his stomach.

'If you push someone and they split their head are you to blame?' said Ricbert the Elder.

'It cannot be murder,' Imma said uncertainly, 'I did not mean to kill her. Why would I? She nursed me when I was a baby she told me, she told me,' the boy cried desperately. He collapsed in a heap of sobs. He felt the heavy weight of his uncle's hand on his shoulder. It was like the weight of the world. 'Nobody is blaming you for the death of Beadhild,' the familiar voice said soothingly, 'for how can we know for certain? How can any of us know?' Aldwulf shouted, and for a moment it was apparent to those listening that he was talking generally, almost to the stars above, rather than about particular events.

'What the boy has done can hardly have helped matters,' Ricbert said sarcastically.

'No,' Aldwulf agreed sadly, 'no, this much we are as one on.'

There was an uncomfortable silence, punctuated only by the shuffling of feet, a couple of embarrassed coughs, and then another shout, this time from outside the humble meeting hall, for the witch's bastard to be tied into a sack and thrown in the river.

'You must make it *right* Imma,' Aldwulf said emphatically, 'and we will think on your punishment; by rights you should have a grown-up punishment.'

'It is an odd trespass,' Eost remarked with a shrug, 'there is no older example and,' she added derisively, 'blood marks do not make a man as is plain; he is a silly irresponsible boy.'

Ricbert the elder raised a hawkish eyebrow but said nothing.

'The boy must make offering to the Goddess, as Aldwulf has already suggested,' Eost concluded, 'his own luck has deserted him that is certain and it might be bad for us this rising. Poor Beadhild, after labour, on the Mothers' night, well …' Eost put her palm to her cheek. 'It is an unknowable thing and unlikely to be bad witchcraft, as I keep saying and *kept* saying.' At this she raised her voice addressing the gathering behind her: 'Much notice they took, and the way some family acted, that was more like evil spelling.' She shook her head, looking at Aldwulf. Ricbert cleared his throat rather obviously and there was some general muttering at the back. Then the sound of a few people leaving.

'Think Imma,' Aldwulf said to him, 'whatever Mother Eost may say, you were man enough to prevent something terrible.'

The boy looked up with tearstained eyes. He wiped his nose on the back of his hand.

Eost was nodding. 'I do not have a problem with that,' she said.

'What of our neighbour, Saethryth?' Aldwulf enquired. 'You saw her home, Eanfled?'

'Yes, father,' Eanfled replied, 'understandably she is shaken and her door will need mending. She wished to be left alone.'

'We shall go see her in the morning and set things straight,' Aldwulf declared.

Ricbert the Elder stood up. 'I need a drink,' he said, making to leave, and this was the signal for the hall to empty, with some of the men heading across to the other hall and the women mostly back to the houses. The night was filled with the chatter of confused human beings. Only Mother Eost and Imma's adoptive family were left.

'I will make it right with the Lady Earth,' Imma assured them, 'I will make it right.'

'You must not violate her shrine,' Eanfled warned. 'Let the river take your gift.'

Chapter
14

Frida always snored in the exact same way. It identified her as surely as any birthmark. The air was drawn in like a comb scraped over the edge of a table; then a rapid exhalation like somebody fat had stepped on a bladder of air. Imma lay awake listening to it. His mind raced and the same cold stone was in his belly and his heart from time to time fluttered like a frightened sparrow. It was not yet light when he sat bolt upright on the makeshift pallet that was his bed and stared with rapidly accustoming eyes around the room.

He had not heard his uncle come in but he recognised the hills of his body under the blankets. Icicles might have formed on the bed frames but some heat in Imma was strong; he did not even shiver as he disentangled himself from the twist of blankets and furs which cocooned him. He already had on his tunic and leggings, thick woollen socks too. For a body could hardly sleep naked at Yule. Everybody went to bed dressed, some of the old folk even winding scarves of wool around heads, hands, and feet which ached with the cold. A few would keep a low fire, which invariably went out, or they would lie awake worrying that should a sprite come whistling through a gap in the timber the unwatched child might crawl from his box and set light to a blanket. Imma wanted to set off before the village woke up: the last thing he needed was a gormless audience for his making amends. As quietly as possible he made ready to leave. Into a woollen bag he put certain essentials for survival: a fire steel and flint, a good stash of dry kindling, a small sack of roasted barley, and a number of strips of dried mutton. He let the lid of the food trunk fall back and cringed at the noise. Sure enough it woke Eanfled. The rest of the family would have carried on sleeping had they been tossed onto a fire.

'*Imma,*' she hissed. '*Imma,* what are you *doing?*'

He stepped across the room and kissed her on the cheek. 'I want to leave now,' he whispered. 'I have to leave now.'

'Wait until it is properly light.'

'No I have to leave now, you don't understand,'

'What don't I understand?'

'That I have to leave now.'

She sighed. 'You are a silly boy,' she said, as he rested his head on her bosom, which rose and fell under the furs, setting him adrift on a gentle sea. The sparrow of his heart alighted and the cold stone in his belly dissolved, and for a few moments he was free. She was gently twining his hair through her fingers.

'You should get married, Cousin Eanfled,' Imma said in a loud whisper. An owl hooted, so close by it might have been sitting on the bedpost.

'Thanks for your advice but I think I have enough to do.'

'I mean it,' the boy insisted. 'You are too beautiful not to be married.'

His cousin did not answer and simply carried on twining his hair; then she stopped and let her hand rest on his head. There was a loud sigh and then she sat up tipping him out of his boat. He thought he saw her wipe her eyes on a corner of the blanket and then somehow the stone had formed itself again. He never seemed to say or do the right thing. He looked away in anguish. She took his hand. 'You have not upset me Imma,' she assured him. 'It was a lovely thing to say, but you must understand folk do not see the world as you do, they do not see it through your eyes, do you understand?'

'Not really.' The boy shrugged. 'Surely if I see a tree, folk see a tree?'

'*That,*' Eanfled whispered, 'is exactly where you are *mistaken.*'

He did not understand but she seemed happy again and that was enough for him.

'Anyway, young man,' his cousin remarked in an undertone, 'why should not a plain woman be married, does she not deserve the same chance of happiness?'

'I suppose so,' Imma agreed, 'but I suppose it depends on *how* plain she is.'

'*Imma,*' Eanfled hissed. 'It's good to know you are not *so* different after all.'

They wrapped the offering in a light blanket. Eanfled and her sisters had prepared the basket and it smelled of what it contained: dried fruits and flowers and a drizzle of honey. 'This already belongs to the

Goddess,' Eanfled told him. 'You must look after it as if she gave it to you for safekeeping.'

'Will it float?'

'Of course it will float,' she answered softly but indignantly. 'You've seen the baskets at festival. Edwin makes them watertight; they are like little boats.'

'With my luck it will probably sink.'

'Do not tempt fate Imma,' his cousin warned, 'it is a most stupid thing to do.'

Aldwulf turned over like a whale surfacing in the fields of ocean. He blew skyward such a fart that Eanfled and Imma were amazed the covers stayed on him. They both shook silently with laughter. Eanfled had to hold on to a chair to support herself. Then she slipped the strap of the woollen bag over Imma's head. 'Are you sure you need the bearskin?' she whispered. 'It is very cumbersome on you ... perhaps another cloak?'

'I feel grandmother is protecting me when I wear it,' the boy answered.

His cousin nodded. 'It is a fine gift,' she noted; 'the Earl was very generous.'

'The dawn will wear a grey mantle today,' she observed as she stood on the step of the house to watch him leave.

A bleak mosaic formed the landscape. Imma was warned not to step ashore in case of wolves and lastly he was given another reminder that the Island of the Earth was sacred.

'The wolves on the Mothers' Night have not been heard since,' he said, 'they have probably moved on.'

'You know the forest well,' said Eanfled, 'but don't let confidence make you cocky.'

'It won't,' the boy assured her. 'It will be nearly light before I get there.'

'Be quick, be careful,' Eanfled warned. 'Row straight home.'

With that she closed the door which, scraping over the threshold, sounded loud in the silence. Now the prospect of making his way riverward was a severe punishment in terms of fear. As his cousin must have known only too well. He would not regain the love of the Goddess merely by grovelling at her feet; he must win her respect by the accomplishing of a deed. In front of Leda's house he paused. The wooden building loomed at him out of the dusk. In the sky he saw neither star nor moon; to the east there was a faint profile of the resting dawn in pastel grey. The snow creaked under his boots as he turned away, holding the basket carefully, the tail of the bear fur dragging after, his ears and nose already twisted by the cold, and his eyes full of determination to accomplish what he had set out to do.

Imma then saw the pregnant moon hanging over a clearing in the blue dusk. She was watching him, seducing him with ideas of magical power. She had an unbreakable loneliness. He wanted some of her cold forbidding light. He did not want to hurt or be hurt again.

Upstream of the Island he made the offering. The small boat pitched as he lowered the basket gently to the water. He almost lost his oar. The forest was a tangle of witches in the twilight. Rather than return straight home as his cousin had desired he started paddling downstream as ashes were scattered in the sky. In sluggish pools there was ice over the black water.

He floated slowly alongside the Goddess, sometimes pushing with the paddle, sometimes letting the boat drift, and when he did this, lifting the stubby paddle out of the water, only the river flowed gently onward, while his mind seemed to stop. He had to pass the Island's length to travel to the hall of Angletheow, which stood at a bend in the river above Gipeswic.

Small baskets clogged the shoreline and any offering made in the dead-time became a feast to the many birds nesting there. Imma felt a terrible desire to trespass again. So when his boat drifted naturally, like one of the sacrificial baskets, into a hook of the Island, he did nothing to prevent it. Imma had been told by his grandmother that a man's life was like that of a worm around a stick. The stick was a person's fate and it could not be unmade, except perhaps by the most secret fire, and the worm that curled around the stick, sometimes curling back on itself, but always climbing generally upward along the lines of weird, was a person's choice. 'In other words your will Imma, what you choose to do or not to do.' He was trying to decide whether the stick had led him again to the shrine, or whether it was the worm, when all at once the unmistakable sound of moaning reached his ears. It was not at hand and it was not distant but it came from the Island. It was not an unnatural sound. It was a human sound. Imma was familiar with it and yet the fact of it here, at the Island of the Goddess, was not possible. Yet, like the beating of his own heart, there it was again. A body that in all likelihood had short time to live made that sound.

He did not know quite what to do. One voice said float silently away. There was a desperate moaning again and then a kind of grunting like a sow in labour. Some kind of enchantment was at work changing a man into a pig. An elf-witch might change a man into a pig if she felt like it. 'An elf-witch has changed my father into a pig,' Leda said to him once. 'She has not,' Imma had answered. 'He is still a man.' '*No*, he has been turned into a *pig*, can't you see that dimwit!' Leda had said angrily. Some magic was at work though because Imma was spellbound. Against all common sense he scrambled ashore after roping the boat to a branch and clambering onto a useful fallen tree. He must know what was making that sound. Imma hesitated but then the noise started again and it was plainly the throes of a body bewitched by sickness. He was about to take up the paddle as a cudgel, which he had thrown onto the bank, when the noise stopped and a silent calmness fell along the river. A flock of rooks in the highest treetops began to call out, *caw, caw, caw*, and there was a great flapping of wings and fuss about something.

The woodland on this part of the island was thick and, away from the water, oak and elm held sway. Imma followed the noise, not caring what twig he snapped, or bush he crashed past, as it was obvious whoever it might be was being given a ride on the moon. It had not occurred to him that the sick man might not be alone and only now as he broke through into a small clearing and laid eyes on the man for the first time was he thankful that the man, who was clearly in a fever as Imma had suspected, appeared to be alone.

He was a man old enough for battle but not enough for a proper beard. Perhaps sixteen Yules. His face, which was soft of line and with a dimple in the chin, was like a scrunched-up washing cloth, feverish and full of pain; his eyes were so tightly shut he did not notice Imma standing at the foot of him. His blubbering and babbling was such he did not hear Imma. Neither was he aware of anybody when Imma shook him by the shoulder. It was a nasty dart the youth had taken. His clothes were like the wrappings of a buried body but he had a long warm cloak and, filthy as it was, it must have kept him alive because his fire was out. He had made a dismal bed out of a pile of dead bracken.

He opened his eyes and a terror came into them. He grabbed Imma around the neck. It was as well some helpful spirit was nearby. The youth rolled away clutching at the sides of his head as if an elf was beating it in with a stone.

Imma fetched some water, hooking out his skin bag from the boat and filling it from the river. The water was so cold it was as though a demon handed it to him with black claws. He washed the stranger's ghostly face and tipped his head so he might sip from a handful of water. He was like a frothing dog at the water. Chills shook steadily from him and his skin fried like bacon in its own grease. Imma draped his cloak over him but the bearskin he kept for himself. He gathered the driest twigs and branches he could find and made a nest in the same patch the youth had used for his fire. It was wet and black with a sprinkling of snow. Imma first cleared some of the ash so that it did not smother the flame. The sparks he struck from his fire steel leapt dutifully onto the tiny heap of fern leaves and birch bark. This dry tinder he had taken from his fire purse. Once it was smoking he patiently blew life into it. Birch bark was like honey to the fire child. The fire was smoky but as the damp left the bigger sticks it began to burn nicely.

Imma stayed as still as the winter birds were in movement. The Sun Goddess woke and stars bowed down before her. The remaining leaves of the trees seemed of beaten gold where the cold sunlight fell across them. Imma watched the struggling face for signs of the fever leaving. Trespass or no, the loom of time had stitched him to the Goddess once again, and he would swear later that he had seen her as a vision of summer in the snow, much as he had seen Leda in dreams, and her eyes were soft as everybody said they were, dark as the colour of the fallow, and her gown was all of green, and her hair shining as the living grain. As he was making breakfast of a dried deer rasher and taking great gulps of water to help it down the stranger woke up.

Imma picked out another rasher from his bag. 'My name is Imma. What is yours?'

The youth put a hand to his head. He drew the extra cloak Imma had given him around his shoulders. He muttered something in a foreign tongue, which seemed to Imma like a sort of singsong curse. Then he grimaced and said: 'My name is Daniel.' His Anglian accent was that of the kin and therefore he could not, Imma thought to himself, have come so very far.

'*Daniel*,' Imma replied, pulling the bear fur close around his shoulders; 'that is an odd name.'

'And Imma is not?' Daniel suggested. 'I mean what sort of a name is Imma?'

'It is my name.'

'And Daniel is mine. Shall we leave it at that?'

'Yes,' Imma agreed.

He set his little black cauldron at the edge of the fire to warm the water. Into it he dropped some dried nettle leaves.

'You have everything in that bag of yours,' Daniel observed. 'Were you raised in a wood?'

'No, in my village.'

'In your village,' Daniel repeated. He lay back cradling his head between his elbows. 'My head is banging away like a ram at a gate.'

'Here drink this,' Imma said, hooking out the cauldron with a stick. 'Let it cool though.'

'What is it?'

'Stinger tea.'

Daniel frowned.

Imma laughed. 'Drink,' he said.

'Next time piss into the pot and be done with it,' Daniel said, finishing it up.

He told Imma what he could remember of his fever. He had seen a fearful demon called *Satan*. And this demon was like a king among demons and he ruled over a place of evil which sounded to Imma like the *Hidden Place* but then he said the demon looked like the barbarian king and that the barbarian king was coming to get him, the barbarian king or one of his bloodthirsty devils, and Imma could not understand. Then Daniel told a story about an unhappy man who lived in a dry place who even though he was a good man, a wholesome man, a god had allowed a dreadful nightwalker to attack him and the man had been laid low with sores as if he had been scraped to death with a razor shell.

Daniel ranted on awhile and Imma was unsure as to whether his illness had returned because new drops of sweat were wrung from him and his grey eyes were wild with a look seemingly turned inward. He kept calling Imma a 'barbarian', which Imma did not mind because he did not know what it meant. Then he went on about the Angles not knowing anything, about them being slave-masters and bastards, but it was them who were the slaves of this cruel demon called Satan. Clearly the illness had returned but when Imma went to feel the heat of Daniel's brow his hand was knocked away. Finally the strange youth drifted again and his skin was cool as the holly leaf Imma twiddled out of boredom.

He marked the progress of the winter sun and thought about leaving Daniel to the care of the Goddess. Yet it must have been the Goddess who had brought them together. He pulled up the leg of his woollen trouser and looked at the scar where he had been savaged. There was an ugly pink fold as if a large lugworm had knotted up and died under the skin. In the chilly afternoon light Imma took a nap wrapped snugly in his bearskin. He dreamed of many things he did not remember when he woke but he had a feeling of floating, like a blossom on the surface of a river and the water elves sang songs in his ear. He wondered if he might be dying in the ice-cold grasp of the river.

The Moon Goddess had pulled a shawl around her shoulders when Daniel sat upright and declared he felt better. He asked how it was that Imma came to be here and Imma told him it was a long story. It was the sickness leaving Daniel and not the moon who blanched the life from his face so that it was the colour of whey. The firelight gave him a brand of health but if he withdrew into the shadow it was a frightful ghost that looked out.

'It might yet return,' Imma warned.

'No I will die of hunger first,' Daniel said grimly. 'You might die before me.'

'We have broth,' Imma told him. 'I have put barley meal into it.'

'What a couple of fattened porkers we are.'

'I am not eating it from choice.' Imma shrugged. 'Accept what is given. Where is *your* food?'

Daniel smiled. 'The Lord has sent a heathen to mock me.' He pulled at the skin over his ribs. 'I might hire myself out as a wall hanging.'

'Need a woman to dye some colour into you first,' Imma said, laughing.

'Every man needs a woman to do that ... or so they say.' Daniel wiped his hand across his lips and patted his stomach. He watched as Imma refilled the cauldron with water. The cauldron was so small there was not enough broth in one batch for both of them. He was about to add a rasher of dried venison when Daniel asked to taste it. 'It is very tough,' Imma advised, 'but in a boiling it softens.'

'We should eat our shoes instead brother,' Daniel remarked, chewing at the rasher.

'I told you it is best softened.'

'I have owned tanned belts that were more tender.'

Imma told of his grandmother's death and the Earl Angletheow's promise. He invited Daniel, who had asked many questions, to come with him now that he seemed better.

'I trust you when you say your grandmother saved the life of his sister.'

'Why should I lie?'

'Indeed why should you.' Daniel smiled. 'You say there is a mass-priest there?'

'Not there, but at Rendlesham, in the hall of the King.'

'At least he was there a few months ago?'

'I came back with my grandma in the month of Going-before-Yule.'

'You are sure what I mean by the word *priest*?'

'He had a sign around his neck like this.' Imma showed by crossing his fingers. 'It was a rune of wood,' he added.

'Like this?' Daniel asked, pulling the cross from his tunic.

'The very same,' Imma replied; 'except it was of a shiny black wood.'

'So …' Daniel said, 'we are actually in the shrine of your goddess?'

'I told you already.'

'Hmm,' Daniel said. He put out his hands toward the fire. 'Night comes again,' he observed, looking up. Then he shuddered visibly.

'As the day ends it is not unusual,' said Imma, taking a sip of broth and burning the tip of his tongue so that afterward there was a tingle in it.

'You are *unmistakable*,' Daniel remarked. Imma merely looked at him. 'Hair as white as a swan's wing, little snub nose like a gosling's beak … my Lord, I wonder that a swan does not land on your head and try to love you.'

Imma was grinding an unpleasant bit of gristle.

'My hair is white and yours is brown,' said Imma through the gristle, 'what does it matter?'

'More than you think,' Daniel told him. 'How much is yours worth in a blood price?'

'No idea,' Imma replied. The gristle almost had the beating of him; it was a relief when he was finally able to swallow it.

'I can tell you it is worth more than mine.' The frown that had darkened Daniel's face lightened into a smirk as Imma made a loud slurping of the broth. 'What about the King?' he enquired; 'does he not come into your village and take slaves?'

'Why should he?' Imma answered, wiping his lips with the back of his hand. 'He gets all he needs from the ships and there are many born at hall. We are kin. We pay the Earl tribute in cloth and sheepskins and corn and apples and he is happy. In a hard year we pay less because he is a good earl. If he was a bad earl we should starve. It is just a fact.'

'Have you ever been across the *Waterland*?' Daniel then answered his own question: 'No, of course you haven't.'

'Where?'

101

'The Waterland ... it is over the other side of this forest.'

'The other side?'

'Yes, the other side.'

'I did not know there was an other side.'

'What?'

'I did not know there was an other side to the Motherwood.'

'What did you imagine it went on forever?'

'No I ...'

'Imagined it went on forever.'

Imma shrugged. 'I suppose so.' After all, the to and fro of his life and that of the entire village went on this side and downstream to Gipeswic. He remembered something: 'Is that where the *North Folk* live?'

'Who are the North Folk?' Daniel was chewing on a stalk and regarding Imma intently. An owl was hooting way off and near to there was a harsh unfamiliar chirring sound. No more snow had fallen but it seemed even colder away from the fire's heat and the air had a brittle quality like an icicle. The moon was riding high over the shrine of the earth and giving light to her.

'They are folk ...'

'Who live in the north?'

'Yes,' Imma said, giggling. He watched as Daniel unfolded himself and stood up. His legs were so thin it was like seeing a tangled crane-fly take-off except that Daniel did not take-off he sat straight back down again. 'The spirit is willing but the flesh is weak,' he whispered, barely enough to hear. 'I cannot walk a step.'

The chill ground and bracken beds made for uncomfortable sleeping. Several times, despite the warmth of his bearskin, Imma woke with the horrible feeling of being pressed under a flat cold stone. The monstrous stars of Ing were fiery overhead and under the flickering sky the bare trees were like the most outlandish folk. Imma poked the blaze from time to time with a long stick and watched the leap of the fire child. Once he had been shown a rock with a magical pattern on it. Eanfled had shown him, for Aldwulf had bartered with a trader, and the rock came from a far sea and it showed the thumbprint of a giant but to Imma the pattern was like that of a large water snail as if the water snail was somehow living in the rock. And this was how Imma felt during the sleepless winter night. Sometimes a dark shape sat up and began murmuring to itself in a foreign tongue. It was quite beautiful and unearthly to hear it. At one point Daniel said quite loud enough in Anglian that if any more snow fell it would make his tomb.

The Lady Dawn had barely risen in a grey pearl gown when Imma opened his eyes and saw Daniel sitting up and staring at him from the other side of the dying fire. Imma stood with difficulty, slapping at his body and at his legs which were cramped with cold.

'I am weak but feeling better,' Daniel said in a strange voice; 'let us go to your earl. If we stay here much longer we shall die.'

Imma nodded. It was an obvious truth. Even though his hands were wrapped in the sleeves of his Yuletide tunic he could barely feel them and his feet were so numb he had to look to see he had socks. He stamped some feeling back into his feet. 'What about breakfast?' he asked.

'We can chew some venison as we go.'

Imma quickly gathered together his things and slung the bag over his shoulder. He let Daniel lean against him and somehow they managed to stumble to the river. It took a warrior's effort to get the barely-recovered youth into the boat. 'Thank you for saving my life,' Daniel whispered as Imma pushed off with the oar. They floated downstream through a spectral twilight. Apart from the call of an occasional bird and a rustle at the bank there was scarcely a sound. When at last the sun began to spangle through the forest the trees were crystal white and brilliant.

The hall of Angletheow was as large compared to the houses that surrounded it as the Earl was himself to the average man. It was bluff, oblong and worthy like the mighty warrior but lacked the fine carving of the great hall at Rendlesham. There was no doubting it was as ample as the hides in which it stood. The Earl's clinker-built ship was moored in the deeper river and there was a small creek which, cutting through the bank, ran close by the hall.

The sight of it filled Imma with awe and he was gripped with a fear the Earl might not remember him. Without a word he let the boat drift by the creek.

'Is that not it?' Daniel asked. 'Is that not it?' he repeated, pointing with a limp arm.

Imma nodded.

'Then why are we leaving it behind?'

'It is the Earl's creek,' Imma answered, 'we might get in trouble.'

'Shall we moor when we reach *West Frisia*?'

'Very funny,' Imma said, now steering the tiny boat around with his paddle. This was the last of the freshwater river before the brackish tide at Gipeswic and out on the river there was a stiff breeze which blew across the little prow as Imma turned it. This and the fact that he was now against the current made achieving the creek difficult. The water meadows were empty of cattle and the banks of the river dead of flowers. Patches of snow lay on the fields. It was the month of After-Yule. The sky was a cold faded blue but the Sun Goddess shone as happy as a carefree girl. At the creek a watchman of the hall signalled to them. He caught the rope that Imma threw him and pulled them into the bank.

'Why do you want to see the Earl?' he inquired, after both Imma and Daniel had scrambled ashore. He looked them up and down. 'You look like two beggars who have stolen a boat.'

'The boat is mine,' Imma said crossly. 'I am from Wulfingstow in the hundreds of Lord Angletheow and I come to claim a debt.'

'You are young to make such a claim.'

'He can't help that,' Daniel said.

'You are a foreigner,' the watchman said, 'what do you want with the Earl?'

'I don't want anything from him. He is not in debt to me.'

'Wait here,' the watchman ordered.

'I hope the Earl is at home,' Imma said, as the watchman strode across the field.

'He will probably hang us,' Daniel said ruefully, raising an eyebrow. 'I wonder why this earl builds his house here on the low ground; he must be flooded every other day.'

'Young leech!' the Earl bellowed across the muddy field. He waved for them to come over to the hall. A large area of snow between them seemed to catch fire. A woman was at the doorstep with him and from behind her skirts two children peeped. Imma and Daniel started walking over the soggy pasture and halfway they met the watchman who was coming back. 'I never saw the Earl so pleased,' he remarked as he passed; 'you are like his long-lost son.'

Angletheow strode forward and gave Imma such a slap on the back the boy nearly fell over. 'You have come for a visit. You are always welcome. Your uncle knows you are here of course.'

Imma looked at his feet. He suddenly felt hot and sweaty in his bearskin.

The Earl looked at him sceptically. 'What is this mischief?' he inquired.

'Angle bring them in for some food at least,' the woman said from behind.

'Come in, come in,' the Earl cried heartily, 'you and your friend. This is my wife the Lady Urse and my two boys. Don't ask me where the girls are, my eldest though is inside. If you want to know all their names ask Urse for I can never remember them.' The two boys, both of whom were younger than Imma, really were like chippings from the massive block of their father. Angletheow today was dressed in brown leggings and a comfortable tunic of faded yellow. His warm cloak was of the same weld. He could have been a farmer except for his noble bearing and the styling of his hair. His powerful neck was as broad as his head. There was a scar on his cheek that ran to his throat and was obviously where a blade had tried to do for him. For some reason Imma noticed then that his eyes were bluer than those of the Lady Ealhhild whose were softer and had a violet shade.

'Ignore these thanes,' Angletheow cried, as they went in. It seemed the front part of the hall with its large partitions was given over to favoured warriors, some of whom were presumably the warlord's men from Rendlesham. His brother Lord Aelfwine stood and bowed. Angletheow stopped to talk to him and waved that Imma and Daniel should follow his wife and children.

'Come down to the family end,' the Lady Urse said cheerfully, beckoning to them as they trailed after her. The *peace-weaver* of Gipeswic was as big-boned as the Earl. In size they were more like a stallion and his mare than husband and wife. Her cloak clasp was a stunning circle of gold and her dress of a queenly blue. She wore a fur cloak from some unfamiliar animal. When she reached the family part of the hall she dropped her light linen scarf to her shoulders and Imma noticed that her hair was braided in a style he had not seen worn except at Rendlesham.

Cold meat and bread, fresh water, and a jug of ale were brought to the table. Imma and Daniel ate as if at any moment it all might disappear. The Lady Urse watched them with amusement. She beckoned to a nearby chattel and, before they had finished eating, new clothes had been brought for them. 'You look ill,' the Lady Urse suggested to Daniel, 'put on these warm clothes.'

A few windows on the eastern side were thrown open despite the cold and the sun fell through them. The central hearth was a golden blaze. The inside of the hall was a pattern of dark and light. There were several embroidered hangings and a number of linden shields around the room but the posts and beams were plain. Imma had seen the King's hall at Rendlesham and the Earl's was beside it like a giant cowshed; but it was, like the Earl himself, filled with dignity. Imma liked it. He had planned to ask Lord Angletheow if he might learn the metal trade at Gipeswic. He wanted to be a smith like his father. He had worked it all out. He would learn the trade, save a bridal price Leda's father could not refuse, and return to Wulfingstow to fetch her. He pictured arriving heroically on a horse, because he would be rich enough by then to have one, and he would grab her and swing her up as he rode past. He would not even bother to get down to give the gift to Urswine. He would throw a bag of gold at him as they galloped away. He would shout his thanks to Aldwulf and Eanfled and that would be it. He and Leda would then live happily at Gipeswic. He was trying to decide whether it would be better to arrive at sunrise or sunset when the Earl strode up and told them they would sail for Rendlesham that afternoon. His sister, the Lady Ealhhild, had become very attached to Imma during her illness and would wish to see him.

'I am glad we are to Rendlesham,' Daniel said, 'I should like to see that priest you told me of.'

Imma nodded and looked over the side at the water purling around the prow. He had the feeling he sometimes got: that the stubborn stick of a person's life had the beating of the worm that curled around it. Though it was not so bad to let things flow where they would and Imma was happy enough to sail with a rapidly recovering Daniel in the Earl's fine ship. It was exciting and he watched with sparkling eyes the rigging of the broad square sail when the ship was on the tidal Gipping. The strong breeze blowing over the river filled out the sail and the sail was like his own heart puffed with pride. Lord Angletheow let him help steer the ship as it rode the waves around to Rendlesham. Daniel smiled oddly as if he too were unsure where life was taking him. Imma was looking forward to seeing the Lady Ealhhild again. She was the most beautiful queen in all the lands between the seas. It was a simple fact.

Chapter
15

Birdsong shivered from the branches and from a distance across a fielding of moon it seemed a hundred cockerels competed for one hen. Father Julian had walked wearily from the woods after his morning toilet when something occurred which seemed to ease all the trouble in his pinched and pockmarked face. He caught sight of a man leading a small horse carrying a young girl. As they broke through the bands of mist, which hung over the shallow dip, the scene had the effect of a mystery play on the monk. And when the figures drew closer and he plainly saw the ragged girl was too young to be tending anything in her womb other than hope and that the man was an enormous shambling ox with matted fairish hair there was a part of him which still knew these humble people to be Mary and Joseph. The child was a repository of miracle like the Madonna, her honourable father a craftsman like Joseph. He recognised them immediately as the cooper and his daughter from Gipeswic. The child he had baptised. She rode on a small pony which had a silver sheen to its flank like beech bark. He ran his hand over and over her dirty foot. He had hesitated in touching it, afraid almost of contaminating a transfiguration, but once he had touched and felt there flesh and bone he could not help himself in examining it again and again. He even had to press each toe between his index finger and his thumb; the big toe had a cracked and crumbling nail; it was more real to him than any relic. There was another with the Holy Family not even Julian's frame of mystery had cast as an accompanying angel. A watchman from the gate. 'We must take her to the King at once,' Julian said to him breathlessly. The watchman grunted and walked on.

Julian's eye ranged across the morning with its pale blue sky and God's candle behind a thin stand of birch trees. People were about the morning chores. There was the first ring of a hammer on metal and the dull chocking of a mallet on wood. Little ochre people crossing the fields and all for a sublime purpose: God's purpose.

'*What is the meaning of this?*' Radwald demanded as the deferential giant with his waif-like daughter approached the mead bench. All had stood from their breakfasts with amazement. The Queen herself was absent for it was her habit to breakfast in her own chamber. It was the King, dressed in a wide-awake red tunic and cloak, and his closest thanes, together with the men from Kent who stood dumbstruck. Of the Kentish thanes only the Ambassador and Heoden the poet had seen the baptism in the river and the widest eyes were reserved to the soberly attired poet alone. He always wore black or grey as if in his clothes he wished to reflect the melancholy nature of his songs. Ambassador Uric whose wardrobe was as varied as the island weather maintained a fixed expression which betrayed only the meanest hint of a smile. Today he was in scarlet, a dye of cultivated madder which to the royal Angles was a singular temptation since the noble red of their own fabric was from the wild, rarer and less brilliant plant; but the King's tunic was a gift from Kent and the shade of Uric's own relatively duller, as if even over this he had taken pains. His sandy-coloured hair, which it was his habit to wear bobbed to the jaw, had grown longer and he had drawn it into a tail so that the bones of his face appeared more prominent than usual.

'Lord Radwald,' said Father Julian, 'this is the girl who was born again in water.' He beckoned that she should come closer and her father gestured to her with open hands as if he released a bird to the air.

'How can a girl be born again?' the King inquired. 'Should she climb back into her mother's womb?'

'*Nicodemus*,' Father Julian murmured and put his hand to his cheek.

'Come here girl,' the King ordered. He bent down and squeezed her lower leg and, although a man of the world such as he could hardly be too credulous, it was in fact a look of utter incredulity that showed on his upturned face because the fact of her healing was plain.

'The morning is here and darkness is lifted,' Father Julian cried joyfully.

'The morning is here and darkness is lifted,' Uric echoed, clapping his hands in a dramatic manner.

The other thanes and the attending slaves contributed only a stunned silence.

Radwald nodded. 'The magic of your rite is strong Father Julian.'

'It is Christ who has healed her out of love.'

'Proclaim it to the kingdom!' Uric cried.

'Such things have been known before,' the King countered.

Julian beamed with pleasure. 'Lord, have *you* seen such a thing before?'

The rays of the recently risen sun slanted through the eastern door and highlighted the dust hanging in the air. There was a cold clean look to the light which contrasted with the sullied light of the central hearth and with the smoky shadows that everywhere moved about the palatial room.

'What is your trade man?' the King inquired.

'I am a cooper, lord.'

'Yes I remember now,' the King mused. 'Why have you come here?'

At this the giant threw a quick uncomfortable glance at the Ambassador. 'Please, your lord to show you my daughter that she be well.'

'Why has this suddenly happened?'

'I know not your lord.' The man dropped his gaze to the floor. Apart from this the only outward sign of his agitation was to be seen in his thumbs and fingers which rubbed nervously together as if he continuously sprinkled salt on his dinner.

The King, with a considered walk, made his way down the length of the hall and stood gazing out the open doorway. Nobody else moved to follow; all the good people in the room merely turned their heads to watch.

'See how the King is bathed in light!' Father Julian exclaimed. 'God speaks to you my liege in tones of light.'

Radwald answered with a troubled look. It was true there seemed a heavenly quality to the light surrounding him. He plucked curiously at the strings of winter sunlight as though he really wished to bring a tune from them. He strode back to the head of the table but he did not sit down. Instead he remained standing with his arms resting on the high back of the chair.

'I seem to remember a vision of this Counsellor Uric?'

'I knew that it would happen.'

'You had a daytime dream?'

'My dream is only that the true religion might save my kinsman's soul.'

'You speak like the priest.'

'Alas it seems these days I must speak for him.'

'Why?'

Uric glanced with no small amount of derision in Father Julian's direction. 'He has become too mystical to spread the good news of the saviour to others that are in need of it.'

'You presume too much Lord Uric,' said Julian.

'Do you deny you would rather be in a desert?'

'I do deny it Lord Uric. I do deny it.'

'What pray do your starry eyes make of this girl?'

'She is a sign as real as Lazarus; as eloquent as the burning bush.'

'She is a twin Father Julian. What do you make of that?'

'I do not understand ...'

The King slapped the back of the chair in obvious delight and his well-groomed locks shook with laughter. In accord with the King's reaction the other thanes also began to smile and the mountainous Hengest of Kent who dwarfed even the cooper from Gipeswic stamped his foot in pleasure. The boards of the great hall shook and an audible tremor passed through the plates and cups on the table. In common with the natural order of a hen coop the servants and chattels also then began to laugh. Only three people did not appear to enjoy the joke: Father Julian certainly, and also the craftsman and his daughter whom only a short while before the monk had seen as a timeless enactment of the Holy Family.

'You make a mockery of the Lord's miracles,' Julian spluttered. He was almost apoplectic. Something which did little to put a lid on the hilarity that was boiling over.

'I do not mock *his* miracles Father; I mock only yours.'

The priest fell silent and he had the look of one who is abruptly tipped into recognition.

'You have stabbed under your own arm Lord Uric,' Radwald cried when he was sufficiently recovered.

'On the contrary lord.'

'You had me believing this magic.'

'We bring you something different from magic.'

'What?'

'Faith in a higher purpose.'

'Faith?'

'A follower called Thomas did not believe that the Christ had risen from the dead.'

Radwald furrowed his brow. 'Go on.'

'He said he would not believe unless he touched the wounds of the risen Christ.'

'A reasonable man.'

'Reasonable yes, but doubting.'

'Did the Christ god then appear to him?'

'Yes.'

'Are you familiar with this story Father?' Radwald said, turning to Julian.

'Yes lord. Only it is not merely a story because we have the witness of one who was in the room when it happened. Our Lord allowed Thomas to put his hand in the wound of his side.'

'He then believed?'

'Yes.'

'As I say a reasonable man.'

'Tell me my liege,' Uric said with a smile, 'if you were commanding a shield wall ... one that had never fought for, or knew of you before ... would you rather an army who believed at the outset you could lead them to glory or would you prefer a wall of men who were unsure until after the battle?'

'The former of course.'

'It seems then,' concluded Uric, 'that evidence is not always everything.'

The thanes fell silent and to everyone's surprise the King strode magisterially the length of the hall again and stood once more in the sun. After looking up into the light and grabbing bars of it in his hands as if to climb a ladder he turned on his heel and regarded them. 'As my lady points out to me,' he said loudly, 'there is nothing remarkable in a risen god but a risen everyman *that* is something to be feared.'

Chapter
16

One morning, before the sun had risen, Father Julian woke to find the fulsome woman who serviced the Ambassador in such vile ways whispering at his ear with a cloven tongue. He reached forward to strike the image from his bedside but she caught his wrist and, pulling his fingers out of the fist he had made, made a cup for her breast with his palm. He knew it to be witchcraft for how could the warmth under her nipple come to him through a dream with such heat that in the tomb-like air it scalded him. When she trapped his hand between her thighs it felt as though he had thrust his arm into a fire. The monk fell upon the woman with such ferocity that she was forced to hold him off until she relaxed and received him easily. The musk of her was strong and her sweat was tart. He licked it from her in a sorry gratitude. 'You are such a woebegone man,' she whispered. 'So woebegone.'

They lay together until the dawn rolled aside the stone of a sepulchre and let in the light. Sitting up she drew her hair in one bright stream over her shoulder and it fell across her breast. The colour of it was not brass and it was not gold. It was a creamy brown like the colour of fallen bracken when it made a carpet for the woodland under a winter moon. She gathered it into a tail and banded it with a tie of grey cloth. When she rose to leave there was a damp patch where the crux of her had lain and the scent of her was still fetid in the fur of the coverlet.

'You have a smile on your face Father,' Heoden called from across the hall.

In answer Julian pulled the coverlet over his head.

The poet laughed. 'You have seen the only god worth knowing. Why hide your head?'

'You have amazed me priest,' Hengest shouted gruffly. 'I never thought there was enough blood in you to fashion a weapon without fainting.'

'Shall we tell Uric that his strumpet meets with your approval?' Julian recognised the voice of Breca. At least it sounded like him. He had a gravel-like tone to his voice. Not as gruff as Hengest and not as cultured as Heoden. The other younger warrior of the Kentish party, Godric, hardly ever spoke. He would merely look Julian up and down as if he disapproved of him.

'Do not worry Father,' Julian heard, and it was the singer again, 'our illustrious leader beds in the King's hall; Earl Angletheow himself has the privilege of hearing him snore.'

'I know that storyteller,' Julian said, rising with a pelt around his shoulders, 'why tell me something I already know?'

'Ah, so it is your own little arrangement then?' said Heoden, standing up.

'I have arranged nothing,' Julian insisted.

Heoden pursed his lips as he tightened the belt around his tunic. 'Be sure Uric has finished with her that's all.' After pulling a hooded tunic over his head he picked up his harp and sat on the floor with it, sounding out notes, and fiddling with the pegs as he tuned. 'That's free advice,' he added, glancing up at Julian, before going back to his lyre. The lyre had four strings and was made from a blondish wood. Heoden, when he was evidently satisfied with the tuning, which had taken him considerable time, and which to Julian's ear hadn't seemed to make much difference, sprung up like a hare and, following his Kentish compatriots, left to breakfast in the King's hall.

Alone, the monk fell back on his pallet in a melancholy reverie.

It was the wakefulness of fertile gods. The loins of the world were stirring; the buds were breaking into green along the boughs; songbirds battling in the eaves were heard; the drilling knock of a woodpecker sounded among the stretching trees; and maidens in every hundred were dressing radiantly in expectation. The festivals of a flower goddess the locals called *Eostre* were at hand and weddings were sprinkled like daisies across the leas. 'When the Lord expelled our parents from that holy garden,' Father Julian thought to himself, 'in his mercy he allowed some happiness to the east.'

In his youth at the mountainous Cassino monastery there had been a herb garden with a small marble fountain. In the bowls of this fountain rain would collect. Often he wandered down the slopes to watch the mosquito larvae wriggling and feeding in the stagnant water. He was an observant naturalist and, in the absence of any non-devotional literature, would make notes and small sketches on pieces of spare parchment. He noted, for example, that the larvae seemed of two main types, one of which would swim freely about the puddle, whereas the other would be seen suspended from the surface of the water as if some part of it required contact with the air. The pupae were like locomotive seeds, punting about with seemingly little purpose, but then in a moment they would become still and at one with their deepest nature, letting a ripple carry them where it would. As an observed case split so also would the dial of time itself, so that a callow monk in the garden at Cassino, did not notice its passing. The tiny crumpled fly was like the palm of creation unfolding. The fly would sit with legs the thickness of an eyelash testing the tension of the water and the water was like the silver skin of an archangel. In a rhapsody of movement the fly would pull free of the glue of the puddle and across the mountains the clouds were cleared by an almost entirely spiritual breeze. In such pellucid moments Father Julian might have said no to the apple. But there were other times when his hopeful reasoning deserted him and it seemed that he could feel the splinter of Eve in his flesh and it was as real as the thorn of the wild rose he held in his hand. The flower of the rose, blasted by the unmerciful sun, dropped its wilted petals over his clenched fist. It felt to him that he, Julian, had strangled it, but the rose left a large ugly thorn in his open palm. He had been able to remove it with his teeth but when he wandered down to bathe the wound at the fountain he found the bowls dried up and only a desiccated residue of what a month before had been a green pond of rich organic purpose. It was then that he had gone to the stream with a pitcher and met the rib of Adam.

The girl was small and dark and the possessor of an Arabic beauty, with a nightingale's eyes and a slight predatory hook to her nose. She offered him bread in which she had baked olives as exchange for a few cuttings from the herb garden. They sat in the shade of an almond tree and shared the bread, which they washed down with water from the stream. The water was clean and cold and slightly metallic as if an iron key had been dunked in it. The bread was soft and fragrant with the tang of olives. As they sat a cool breeze ameliorated the exhaustion brought on by the afternoon sun and made each moment perfect. Julian dreamed of marrying the girl and of having a child though he had not spoken above ten words with her.

A patriarchal reedy-looking monk by the name of Jerome, who the brothers often joked would outlive Methuselah, happened to pass by the almond and upbraided the young Julian for sowing serpent's teeth in a still fallow soul. The girl, skittish as a blackbird, flew behind the protective trunk of the almond.

'It is good Father, it is good,' Julian had said, 'do you not see? I have met *Rebekah*.'

'You have *Satan* in your eye Brother Julian,' the old man said testily, 'cast him out.'

'No, I have shared a simple meal with Rebekah, and God sits at our table,' Julian insisted.

'One of us is mad Brother Julian and I do not think that it is me,' said Jerome sardonically. He called to the girl who came out from behind the trunk. The cool wind loosed a few leaves in a humble shower over her head. She brushed one from a braid of ebony and her look was toward them but ever downward as though she were not worthy. 'Child, what is your name?' Father Jerome asked her.

'Magdalena,' the girl whispered.

Father Jerome cocked his ear at her. 'What is that you say child?'

'Magdalena,' the girl said, more clearly this time. 'My name is Magdalena.'

'You are well named I think,' Father Jerome told her; 'and do you not have chores Magdalena?'

'Yes I have chores Father,' the girl said, scuffing the toe of her sandal in the earth.

'How old are you Magdalena?' Julian asked.

'I am sixteen, Father.'

'You are not married?'

'I am not married, Father,' the girl answered, glancing briefly up at him with a blinding smile which made Julian feel he had ascended to the sphere of the sun.

'And why not?' inquired Father Jerome.

'My mother is dead and my father needs me to look after the family; he is not in any hurry to send these hands to lift and carry for anybody else.' Magdalena looked away and then glanced behind her down the hill, in the direction of the village.

'Why are you nodding Brother Julian?' Jerome chided. 'The village has a priest.'

'He is not a holy man, Father,' said Magdalena.

'How would you know that child?' said Father Jerome indignantly.

'Sorry Father,' Magdalena answered quickly, 'I am truly sorry for saying, I mean …' The girl blushed in confusion. Father Jerome fixed her with a blistering eye. 'I came only for some herbs,' Magdalena insisted, 'you have such a beautiful garden … blessed by God,' she added.

'We are all blessed by God, child,' Father Jerome instructed her.

'Some are surely more blessed than others, Father.' For a moment her aspect changed and her features gathered like a tiny cloud around the spark of her defiance.

'Look you brother,' Jerome said, laughing, 'it is not often we see Lady Philosophy in the guise of a peasant girl.' He regarded the girl critically with no small degree of repugnance.

'They say Philosophy is beautiful.' Julian smiled. The gaze of Magdalena met his own but then she looked away shyly, biting her lip as if she saw something in the far distance.

'Be gone child,' Jerome commanded. 'View your reflection in a piece of glass. Do you question God's care of you?'

'I am happy, Father,' the girl said. 'I do not question it.'

'Then do not question it when you are unhappy.'

'No, Father,' Magdalena said sheepishly.

'Now be gone,' Father Jerome said peremptorily, 'before I use this stick on you!'

The girl turned and fled, her patch of summer dress billowing out as she ran.

'Your herbs and your basket!' Julian cried, seeing the basket by the almond.

'Do not encourage the girl,' Jerome warned, 'I think it lucky I happened by. You have fleshly matters for reflection Brother Julian.' The old renunciant tapped the younger man in the groin with his stick. Julian stepped back quickly in horror.

'With respect Father Jerome,' Julian protested, 'I know my path; it is with Christ.'

'Let us sit down a moment,' the venerable monk said, 'and enjoy the shade of this goodly tree.' His movement accorded well with the summertime but his physiognomy had a frozen muddy character. The numerous ruts of his face seemed to have been laid down by a hundred cartwheels.

Julian reached up and plucked a leaf from the almond and then sat down beside his mentor. As he listened he passed the leaf to and fro under his nose and although it was too late in the year for blossom and too early for fruit the leaf smelled to Julian of almonds and flowers. In his mind he saw Magdalena run down the hill, her calico shift and the movement of her legs, the dark river of her hair, and it was as if he had been abandoned in Eden, the condition of his soul unspotted, to wander without aim the pristine valleys with no hope of finding again the bone of his bone, the flesh of his flesh. Almost without thinking he reached above him to pluck at the fig he saw there but his fingers closed on air.

He then began thinking of other things to take his mind still further from the *succubus* Leoba who seemed ever there and ready to occupy his thoughts if they should become slothful.

It was long before he first landed in Kent and it felt strongly like a place of saintly light. He had wandered for a time that may have been forty days. High in the mountains, which lay under snow in winter and broiled beneath the summer sun, was a cave in which a famous ascetic lived. Julian, when the down was still soft on his cheek, had trekked the long way to visit him, hoping to receive wisdom. He had the restlessness diagnosed by St Augustine. It was insoluble the mystery why one man sought union with God in this life while others were content to wait until death. The eremite had the desert in his eye and was like a barren cactus plant. His life was all spines without the beauty of a single flower but he could break rocks with the intransigent will that kept him upright. He had a reputation for throwing stones at any who had the audacity to approach him. This he did at Julian also. A large stone hit the pilgrim on the knee and with a cry of pain Julian lifted his staff out in front of him as though he were carrying a cross. Perhaps the mantis saw this as a sign because he allowed Julian to enter the cave. Not one word would the saint say to his new pupil so that Julian was forever unsure as to whether he had even been accepted but he was certainly suffered to live for a time in the cave.

The eremite prayed from sunrise to sunset taking nothing but a mouthful of bread or a sip of water. Peasants from the nearest village would leave a napkin of food at the foot of the incline; for the eremite was a holy fool and took the sins of ordinary men and women upon him like a willing hunchback. At certain times, when the light was unearthly, Julian felt he saw through the mortal nature of his teacher, so stretched was the saintly skin on his bones. The eremite did not pray aloud and somehow Julian knew that he did not even speak a prayer within his mind because the saint was an adept and prayed in a transfigured trance

117

with each and every beat of his heart. How was a loving God not to hear?

One summer dawn the ascetic was kneeling on an outcrop of rock, his hands lifted in prayer, his body swaying like the insect that is called also a mantis, when the sun rising over the hills made golden apples of the cones hanging from the mountain trees, and the world was full of the song of birds praising heaven and a waking chatter of cicadas and drifting across a distance the clang of a monastery bell calling the monks for matins. Julian heard the doleful bell that was so familiar to him and it rang against his heart; but a higher path spoke also to him. He had no doubt the eremite partook that morning of some glorious communion because Julian knew not whether the material sun was behind the figure he gazed at or whether it broke from inside the man like some uncontainable energy. The saint had flown the rock that morning like a dove of fire.

Soon after the ascetic was troubled by unclean spirits which crept as shadows on the wall of his cave. There were tricks of the late afternoon sun which played around the cavern entrance but shadows of desire stole deep into the hideaway and found him there. There was a scrubby clump of thorn nearby and the eremite used it as a cleanser. He used it until the skin was stripped from his stomach and his back. He would not allow Julian to bathe his wounds with even a drop of fresh water. He seemed at moments like a defiant Christ but to Julian he had a stubbornness that refused even a little water offered with love. Although the air was cool high above the valley which opened a grateful mouth whenever there was a drop of rain it did not prevent the wounds becoming infected. The eremite thanked God for his further suffering and it was like watching the corruption of a corpse as it twisted in the grave. Such was the eremite's wish to utterly destroy the body.

When Julian could stand it no more he lay in wait at the bottom of the incline and sought help from a grandmother who came to leave a cut of bread and a few berries. The old matriarch required considerable assistance to make the climb. A sharp stone caught her on the temple as she appeared at the opening of the cave and the eremite cursed her into a pit of sulphur. Julian sat with her out of sight and washed the cut. Then the two of them prayed together. It was obvious the eremite had become a madman.

Several days later he died and Julian carried him like a flap of rotting skin down among the foothills where he buried him and knotted a cross for him out of cypress sticks. At the final resurrection God would find the bones at the foot of the mountain and raise them up in glory. Father

Julian meditated often on the eremite's fortune in the light of providence but it was not given to human beings to understand the ways of God.

Despite Julian's attempts to keep her from his thoughts the Ambassador's slattern became a regular visitor to his pallet. Sometimes she would stay and talk after the other thanes had left. One morning he was watching her, as had become his custom, while she dressed. She was fastening the shoulder of her grey gown with her iron brooch. 'It is the ghost of an owl,' she told him. 'It is not one of your devils, no matter how I see you look at it.' She had been a hunting owl when she kissed him with a cold glitter in her clouded eye. Then she was only Leoba confining a few narrow rolls of flesh in the fabric of her dress. She even asked him if he were hungry. She seemed like a little girl when she said her tummy was rumbling as if her throat had been cut. She persuaded Julian to put his ear to her stomach where sure enough the juices were squishing around like a Roman grape-treading. The scent of her was like must clinging to the winepress.

'Yes you need a breakfast,' Julian had agreed, getting up and taking her hand.

'What?' she asked as he looked at her.

'Nothing.' Julian shook his head. 'I was thinking that is all.'

'Too much thinking is bad for a man,' Leoba said. 'It makes him unhappy.'

'It seems to me you do plenty of thinking yourself Leoba.'

'I said for a *man*,' she answered with a slight flare of the nostrils that he knew well enough now was the signal of an ample smile.

'How did you come to be here Leoba?' he asked her. 'I mean here at the King's hall?'

'You don't want to know all that,' she told him. 'You keep asking but it is as ordinary as this scabby old dress and as patched and sewn as it too.'

'I do want to know,' he insisted as he tried to pull her down again.

'I must get back and clean the shit out of that cattle byre,' she said, pulling her hand from his. 'A fine life you have idling around all day but it'll be a birching for me if I don't get back.'

He let her go. 'Leoba,' he called, and she turned and stepped toward him.

'I must go,' she hissed.

'I think I have fallen in love with you.'

'For a clever man you are an idiot,' she gasped and turned on her heel. All the same a moment before she disappeared out the door Julian saw her glance over her shoulder.

He reflected on the slippery nature of the human person. How difficult it was to skewer down. One could not pin it like this hand on a block of wood. Who was *Leoba*? The supernature of an owl, the bony frame with its scarred and trembling masks of flesh, the little girl with an upturned face in the house of her widowed mother, the imprisoned drudge with chapped and calloused hands, the Ambassador's whore with her quick but furtive intelligence, his lover and his only friend. All of these and none of them also.

'Do not go to him,' Julian would entreat her. 'I cannot stand it.' For Uric had resumed his interest in her.

'You know that I must,' Leoba told him. 'Or he will kill us both.'

There was a splinter in him that felt Leoba wanted to go to the Ambassador, a part of her that was in thrall to him still, and which was the primary compulsion she obeyed rather than fear of what the seemingly amoral Uric might do.

He thought of taking her to Canterbury and from there they might sail for the sunny land of his birth. They would be married and he would become a repentant serf raking through the grit of the foothills. He would make it right in the eyes of God. He would smile at the memory of the Benedictine chapel where he had laid eyes on the mason's tools, the mallets and the sharpened chisels and the thought that he could not dismiss as temptation, the desire to re-enact his own day of love. He made a kind of putty from olive oil and dust and used a small lump to hold the nail upright on his open palm which he then rested on a small block of wood. Kneeling on the cold flagstone he prayed hard for God to drive it straight. In his right hand he held the mallet. One indomitable blow and the cry rang around the church. He awoke in the infirmary. His left hand was swaddled like Luke's baby Jesus, relaxed and quiet above the linen counterpane. He could lift it and examine it and it was real to him, a calico wrapped object on the end of his arm. A spot of brownish blood lay in the centre. This then, the cicatrix in the middle of his palm, was God telling him that the vow he had made was real. In short it had existence in eternity; not like the life a man lived on the earth.

He no longer wore his monk's dark habit. Instead at night he merely rested his head on the folds of it and when he saw himself in dreams he was always wearing it like a spiritual pelt. Similarly he had allowed his hair to overgrow his tonsure. Leoba had tried in vain to create some sort of order by cutting the hair around his temples and at the back of his head with an edge sharp enough to pare a single strand. She used the same knife when he would importune her to shave his beard. He enjoyed offering up his neck to her like the white throttle of a goose.

'What would you do if this were Uric's neck under your knife?' he had asked once.

'Ha,' Leoba said with a grin. 'And you told me *I* was the demon who corrupted *you*.'

The chapel of Benedict was a deeply holy place in which the breath of God breezed through the unglazed windows. The chapel contained a Roman light through which Phoebus despite his smashed altar still deigned to shine. Many was the time a glorious lance of sun shattered against the sacred tomb. What further proof that however much poets persisted in personifying the sun it was God who had hung the big light in the night-times of the sky and made from it the day. In the devil's patch the truth had been planted and Satan banished by the most holy servant of the servants of God, Saint Benedict. As Father Julian had hoped once to do in this the land of the pagan Angles.

Chapter

17

A single star hung across the calmness of the water. A glimmer had appeared, a paler sort of dark, like a fold of silver nightgown stirring, and the slow wind whispered in the ears of the spellbound crowd at the shore. A thousand small baskets each containing a single tallow to imitate the star had been set adrift toward the east and so the dark waves were lighted and made full of meaning. It was beyond the skill of any *scop* to remember this moment as the kin felt it. In this sacred play time was felled and it was as if folk were witness to the beginning of life itself. As if they were watching the folds of the Lady Earth break from out of the first ocean, seeing the first creatures form from out of the dust of stars, seeing a fish flap helplessly on the shore and then miraculously take breath and wing into the sky, and more than this, seeing the first man unfold from the palm of the Great Goddess and step upon the earth. So the star was delivered to them. The shingle was thronged with the shadows of five thousand kin. Human expectation manifested the living air the way it is before a thunderstorm. And then, as the Lady of the Sun shook the first tress of light at the horizon, Lord Ing walked a white horse forward out of the waves and returned to dwell among his people.

Father Julian did not exactly care for the celebrations of Lord Ing. Alone with his thoughts at dawn he had the deserted closures more or less to himself. He had trotted like an eager hound down to the milking byres and found them empty. It seemed every woman in the land was tied to this returning abomination. The great pagan god had only to reel them in at his pleasure. At this very moment his own Leoba, his own sinful darling, was somewhere by the side of the sea awaiting this blasphemous gesture. Soon they would be back, and many more beside, every man, woman, child and their dog, would be back thronging the enclosures with their futile festivities. The air would choke on the stench of charring meat, the bellow of confused animals lined up for slaughter, the endless loaves in batches being brought from the kitchen ovens, great hearths set up across the green, huge cauldrons of broth for the poor and hungry, for on this day the brotherhood of the King's hall, which was a privilege earned only by relation or valour, was open to all. And how life's exiles flocked to pay homage to the phallic king.

Soon enough the revellers returned from the side of the foaming sea. They had rushed inland, as one bright running wave, several thousand strong and had burst irresistibly over the defensive palings which surrounded the royal halls.

Father Julian found himself washed from the pile of logs where he had been sitting and spun around like a cork in a human whirlpool. Such was the delight and merriment of the crowd. Then the agony of his aphelion was at an end as Leoba discovered him among the joyful chaos and seemed to gather him up as easily as a mother her newborn babe.

People sat in large circles breakfasting on breads and skillet-fried gammon. Many were still drunk from the night before. A chattel brought Father Julian a two-handled goblet of mulled and spicy wine from out of the King's cauldron. It was a source of embarrassment as he sat with the common herd that the chattel had found him out.

'Counsellor Uric sends this to the happy couple,' the serving man grated.

'Thank him kindly,' Father Julian retorted. 'Tell him his attempt at a joke is appreciated.'

'No, say nothing to him,' Leoba warned.

The serving man, of a singular appearance which took in bulbous eyes, a hammered nose, and hair like an upturned willow basket, lingered a moment with an unpleasant leer as if the weight of an ingot of lead depended from the side of his mouth. 'The warrior of Kent said to be sure to take a side each when you sip … a *loving cup* he called it.'

'Did he?' Julian answered grimly. 'Well you can tell him …'

'Tell him nothing,' Leoba insisted again.

Still the slave remained, clearly waiting for them to drink it. Others in the breakfast circle now began licking their lips and asking Leoba for a sip of the wine or at least a scent of it. All one old man wanted was a sniff and he would give it straight back. He assured Leoba and Julian of this. 'I can think on it,' he waxed oddly, 'is it like a painful memory of love?'

'What's that old fool going on about?' another asked his neighbour.

To everybody's surprise Leoba took the cup and dashed its contents onto the grass behind her. 'Who knows what's in it?' she declared defensively. The assembled circle looked quizzically at her. 'Why should we drink wine when all you have is ale?'

There were nods all round at this.

Still the serving man stayed, lingering above them.

'Remain there any longer and I shall have to employ you as my conscience,' Father Julian said acidly, looking up at him and squinting because the sun was in his eyes.

'The Kentish warrior said ...' the chattel began.

'*The Kentish warrior said, the Kentish warrior said ...*' Leoba took him off in a mordant tone and was rewarded with broad grins and laughter from the circle.

'The Kentish warrior *said*,' the servant repeated carefully, 'to make sure she washes your feet with her tears and wipes them dry with her hair.' With that he left.

'What did he mean by that?' Leoba asked.

Julian shook his head. 'Do not worry,' he reassured her, 'Uric has the satire of an educated butcher that is all.'

Chapter

18

In the salad days of King Radwald the showing of the Lord was delayed at Rendlesham while he toured the land of his inheritance. A flock of women followed him and, as he passed through the villages, any there were that felt a pull toward him were garnered into his harvest. At certain settlements he threshed a grain of gold from a favoured handmaiden. A substantial gift would be left for the village, the glitter of which, farmers were unlikely to have seen. The King was also received on occasion by a priestess at the woodland shrines of the radiant Lady Eostre.

The subsequent midsummer wedding to the young Ealhhild, who had been the virgin bride of Radwald's father Tyttla, that great earthshaker who had successfully secured the borders of his people, was a necessary sacred event. The Lady Ealhhild, who had been spliced to the old King at only sixteen winters, had not given him another child. Most ordinary people had at best a hazy understanding of the bond between the king and the land. 'It is holy,' they said. 'Yet some years they do not seem to be wed.'

One who declared it was both close and holy was the Queen herself.

'You are a blessing to her young Imma,' the Lady Ealhhild said, turning from the elegantly chiselled doorway where she had been gazing down the grassy slopes, which were thronged with people at their breakfast. The frame was patterned with beautiful knot-work. 'And to me,' she added. 'You are a boy of singular gifts. I thank you for taking Swanhild all that way to see her father return. The snow lay on the ground when my brother brought you first to see me. Look now it is all but midsummer.'

'It is nothing Lady Ealhhild. She is very light, like shouldering a sparrow.'

'She is determined not to put on weight,' the Queen said with a sigh. 'Where is she now?'

'With the wet-nurse.'

'Thank the stars for that nurse,' the Lady said, advancing into the room. 'The days stretch their ends toward the summer as I said and today the King brings my bridal gift and this bower shall serve as my father's house. It was hot as a dragon breath the day Radwald and I were under the marriage arch … there was a suitable heat you could say,' she added, laughing and directing her remark not really to Imma but to Nurse Gudrun who sat with doubled back at her spinning like some crotchety old spider.

'Aye there was always heat between yourself and Radwald,' the old nurse agreed, nodding and glancing up for the moment from the twist of the weighted bobbin.

'Folk say you are as fresh as a newly opened flower,' Imma said to the Queen. 'Is it because you are the Goddess?'

The Queen smiled in a motherly way but did not answer.

Her gaze made him feel silly and he pretended to have an itch in the small of his back. 'Rub your back against that post,' Nurse Gudrun advised, 'if you have an itch there.'

'You do have an itch I know it,' the Lady Ealhhild then said, and looked at him, as she often did, in a way that made him feel she could rummage through his feelings as easily as if they were yarns in her embroidery basket. 'I could hand you a wedding gift when the time comes but would you then be man enough for her I wonder …'

'I should like to earn it in the metal shops,' Imma said.

'Yes, you have told me. Well that is simple to arrange.'

'It was my grandmother's wish.'

'That you repeat the life of your father?'

'That I learn his trade. Although he was only a village blacksmith.'

'I think you have other skills,' the Queen told him.

'I should like to make a jewelled sword for the King.'

The Queen nodded, although it struck Imma, not really in agreement. He had asked her as often as he dared about becoming an apprentice but each time he had done so she had been evasive. He had no idea why. 'A skilled smith is something of a magician,' the Lady Ealhhild subsequently declared, 'he has the wonder of Wayland about him; he shows you truth in a flawless shape but I have learned that real perfection is the perfection of *balance*.' She laughed, as the look on Imma's face

126

must have shown that she had catapulted a rock over his head. 'Would you not wish to be initiated into the womanly mysteries?'

Imma shook his head doubtfully.

'It is possible for a boy,' the Queen said, still smiling. 'Under favourable circumstances.'

Silence fell in the chamber. The old nurse rose stiffly, but cleverly she swung the bobbin from one hand as she bent to toss another faggot on the fire. The Queen's chamber was not furnished with the usual firebox but had a clay-bricked hearth of earth against the wall opposite the door, with a great iron plate to protect the timber. The high gabled hall had three similar hearths together with a central roasting pit. To Imma these amazing sources of heat and light were as though he gazed on the wonders of giants. He did not really take in the privilege of attending the Queen in her bedchamber. It always reminded him of the time Leda had fetched him into the women's hall at Yuletide; the night Beadhild had died.

'My brother seems to have taken a special liking to your friend?' the Queen suggested, sitting down in the great carved chair. 'Be a good lad and pass me that fur. Thank you.'

Imma stood awkwardly while the Queen stuffed the fur behind her back for comfort. Her gown, which brushed the floor as she walked, was the colour of river mud and around its hem yellow birds of the most exquisite needlework pecked and strutted like waders on an estuary shore. She wore a smoky-grey coloured jacket and its effect was similar to a mist above a bare earth. Imma had never seen the like of that mantle. It was full-sleeved and seemed of a sort of stiffened linen with little hoops of thread to catch over the wooden toggles the Queen now suffered him to fasten. 'My fingers are cold,' she complained; 'lately I seem never to gather enough heat.' Nurse Gudrun looked up momentarily from her spinning. A chambermaid with a sullen look appeared at the door only to be waved away. 'She wants to be at the festivities,' the Queen observed. 'Now I have allowed her perhaps she will manage a smile.' She motioned for Imma to sit on one of the sheepskins at her feet. Imma noticed the Lady was wearing coarse woollen socks. 'I shall be removing *these*,' she said, laughing and wiggling her toes, '*before* the King's arrival … a woman must continually spin illusions which,' she added looking directly at Imma, 'can be very tiresome, although of course it may also be fun.'

Her subject looked at her blankly.

'Tell me,' the Queen inquired, brushing a few imaginary crumbs from her lap, 'do you think of your lady-love at night?'

Imma was unsure what to answer.

'It is a simple enough question,' said the Lady Ealhhild.

He looked down at his hands.

'Do you think of the girl you are fond of at night or does she come to you in dreams?'

'You mean do I think of Leda when I am in bed?'

'Has your mind flown out of the window like a bird?' the Queen cried, exasperatedly.

'Yes, I mean no, I mean yes I think of her and sometimes I see her when I sleep.'

'We are finally getting somewhere.' The Lady Ealhhild sighed. 'When she visits you, are you aware of anything that happens?'

'Happens?'

'Yes *happens*.' The Queen threw up her hands. 'I shall take that vacant look as my answer.' She beamed at him. 'I have thought on it and I shall allow your wish to learn the metal rites but you are to remain close to me and help with Swanhild as if she were your baby sister as, indeed, you have been doing … is that agreeable?'

Imma nodded. 'Thank you Lady Ealhhild,' he said, rearranging his cross-legged position. He began picking at the threads of the sheepskin. 'A fine rug we shall have with you sitting there,' Nurse Gudrun said from her corner. Imma merely looked at her but his fingers stopped pulling at the threads. He felt extremely homesick all of a sudden.

'I did a terrible thing,' he said.

'Hmm.' The Queen appeared lost in thought. She yawned revealing a set of almost regular white teeth. Imma wondered what she cleaned them with to get them so white. They were quite the whitest teeth he had ever seen. It was as much as he could do to keep his own teeth free of rubbish. The teeth of most of the people he knew, especially the elders, were like the old speckled stones of a forest. Still the Queen was known to have magical powers; perhaps she used a thimble of them on her teeth. But she had heard him.

'And what was that?' she inquired, after she had evidently waited a suitable time.

'I can't really say,' said Imma, beginning to pick at the rug again.

'You are a strange boy. I am sorry, but you can't do that. It's hardly fair is it?'

'No, Lady Ealhhild.'

'Well?'

Imma glanced over his shoulder almost hoping someone would come in.

'You obviously want to tell me or you wouldn't have said it.'

Still Imma hesitated.

'As you wish. Perhaps it is better you have made a fresh start. I owe your grandmother my life and the life of my daughter. She gave her own in grim battle for me. I asked my brother to look after you. He went to your village as you know and offered you protection; he gave you a gift to underwrite his oath, but you chose to remain with your uncle. We of course respected that. Then you come to claim what you are owed to win a bride. What more is there to say? Here you are and today is a day of new beginnings. I too am born again and in renewal there is hope, the remedy of life. All of us are pursued by memories we would forget. Do not let them hag you Imma.' The Queen stretched out her feet and turned them this way then that as if admiring the turn of her own ankle.

'I cannot say for your *sweetheart*,' the Lady Ealhhild said when Imma had finished his tale. In a moment he had poured out his heart. 'As for the *Goddess*, perhaps I can help you. She may tell in a spill of runes if we approach her in the right manner. We will go to her sacred pool and offer her a gift. She may speak to you.'

'And if she is angry?'

'She is a tallow in my heart Imma and I feel nothing but love regarding you.'

'A mother forgives when a friend won't,' the boy said unhappily.

The Queen nodded. 'Nurse, can you yell for some breakfast?'

Imma was uncertain whether it was the chair or the brittle leaf of her skeleton that complained when the old woman got up. She was old enough to have been at the naming of his grandmother. Excepting the curse of labour women stood strong on life's battlefield. The cord held their ships long and fast. A soldier who had covered himself in glory for his king was swiftly cut down by a fever. Imma had seen it. He wanted some of it. He wanted some of this womanly power. The Goddess might give it if the Queen vouched for him. The Lady Ealhhild could make everything right. He believed in her utterly.

'If the Goddess wants you to be with this girl then it will happen,' the Queen said flatly. 'I have a feeling there are other plans for you. We will see. But today, after we have had breakfast you will enjoy the celebrations in the wood. Please take Swanhild. I must bide for the King. Last year my father was here. Today he has left me behind with the parting talent of the dead. You know this token of course.'

'I know it Lady Ealhhild,' Imma said with a frown. Without thinking he fell forward and clasped his arms around the knees of the Queen. He felt a gentle hand stroking through his hair and she must have bent over him for he felt the ends of her hair tickle lightly against his neck.

'A warrior with his guts hung out for the crows calls in vain for his mother,' she whispered as Imma sat back on his haunches, wiping his eyes with the back of his hand, 'or a common thief on the gibbet; it is the Goddess he whimpers for. It is natural. Man is built by woman and at the crisis wishes to return to her.'

'And a woman?'

'A woman is also born of a woman… *obviously*, and feels the same need but unlike a man she has more commonly the power to become her mother.'

'Leda used to say she was fearful of turning into her mother,' said Imma, wiping his nose on his sleeve.

'Let me introduce you to a suitable cloth,' Nurse Gudrun said wryly, handing him a square of unbleached linen before tapping slowly back to her corner. The handkerchief was warm – it must have been in the old nurse's pocket as she sat by the fire – and it had a faint scent of freshly baked loaves. It was soothing and he determined to keep hold of it if the nurse let him.

'Leda means the little nature of course,' the Queen said, showing a snowfall of teeth. 'Not the elemental nature.'

'A man must become his father.'

'It is most usual for a man to become his father but these things are not bound in ropes.'

'You mean a man may become his … *mother*,' the boy said uncertainly.

'Or a woman her father, yes of course, but you must understand that mother and father, man and woman are only useful images, shall we say *symbols*, for what is beyond an image … but I see you do not grasp what I am saying. It is no matter. Perhaps it is easier to think of mannish and womanish *aspects* like left and right hands …' She put them out in front of her, palm down and he was amazed not so much by what she was saying, which still he did not understand, but by the fabulous rings on her long graceful fingers and by the sacred patterns on the slender fragile

130

hands and by her crafted fingernails which were long as cat's claws. No woman he had ever known could grow her nails like that because they would have broken against a hundred tasks. There was not a thread of dirt around them. Her royalty was spectacular to which not a speck of common or garden mud could cling. He was in another world talking to the Goddess. He felt that whatever he would ask she would be able to give. Her words were like molten beads of silver in the crucible of his skull. They seemed to dance in a fry of secret knowledge.

'That brilliant green stone is an *emerald*,' the Lady Ealhhild informed him, as he gazed at her blazoned hands.

'It is so beautiful,' the boy breathed. 'It is the colour of cudding grass.'

'Best not feed it to a cow though.'

'Ha,' Imma cried, delighted at her joke. 'And these?' he said, pointing.

'This they call a topaz … see the straw light of it like a winter sunrise.'

The boy nodded. 'Winter sunrise.'

'This one is a golden amber. It was found on the shore right here, in a great ugly lump but see what the smiths have made of it.'

'A coiled hair of the sun sits in it.'

'A single coiled hair, yes. These of course are blood berries.'

'Blood berries,' the boy whispered, entranced by the magical quality of them.

Fishing into her lamb's-leather amulet bag, her slender adroit fingers picked out a stone the same colour as those of her ring: a small berry of the garnet tree.

'This is your *lodestar*,' Queen Ealhhild told the astonished boy; 'every ship needs one.'

Imma's palm closed hotly around it.

'You are welcome.' She settled back in her chair. 'Ah, here is breakfast.'

The Lady broke a piece of bread and fed him a clot of butter, which melted slowly on his warm pink tongue. This was no butter from an earthly cow; surely it had been sourced from the herds of the Moon Goddess herself. A sip of fragrant dandelion and a mouthful of bread from which a few wisps of steam had escaped when it was broken. There was a nutty tasty lightness to the leaven which only the most skilled of bakers back home might have managed. It was almost as good as Eanfled's baking and folk would have murdered for a morsel of that.

'I do not want any of this flitch but Nurse please help yourself.' Lady Ealhhild gestured. 'And feed some of it to this pup …' She pointed, her

131

numerous bracelets talking on her wrist. 'A boy must have the best cuts if he is to grow strong.'

The smoke of the gammon when Nurse Gudrun lifted the lid of the pot was intense. Imma drooled at the smell. He wolfed it down licking every last shine of grease from his fingers as the Queen watched him with evident amusement. Nurse Gudrun retired to her corner and ate with her back to them like an elderly hunting dog. The only sound was the smack of her jaws and the gentle crackle of a low dancing fire.

'Your friend,' the Queen began, again brushing a few imaginary crumbs from the lap of her skirt, which Imma had noticed served as an introduction to more serious topics, 'he wears a cross around his neck like so does he not?'

Imma nodded but in his head he was still breakfasting on gammon and buttered bread. 'He wanted to see the priest. It was important to him.'

'Ah yes our good Father Julian. Has he seen him?'

'He has seen him at a distance.' Imma nodded. 'He says that he is not a proper priest.'

'Father Julian is a proper priest. He has merely been distracted.'

'Daniel says he is a disgrace. Wiping his bum with the good news.'

'How direct. Do you yourself know what this 'good news' is?'

'Daniel says it is the news of his god.'

The Lady smiled. Then she said: 'I can tell you one thing the *news* is about.'

Imma looked up expectantly.

'It is the foot of a man on the neck of a woman.'

Imma was non-plussed.

'There is a story they tell,' the Queen continued, 'that all this ...' And she gestured grandly, 'was the creation of a god of whom the god of the cross, the Christ, the Messiah, the Nazarene, he has many names, is a part or a representation or a symbol ...'

'He died for us Daniel says; but I do not understand how he died for me.'

'He is a sacrifice, like a sacrifice of the old days; he assuages the anger of a god toward us, this god who created the world without a woman's help.'

'How can a man give birth to the earth?' the boy asked.

'You must ask the priest this question for they go further in this manner of thinking.'

She again paid some attention to the invisible crumbs on her skirt. A pained look came into her violet eyes and it was like the dart of silver minnows to the surface of a pond.

'Come here,' she beckoned, crooking her first finger at him, which had a band of gold set with an amber fire. The boy got up tentatively. 'Come closer,' she whispered. He could smell her hair, which seemed washed with water coloured with the scent of wild roses. A patch of briar blossomed in his mind. The Queen sat up straight in her chair and undid the toggles of her jacket. 'Press here,' she instructed, indicating her side directly under the breast. The boy was unsure. 'Do not be timid,' the Queen said. 'Press firmly. What do you feel?' She arched a delicate brow.

Imma had half-expected to burn himself, but instead his trembling fingertips first brushed against the velvet nap of her bodice and then pushed into an unmistakable solidness of flesh. 'I feel the ladder of your bones Lady Ealhhild.' He coughed.

'I am glad that you describe them as *my* bones.' The Queen smiled, indicating for him to refasten the toggles. 'The new god would rob them from me and leave me nothing but a multiple built on the bone of a man.'

'I do not understand.'

'Neither do I.'

For a space there was imperfect silence; the cries and hollers of the merrymaking crowd seemed far away. Nurse Gudrun had shifted around to face the conversation now that her meal was plainly at an end. The empty platter and cup were by the leg of her chair.

'Lady Ealhhild,' Imma said hesitantly, 'if you wished to send a spell of love you could surely send it?'

'Are you asking me for a *love charm*?'

Imma looked at the floor.

'I needn't ask whom for?' the Queen suggested, cocking her head mockingly to one side. The boy did not answer. 'I think a spell has already been cast and you are the victim of it. You are too young for me to invoke such a thing on your behalf. Besides has it not occurred to you that force is force whether by spelling, fear, or howsoever a prick presents himself to a woman. Certainly you would wish your girl to come to you willingly?'

Imma nodded; he hadn't thought of it that way; he felt ashamed.

'Something to stop her liking anyone else?'

'You would guard her like a jealous dog?'

'No I ...'

'What?'

'Would guard her if I was able …' the boy trailed off. There seemed no solving of his anguish.

'How old are you Imma?'

'I will be twelve this Yule.'

'And your girl?'

'She is twelve already.'

'You have time then.'

Imma's look was cast down.

'Your friend,' the Queen inquired, changing the subject. 'Where does he hail from, this *Daniel*?'

'He came from across the Motherwood.'

'The great forest of the Lady Earth?'

'Yes.'

'From Mercia?'

'I do not know this name.'

'They are Angle kin that cleave to a different king, even a different god; the soldier god who uses craft in battle as well as strength of arms. Some say he learned it from the Moon Goddess. *Woden* is his name. Fear him, he is a usurper.'

'Daniel was raised in the house of a foreign priest.'

'He is a native. A foreigner.'

'He said another name but I forget … he was abandoned at the gate when he was a baby.'

'Babies may be untimely, unwanted, *unfortunate*,' declared the Lady Ealhhild knowingly. 'Is there more to his story?'

'Much more.' Imma nodded. 'He said his mother used to visit him in secret.'

The Queen raised her eyebrow. 'Really?'

'He saw his mother raped.'

'By the priest?'

'No by a warrior, an Anglian warrior.'

'The priest would not have been surprising.'

Imma nodded although he did not, if the truth were told, know why.

'The foreign priest was also raped and then had his guts unfastened by a knife.'

Lady Ealhhild frowned. She seemed to shiver almost at the exact time the morning sun decided to shine brightly in at the window. It made ghostly shapes out of the floating dust and the shapes turned this way and that making spirals around the gleams of sunlight. 'I think your friend is escaped property. He has a hunted look about him.'

'All I know is he came through the Waterland and got sick,' Imma said, not enjoying the intensity of the Queen's gaze. He wondered why she sometimes asked him things that she had asked before, as though she had no memory for his answers.

'It is a wicked place,' the Lady Ealhhild remarked. 'No army crosses it without loss.' She glanced at her nurse who, with her belly now full and chores for the moment done, had been charmed into a doze by the dance of the low fire. 'If your friend has run away then he is lucky he met you for as your friend he is free to do as he wishes.'

'He wanted to travel to Kent.'

'Then he may do it. Let him take ship from Gipeswic.'

Nurse Gudrun for some reason startled and began raking over the fire muttering something about the blackened iron poker being as old as she.

'I like him,' Imma said. 'I hope he will stay here.'

'He has a sinuous charm that would be the envy of many girls.'

'They are heading down to the wood my lady.' It was the same stooped woman who had brought the breakfast standing in the light and waiting to take the empty plates. She had a nose that stood out from the miserable rag of her face like a partly wrapped chisel. The old hunting dog was forced to stir herself from the consolations of the fire.

'Go,' the Lady Ealhhild then said emphatically, 'see them make a fuss of the bridegroom. As for me I must prepare myself to accept him. Yes father I shall make myself pretty.'

It seemed from her look that she saw her father right in front of her and Imma, who had never seen him and did not know what he looked like, imagined him standing there, clothed in all his finery, his hair and beard combed proudly, right as if a year gone by could be bought back.

Chapter

19

It was the open display of penises that Julian found most difficult to stomach. They seemed to be everywhere, carved from every possible wood, and in all manner of shapes and sizes. Some were so poorly carved as to be beyond anatomical belief. Only the night before he had seen what looked to be a tiny penis hanging from a leather cord around the neck of a serving woman. He had felt compelled to ask her to come closer to confirm his suspicion.

'That is a man's tail you have around your neck woman,' he said to her, almost in disbelief. The woman had not understood. 'It is a *prick*, it is a *prick* you have around your neck woman!' Father Julian spluttered, pointing out the small monstrosity.

'That it is lord,' the serving woman, a mother of advancing years with her grey hair coiled into a bun, answered gravely.

'You feel that such an appendage is a pretty pendant for a necklace?' the priest suggested.

'My mother gave it to me lord,' the old servant answered, nodding and shaking her head as if unsure which gesture would be most pleasing.

'A beautiful sentiment no doubt.' He dismissed her with a wave of his arm.

Across the great oaken table a row of eyes was concentrated on something at his back. Julian turned and saw the Queen standing there dressed in a gown of vernal green, which even the dim and ever changing torchlight could not repress. Her wheaten hair fell loosely about her shoulders and around her neck she wore a stunning torc of braided gold. Her eyes, which Julian knew to be as beautiful a lilac blue as the sea Aeneas himself had sailed from Troy, were glitteringly opaque and in each of them was a single point of light like a banished star in a black sky.

She carried the great sculptured drinking horn filled with mead and plugged with gold and was serving the Men of Kent and Radwald's thanes and when she was done would then serve the table of the King before resuming her place at his side.

This was no ordinary servant. Excepting her native dress this might have been Minerva in her Olympian glory with the wings of her symbolic owl spread supremely for a halo. For the Queen possessed an argumentative wisdom that Father Julian wilfully put down to demonic sophistries but which, in a more generous state of mind, he conceded was more than a match for either himself or the Kentish Ambassador.

'Is it not the case that every woman has a prick around her neck in some sense,' the Queen said acidly, 'and every man the hoop of a woman.'

The priest merely looked over his shoulder at her. He had long suspected her of witchcraft against him and so the remark she had made was as an arrow to its target.

'Are you to eat that mutton, Father?' Hengest barely waited for an answer before spearing the meat on Julian's plate with his knife. The priest watched with distaste the slapping of the heavy shaven jaw. Grease clung to the warrior's drooping moustache under which he had a fat lip. His huge size had not prevented Breca punching him in the mouth. Some remark Hengest had made about Breca's wife.

Breca's wounded nose was like a trampled strawberry and the purple bruising around his eyes made eggplants of them. Hengest had smashed his opponent's nose. What instinctive lumps they were and now they were friends again. They fascinated Julian as he had been by the natural history of the fountain at Montecassino.

Julian turned his palm and closely examined it: the same small scar showing where the nail had come through. He clenched and unclenched his hand. On cold mornings there was always a certain stiffness to the hand, an intractability which seemed to say: 'I have been *transfigured*; this freely given hand belongs to God.' He thought of Magdalena with the warm wind that summer day blowing through her tangled hair and it had become the affirmation of his existence. Often he dwelled on it and the memory was the window through which he thought he saw God. But then sometimes he dreamed that he was dragged over the nails of a hillside leaving his flesh for a murder of crows. A few herbs from the garden in exchange for freshly baked bread. The wonderful herb garden had a local reputation. God had surely blessed it. And the diligent monks who turned its soil. The crude smells of the feasting hall, roast meat and ale, tallow fat and torch smoke, were ponderous on the air and the sour heat of convivial human beings crowded out the delicate sensuousness of his memory.

He signalled to the nearest chattel for some soup, barely noticing it was the same old crone, until her necklace swung into his field of vision as she set down, somewhat shakily, a bowl in front of him. Simple bean and bacon soup. Heavily salted with a rich and satisfying smoke. Julian had of late become more accustomed to the food he was forced to exist on. The discernment of his palate seemed to have been finally blunted by the rough and ready blocks of taste that formed the staple diet and now sometimes he was prepared to admit certain combinations of these rough and ready blocks worked well. Julian was nostalgic though for the fragrant herbs of his garden. In Radwald's kitchens everything seemed boiled or roasted beyond all help.

The heavy timbered doors were flung wide to the evening. The fine weather had meant ease of roasting and preparation outside and, beyond the door, Father Julian could see a couple of the nearer fire pits and the merrymaking of the crowd around them. Such a hubbub. Be healthy one and all. Aside from the unfamiliar surroundings and the consonantal speech it wasn't so far removed from feasting in a Roman village. He gave to the noisy crowd a paschal colouring. The Dionysian chaos had the similitude of a pattern in it: dark shadowy figures dancing like honey bees around the fires. There was a great shout. Something was happening. With a great clattering a huge spitted pig was shouldered into the feasting hall, followed by what looked like the frame of a roasted goat, and both were hauled over to the giant trestles for carving.

Julian watched as Earl Angletheow came down from the King's table to cut the inaugural slice and people lifted themselves off the benches to watch. He caught the eye of Ambassador Uric who had the honour of the King's table. A short while later he noticed him gone; perhaps for some air. The admired Earl sharpened the knife against a large whetstone, cutting a huge slice from the pig's flank to a rousing cheer. He raised a toast to the god they called *Ing* and looked directly at the King when he did it.

'Be healthy!' the Earl cried to the rafters.

'Be healthy!' the mead hall yelled in unison and there was much clapping and echoing cries among the inebriated guests.

Something else was now happening but a range of hills had risen to block Julian's view. His Kentish companions had stood up and were turning to look. A great hue and cry and more clapping. Julian clambered onto the seat to gain a vantage point.

'What is it Father?' said the poet Heoden, looking up from where he had remained seated at Julian's right.

'A wet-nurse by the look of things. She has tucked away her bub and handed the King's daughter to that slave boy,' Julian answered, getting down again. 'What it means God only knows.'

'She has come to join the feast,' Heoden asserted.

The slave boy paraded the baby around the hall to rapturous applause. He was obviously trying to hide his face in the folds of the baby's woollen. As he passed the bench Julian noted the pale green eyes and snotty little snub nose. His eyebrows were almost invisible. He was like an albino cat but with eyes of jade. The boy had grown taller and his hair, which Julian had been accustomed to seeing long and tangled like a girl's, was now cut short. He was instinctive and feline in his movements. The peasant witch's familiar had risen to become the familiar of the heathen priestess herself. What it was about the boy that made him special Julian was unable to fathom but clearly it had something to do with abominable magic.

'She might be standing and yet she cannot properly lift her head,' Heoden observed, as the boy sat down with her at the King's table. The baby's head lolled out of the blanket with a peculiar leer and the boy quickly put his hand behind the head to support it. The King stared at his daughter with a look of incomprehension. He went on with his meal but whereas before he had been animated in his conversations he now appeared distracted.

'It remains the size of an unweaned infant,' said Father Julian.

'She, Father, *she* is the size of an unweaned infant,' Heoden corrected him.

'If you insist,' Julian said doubtfully.

Chapter

20

Moonlight ran across the floor of the hidden glade as though Leoba herself had knocked over a bucket of milk in the cattle shed. There was a slight mist above the ground as if the moonshine still kept heat from the cow. Her mouth was dry as pegged leather and her palms itchy. She felt she had grasped a clump of poisonous herb by mistake. Her heart galloped like a whipped horse. She had messed with her thick sensual hair, even dragging some soil through it. She knew it was useless: the shit-bespattered slattern, the washed and wholesome woman, the goddess with the coiled and pale brown hair, it was all the same meat to him. She had difficulty remembering how she became glued within his web. Uric had climbed through the window of her mind and upset the furniture.

She had betrayed her Lady and everyday the baby she had harmed lolled and gaped at her in accusation. Often she saw the tiny idiot Swanhild grinding her gums and gazing blindly at the world over the shoulder of the boy who had become her keeper. A bud on the sacred marriage tree of Radwald and Ealhhild had been cankered. The tears were salt and hot in her eyes as she thought of it. Yet she had not killed the baby. She was not a murderess; the blood of her deed might yet be washed from her hand; for perhaps the baby Swanhild felt the sun's warmth and existed the same as anybody in what really mattered. This thought was a solace to Leoba as she lifted her skirts to avoid snagging them on the various branches that lay strewn across her path.

She waited at the edge of the glade under the half-closed eye of the moon. She tilted her head against the trunk of an old oak, which was ringed around the base with honey fungus, its great fat lips brushed with moonshine. It was a good edible toadstool. She shivered and drew her threadbare shawl closer round. Once, a day into her issue of blood, she had attempted to avert him by declaring herself after the manner of women, but he took her the very same. As for Julian he would barely touch her even though her menstruation be at an end; she had to implore him to touch her and spent several perfectly good days convincing him as to her relative state of grace.

She was chewing on her lip, lost in her thoughts and troubles, when unexpectedly she heard a hooting above her head. She looked up and made out the feathery shape of a great grey owl almost hidden in the gloom except for two bright eyes, which were the rich deep yellow of egg yolks. It was the *fetch* of her iron brooch. She was not afraid of the owl despite the ugly fang of its beak. On the contrary it was a comfort to her.

Uric hissed at her ear: 'I said directly after supper and here you are.'

The Ambassador had clasped his hand over her mouth from behind. She had not heard him for he was soft as a polecat on the paths and her eyes widened with fear as the great owl took off at the disturbance and abandoned her with evil under the stars. For once it was delayed. Usually Uric said anything he had to say to her as his erection dwindled but instead he threw her against the trunk of the tree and pressed his fingers into her face. When he seemed sure that she was suitably terrified he released her.

'I have plans for the *exemplary* Father Julian,' Uric said, leaning an arm against the trunk.

'What have you done to him?' Leoba stammered.

'I am tired of him that is all.' Uric smiled. 'And when I am tired of a thing I throw it away. People as things may clutter up a life. It is the 'rising' is it not, when women sweep dust out of doors and bang away at old hangings?'

Leoba bit her lip pensively.

'You are a buxom but well-used woman Leoba. You are all used up what do you say?'

She shook her head slowly as if it would ward off the inevitable.

'Perhaps not quite,' Uric said, parodying her movements.

Ice crystals were forming in her heart as if fear was a demon whose love was insect-like and hard as iron. He took her hand and it became slowly numb with cold.

'You remember the small task I set you?'

'I cannot forget it.'

'You have a conscience; what a regrettable luxury.'

Leoba shivered. 'What do you want with me if not the usual?'

'I am not a paying clodhopper, *whore*; I *own* you do you understand?'

She turned her head because she could not bear it; but he took her by the face again.

'It is night and yet your dislike of me is such that your pupil shrinks to a pin, but you shall not shutter me out Leoba. I have forced my way through those holes in your eyes as I have each and every hole of your body.'

'If you hate me so then let me go and I will away,' the woman said hopefully, sniffing and wiping at her eye.

'I shall when you have done this small thing for me.'

'What small thing?'

'I wish you to take another draught to the Queen.'

'No I shall not,' Leoba cried and her cry rang around the moonlit glade. There was a noisy rustle as if an animal had panicked.

'Some warm milk for her on a chilly morning? You can finish off the idiot princess too if you wish. Call that a *token*.'

'You are mad. They will suspect.'

'They will suspect nothing. A return of her puerperal fever that is all. A black elf has done it and is away.'

'An elfbolt at your madness,' Leoba shouted.

Uric took a step back as if to contemplate her better. He was like a huge hooded crow nodding his bearded and misshapen chin at her the way that ominous bird nods its grey and probing beak at a shambled corpse. His tunic lit only by the moonlight was a darkly foreboding ash but might have been a Kentish purple. His dark blond hair was parted in the middle and newly cut to his jaw. His eyes were like two dabs of tar.

'Why now?' Leoba asked him. 'It has been more than seven moons.'

The Ambassador smiled at her. His left hand was resting on the hilt of his sword.

'An impatient assassin is a dead assassin,' he answered.

Leoba shook her head in disbelief.

'You shall do it.'

'I will not.'

'What if I were to suggest to the King that a bitter slave with a grudge was responsible for the idiocy of his daughter?'

'He will not believe it. He is a good King.'

'His regal abilities are irrelevant,' Uric said, for some reason glancing up at the sky. 'What a beautiful evening,' he commented.

Leoba rubbed the back of her head against the oak in anguish.

'It was the detail of your mother's fate at the fists of those Anglian warriors that opened the door to me Leoba ... so long ago but you can still see it. I know you can see it.'

She chewed on her lip so hard that all at once she tasted the sweetness of her own blood.

'They used her as a rag to wipe their pricks on and then bludgeoned her.'

He was studying her intently like an artisan chiselling at a block.

'A row broke out over possession of you ... the crassness of the wheel turned in your favour or perhaps you think that it did not ... a virginal Saxon from a lonely border farm.'

'It was not the King's fault.'

'Yet you do not believe it.'

'There was a skirmish and our farm was in the way.'

'And no man to defend it.'

Leoba sighed and shook her head.

'Your father would have been killed too had he been there.'

'Of course,' she agreed. 'There is no safety save what your wit may buy you.'

'Well put,' Uric granted. 'I cannot liven up the old wormwood?'

'You cannot. You twisted things so that I imagined the King owed me a life.'

'It was not reason that made you as easy to drive as a plump heifer. It was irrational sentiment that in the absence of your father, the King should have made things right and he did not in the exact same way your father should have been there and yet was not.'

Leoba wondered to herself and not for the first time how such cleverness had been spliced to such a wicked heart. His reason had been painted in light and his feeling in darkness. Such was the image of his character.

'The captain lied and took me for a chattel.' Even now she felt the cut of the binds as she was slung over the saddle of his horse like the carcass of a young sow. 'I cried out to the King when we arrived at the camp that I was kin but he did not listen and then the captain slapped me so hard he broke my nose. With his open hand he broke my nose,' Leoba said and, as she said it, she began to sob.

'You imagine the King will believe you now? Would you trust in that I wonder?'

'Lady Ealhhild will know the truth. She hates the Kentish hall.'

'We return to our original problem. How circuitous is our life. Round and round we go like so many bugs in a puddle. Once she is dead you have my gratitude. Stay here if you wish and continue the life of a drudge or you have my pardon in Kent to do as you please.'

'You would let me go?' Leoba said uncertainly.

'Once the Queen is dead.'

'What is the Queen to you anyhow?'

The glade, alive with echoes of the woodland night, was drenched in moonlight. Everything before her eyes was glossed with a dreamy shine. She owed not one a debt for the life she had lived. She had heard that the trees of Kent were laden with fruit. So many things she had wanted to know she had seen in the clouded jewel he had given her.

'You shall take the milk at first light,' Uric instructed her. 'You do everything exactly as before. Watch out for that old numbskull who waits on her hand and foot.'

Leoba began a forlorn humming as she discarded her shawl and unfastened the brooch of her dress. He would take her as always like a pig takes another pig.

There was a sickening crack and Leoba crumpled to her knees. She clutched at her face. When she opened her hands they were full of blood. She did not scream or cry out, merely moaned sadly, and felt at her face in disbelief as if she did not know how to put it back together.

A great crimson stain was on her breast and it was silvered under the moon. The weight of him surprised her because she had rarely felt it. She was dry as a mouthful of cinders and he would rip into her. Then somehow she was looking down on her own death, as if she was seated in a chair of the moon, and she saw herself reach to her woollen sock and pull out a blade.

She waited for Uric to stand and kill her. Yet he did not move. She pushed him off with a struggle. The blade was buried in the back of his neck. She lay there on the cold ground tracing the profile of the moon with a fingertip. Her chest still heaved as the blood dried across her face. It began to feel like a mask of baked river mud. She found murmuring through her mind the prayer that Julian had taught her. The prayer that felt as though she called out one last time to her father.

Chapter
21

Earl Angletheow left his catamite sleeping and went across the room to the bowl of water that his attendant had placed a moment before on the table. He took a linen cloth from the open trunk and wiped dry his face. He felt at his beard, which grew fearsomely quickly. He selected a carved antler comb and ran it through his hair which he wore shoulder length. He lay the comb down in a gilt-cornered grooming box and picked up another comb which was identical to the first except in size for it was smaller and suitable for a man's moustache.

The Earl then pulled on his soft woollen trousers, dragged his head firstly through a simple shirt of woven flax, and then emerged through his wave-blue tunic like a big bull seal breaking through the surface of the sea. He felt every bit the great lubbed seal as the planks under his foot shuddered and the beams of the bedstead creaked under his leaning. The disarrayed sheepskins revealed the delicate line of his new favourite's shoulder and neck. He was a magnificent heron both in shape and in stature. An elegant strutting bird with an alluring energy which Angletheow had noted through bedraggled feathers. The youth was soft and flexible but his wrist, as the Earl took hold of it, was not a woman's. It was a male wrist but fragile as the bone of a bird. He caressed with a fingertip the silken hairs that fuzzed the nape of the youth's neck. Daniel, as though he breathed deeply of warmth and security, slept on as if drugged.

Angletheow found the Men of Kent waiting for him. His assistant held at arm's length a riddling object wrapped in a brown woollen blanket. A small crowd had gathered and a fine rain spun webs in their hair. The sky was a slab of weathered rock and the atmosphere among those under the press of it was like a little death. It was the let-down after

146

festival. There were gasps from the witnesses. One woman put a hand to her mouth. Another gripped a man's arm. The unwrapped blanket had revealed the gory head of the Kentish Ambassador.

'For the love of a Lady close his eyes,' Angletheow remonstrated. 'Let us go,' he then said decisively to the Men of Kent. 'Where are they?' he inquired of Finn, his assistant in lawful matters, who had a moment before given over the rewrapped head to a woman who had offered the use of her empty washing basket.

'I thank you for the use of your basket,' said Finn to the young woman. 'I am sorry you are not familiar to me.'

'My name is Brunhild,' the woman answered. 'I am a maidservant.'

'A gruesome ball of rags for your basket,' Finn remarked.

The woman nodded as she stumbled into a run to keep up, which the constant bumping of the basket against her hip made difficult.

At the door of the guest hall Father Julian was waiting in obvious agitation. His thin face was the colour of tainted buttermilk. The guards parted at a single wave of the Earl's hand but for a moment they were unsure whether to allow the woman and her basket.

'Let her in,' Finn told them, 'but keep all others back.'

A couple of inquisitive souls at the woman's shoulder tried to squeeze in with her. 'Can't you follow a simple order?' Finn cried to the soldiers. 'Eject them!'

In a corner of the room was a woman whose nose was swollen like a fat blood pudding. Her entire face was a mass of colours similar to those sometimes seen in the sky at first light.

'This woman is Uric's whore?' said Angletheow to Finn. The smaller man nodded. 'Show her the head,' the Earl instructed.

The maidservant stepped forward and at Angletheow's gesture displayed the head. 'I take it you recognise this?'

The battered woman nodded.

'Her name is 'Leoba',' Finn informed him.

'Leoba,' the Earl repeated. 'Good. Well, given that women are credited, and I have to say in my experience justly, with intuition, you might be aware of what I shall say next?'

The woman's eyes were like those of a hare which feels strong hands take hold of its neck. Angletheow was aware of the eloquent silence of the Men of Kent. A grim row of statues waiting for answers and justice. They would take a terrible grudge back to Athelbert. The Earl had always given the Ambassador short shrift but Uric was highly prized in

Kent and now here was his severed head. Not a very gracious exchange.

'No my lord,' Leoba stammered.

'Shall I tell you what we know?' said the Earl. The woman's face was like fractured pottery. Some mad stallion had stamped on her that much was evident.

'You admit to being this man's serving woman in every sense of that phrase?'

The woman nodded and bit her lip so that a trickle of blood ran down her chin.

'Please, Leoba, if that is your name, do not add another wound to yourself however slight.'

She wiped away the blood. There were no tears to speak of remorse. She was utterly dry-eyed. 'Is your mother here to attend to you?' the Earl inquired.

The woman coughed. 'No, Lord Angletheow, she is dead.'

'Get help for her when this is finished,' the Earl said over his shoulder to Finn. 'Some herb for her nose at least.'

The Earl studied her. 'Did Ambassador Uric use you violently?' At this Angletheow made a motion toward the Kentish group to stay them. 'Did Lord Uric use you *violently*? I mean to say was that his habit?'

'It was, lord,' the woman answered.

'She is a murdering bitch who bites the hand that feeds her. She has a stone from him worth more than her life.' It was the unmistakable voice of the warrior Breca. The quality of it was like the drag of pebbles under a wave; harsh but not especially deep. 'Lord Angletheow we *will* have justice.'

'You shall have it,' the Earl returned fiercely. 'Justice is a slippery thing is it not, a difficult fish to get hold of?'

'The justice is simple,' Hengest said gruffly; 'this woman's head in answer and gild in plenty for the worth of his life to hers.'

'She is an Anglian woman and even though she is of small note and has got herself into big trouble we shall decide,' the Earl said to him firmly.

'Decide then.' Hengest shrugged. 'But do it quickly.'

'I want the Queen to speak for me if she be willing.'

All the men in the room regarded the woman.

'I shall ask her,' the Earl replied. 'You still admit that it was you who killed him?'

The woman nodded. 'This is what he did to me,' she cried, putting up her hands as if to cradle her face but not touching it.

'It could have been any man,' said Breca scornfully. 'She is a harlot. I should kill you now *prick meat*.' Then silence as if the sea had stopped moving.

Angletheow turned to address the accused woman. 'In your words tell me everything.'

'So you did not kill him with his sword?' the Earl said when she had finished.

'No with the knife, as I told you, lord.'

'From behind?'

'Yes.'

'That at least makes sense for he was a warrior of reputation.'

'I could not have done for him otherwise.'

'The problem you see, Leoba, is one of forethought. Do you understand that word?'

'I do not.'

'It means that having taken the knife you set out to kill him.'

'I did not.'

'I am inclined to think that you did Leoba.'

'I did not,' the woman insisted.

'So why did you take the knife?'

'I don't know ... I suppose I thought he might finally do for me.'

'Kill you?'

'Yes.'

'Why then did you agree to meet him?'

'Can a slave say no to her master?'

'I see, I see,' the Earl muttered.

'Where is all this leading?' It was Godric, the youthful Kentish warrior. He, like the poet Heoden, was clean-shaven and wore his hair cropped close to his head. Angletheow assumed it to be a Frankish affectation after the manner of the Roman senate. The Earl ignored him.

A rumble issued from the mountaintop of Hengest. 'There is no explanation except what is in that basket. She is a vengeful and lunatic shrew and that is all.'

'It seems so,' the Earl remarked. 'You all admit that Uric used her roughly ... you have on occasion witnessed it here in this room?'

'*Roughly*,' Hengest cried. 'Not like a madman. He used his whore roughly, so what?'

'It is of no matter,' Breca stated. 'We will have her life and our kinsman's price.'

'I cannot let it happen,' quavered a voice that had yet to be heard. It was the accented tones of Father Julian who had taken the accused woman's hand as if they were innocent children about to run out to play together. 'They will have her life and you know it prosecutor.'

'How will you prevent it?' inquired the Earl, who acknowledged the obvious truth in what the priest had said.

'I shall prevent it by telling you she did not do it and that I did.'

'*You*,' the Earl said uncertainly. 'You murdered Uric?'

'He is lying,' cried the woman, looking aghast at Julian.

'I realise you have become entangled with this woman, Father,' Angletheow said, 'but the crime is hers and so should be the consequences.'

'It is not her crime, it is mine,' the priest said wildly, 'I saw him butt her like a furious goat and force her. God *forgive me* a red rain fell in front of my eyes. I took the knife and stabbed him.'

'Why do I find it difficult to believe you Father?'

'It is the truth,' the priest cried, 'I knew she had gone to meet him and I followed her.'

'It is true he left the feast hall early.' It was the poet Heoden. 'I assumed it was because he finds the celebrations hard to stomach. They do not agree with him. But it was a long time after Uric. I assumed Uric had gone a-wenching.'

'It was not,' Julian said, animatedly. 'It is the paschal time and I must follow the dictates of my faith in shunning abominations. I saw Leoba leaving for the wood. It was only her shadow that I saw but I would know her anywhere.'

'Your faith includes womanising and murder I assume.' It was the Earl Eni, the King's brother who, there to represent the King, was a soft-spoken man of winters only twenty two and one who plainly knew the value of listening as opposed to talking.

'Why tell us this now?' Angletheow demanded. 'Why not immediately?'

'It is a damn fool priest with the fog of sacrifice in his eyes.' It was Hengest who made this observation. 'Father, you should allow a woman to grease your spear regularly rather than seeking to deny yourself and your feelings would not be upset like a cartload of apples. The Faith does not deny you a wife so take one.'

'I am a monk of Benedict not some hapless village preacher,' Julian insisted. 'What can you possibly know of the *Faith*?'

'I know that a wife might have saved you this ridiculous trouble,'

Hengest retorted.

'A wife is not water enough for the flame of *your* sin for I have observed you.'

'And I you Father.'

'Much as I am enjoying this discussion,' the Earl interrupted, 'I think we have strayed.'

'You have before you a cowardly man, Earl Angletheow,' Julian admitted.

'We are, at least, back in the realm of likelihood,' the Earl remarked sardonically.

'A man who was prepared to allow a woman to go to the gibbet in his stead.'

'It is a suffering mist clouding your sight Father, not red rain,' Hengest warned.

'What say you wench?' Angletheow demanded. 'Do not look at him, look only at me.'

'Lord,' Leoba stammered, 'Father Julian speaks the truth.' Her chin fell onto her chest and for some reason she felt at her stomach as if she had a pain there.

'Let us be clear,' the Earl said heatedly. 'You are now denying the act?'

'Yes,' the woman whispered.

'She is a filthy lying whore!' exclaimed Breca, his hand reaching for the hilt of his sword. There was a moment of silliness as he struggled. His straps had become tangled and resisted the drawing of the sword, which allowed sufficient time for Hengest and Godric to restrain him. 'She is a *whore*.' He almost spat the words. 'The gallows is too good for her.'

'Perhaps the Goddess protects her,' Lord Eni observed.

'With respect, thane of Athelbert,' Angletheow said, turning to face Breca, 'your single line in this matter is only that she is a whore and therefore guilty. Please calm down for one thing follows on another and before you know it we are meeting on the field.'

'I shall be there.'

'If your opinion of the womenfolk and of this whore in particular is so small then why allow her to be the cause of more bloodshed?'

'Please Lord Angletheow,' Leoba said quietly. 'I am not a harlot I am a cattlemaid.'

'You are in trouble regardless of your occupation,' the Earl cried.

Only a short time before he had blissfully spooned his lover and now here he was firmly in the ordure of a dangerous farce. When the messenger

151

boy had brought him the news that Finn was bringing a murderess up from the gaol-house and that the Men of Kent were cursing the whole of Anglia a melancholy crow had settled on his shoulder. He cared as much for the Ambassador as if an irritating fly had been swatted and whether this blood-caked woman had done it or the absurd priest of Athelbert he was indifferent. In alternative circumstances he might even have congratulated them. But these particular set of circumstances included Uric's kinsmen, the thanes of Athelbert, who waited impatiently on satisfaction. Kill them or deny them the news would reach the Kentish overlord and a big cauldron of trouble would be dragged over the fire.

'Father Julian, the woman was captured as she sought to rid herself of this gruesome prize. She was seen by a watchman who thought she was escaping the King's service. She was in the farther wood and hurrying in the direction of the river … Finn please spell it out for us.'

'I quote the watchman from memory,' Finn said deliberately. 'We were scouting the outer fence when I caught sight of a shape moving between the trees near the river. Under the moon it had the likeness of a grey rag moved by a stick. Some restless sprite we thought it and we crouched low to let it pass unheeded but then we heard a whimpering from it and our eyes were wide with fright but follow it we must and then in a clearing I recognised it as a living woman … shall I go on Lord Angle?'

'In short they rolled the head from the blanket and she confessed all,' the Earl concluded. 'Like a frightful ghoul all silvered by the moon, was it not Finn?'

'That is their finding.'

The Earl took a step back regarding the woman inquisitively.

'Why cut off the man's head, Leoba?' he inquired. 'It seems too much.'

'Do not answer Leoba,' said Julian. 'You did not do it and this show is inferred. A woman out of her wits on a grisly errand. It is small surprise she knew not what she said. Then or now.'

'Your nobility does you credit,' the Earl remarked. 'Heaven knows you are in need of it. But she was almost certainly caught before you even left the mead hall. We can of course find out the exact *watch* … Now I say to you Leoba that my sister may be eloquent but she will not get you out of this unless she invokes a miracle. If you insist on denial the penalty will be the harsher.'

'The penalty for her will be death,' Julian shrieked. 'I stabbed that evil doer and I shall see him in the endless fire and I tell you it shall endure me in that sulphurous prison.'

152

'There are many ways of death,' Angletheow advised.

'Julian it will be the worse for me,' Leoba whispered.

'It shall not Leoba,' the priest cried, tears starting to his eyes. 'You shall be in paradise.'

'That sounds a lovely place,' Leoba said with half a smile. 'It is a pretty thought.'

'I do not know how any Anglian woman, even a chattel, can lower herself to associate with this apple peel,' Lord Eni said quietly.

'Nor I,' the Earl agreed. 'I ask you again wench why cut off the man's head?'

'I wanted his ghost to see what I had done,' the woman said and sniffed. She wrinkled her nose as if she were about to sneeze and picked at the dried blood around her nostrils. 'I wanted his ghost to come looking for its head and I wanted to hold it up by the hair and show it that never now would I be afraid of a man or of the midden of his heart …'

'You wanted to make his ghost suffer?'

'I know not whether there be ghosts, some folk say its so, others no, but I wanted to show it if it came looking … my mind was like, it was like …'

'What was it like?'

'Like a furious waterfall frozen by an icy wind and I knew not what I did and yet I did know.' The woman shrugged and turned to Father Julian. 'Will he be now in the gaol of fire?'

'Why then did you seek to loose this prize from your keeping?' Angletheow prompted, with a movement at the priest that he should be silent. It was the fact of the head that prevented the Earl from seeing her merely as a flesh and blood woman who had walked into a row of hanging skillets and hit out at them.

'I said to myself why Leoba, Leoba, you are mad, lying here with a man's head under your bed, with all oxenmaids asleep and dreaming of their sweethearts, you will be founded, when the ghost comes you will be founded and the game will be thrown up, and then I worried for the stink, for I thinks to myself this hateful soul is not one of those who lie stinkless in their stone boxes, like you tell me of Julian, and then I think I smell it already like a pig's head left on the boards of a kitchen overlong or when wild pheasants are hung up to turn …'

Angletheow was dismayed and it was clear the other men felt as he. It was like listening to the gibbering of the moon on the day he first painted

153

his lips with the velvet flesh of the red berry and adorned himself heavy with the bracelets and chains of a woman.

For she was continuing: '... a cold fear comes over me and it is a darkling blanket and yet I sweats like an ox and I pull the woollen over me like a babe feared of the dark but it seemed as I heard the head speak to me from the straw under the bed and it berates me for being a foolish slatternly woman and it is like the goodly part of me speaks shortly to the black part the part that lusts a man should use me roughly and I cannot understand because it is the head and I cannot understand but that the gouty head should speak up for the better part of me for the dignity of me and then I see the head bobbing like a red apple in the river and I think about what the girls say when they see my face smashed like a clubbed marrow ... why men can you not see I had to put it off to another world?' She blew her nose hard and a black clot dropped to the floor followed by a fresh dribble of blood. The woman wiped it away with her sleeve.

'It is agreed then?'

The Earl nodded. 'It is agreed Hengest, thane of Athelbert, it is agreed.'

'Sentence follows hard on?'

'Sentence follows but first the Queen shall speak for her as she has asked.'

'Is that really necessary *thane* of Radwald?' It was Breca once again.

'I find your lack of respect for our law disturbing.'

'Find it how you like Lord Angletheow,' said the truculent Breca.

Then Finn asked the Earl if he wanted the woman taken back to the prison house.

'No,' the Earl replied, ignoring the belligerence of the Kentish thanes, 'for the moment she might as well keep here. Leave a guard with her as before.'

Chapter

22

The soldier who stayed behind showed his dislike with a cold stare. Father Julian had begged leave to remain and Angletheow had indulged him, saying he cared little *what* the priest did. A taper dish burned on a weighty trunk which was filled with changes of clothing. Natural light shone through the knotholes and weathered splits of the walls.

'What do you look at egg face?' Leoba demanded of the soldier. 'Look at you standing there with your idiot spear. It's a giant to your own I'll wager.' The guard moved as if to butt her with the wooden end of it and Leoba blenched. The soldier spat on the floor.

'Leoba why annoy him?' Julian said.

In answer the woman spat in imitation of the guard. '*See*,' she said. 'Hate is easy.' All at once she fell to the floor in tears.

Julian knelt beside her and took her hands into his own. 'Leoba we must prepare.' She did not seem to understand. 'In case things do not go as we wish.'

'*Death*,' she said, nodding. 'Perhaps tomorrow. The end of all suffering.'

'Leoba you are wrong,' the priest said gently. 'It is not the end it is the beginning and you must carry to the holy mountain and begin the climb for your reward.'

'Is the mountain a happy place?'

Father Julian shifted uncomfortably and glanced toward the door. 'There is a mountain in Macedonia, a place beyond the sea, and it is a holy mountain. Saints abide in its foothills and the light there ...'

'You have seen this mountain?' Leoba said, her eyes widening like those of child.

In the restricted glow of the tallow Julian was able to see them

155

glistening with a wetness that had become precipitately rich. It was hope that had enriched them. 'I have seen it Leoba,' Julian affirmed. 'It is as real as this dark room.'

'Women are happy on that mountain?'

At her question the beautiful image he had been contriving was dispelled and he was forced to admit that women were forbidden on that particular mountain.

'Then how shall I come to it?' Leoba asked, shocked.

'I must begin again,' Julian said, taking her hands once more into his own. 'The image of the mountain is a way of catching sight of something,' he began. 'Forget the mountain. It was my own hope that I related not yours.' He could see she was listening but not comprehending.

'You do not want me on your mountain?' she said uncertainly.

'I do my darling, my fate, but forget my mountain Leoba, you are being too literal.'

'I do not follow; I am only a cattlemaid.'

'There is no cattlemaid, you are a *soul* and you must journey to the place I told you of.'

'As a ghost?' the woman cried, seemingly stricken with apprehension.

'It is you Leoba, your perfectible self, nothing to be afraid of, it is the you I see now.'

The soldier started to tap the end of his spear against the floor. His eyes glinted in the poor light like those of a fox.

Leoba bumped her head gently against the wall. She wound a strand of hair around her finger and stared absently across the room. 'My hair would be a hovel even for birds.'

'Do not pin it back Leoba,' Julian breathed.

She turned on him acidly, shaking her head. 'You insist on carving a goddess even now.'

'I have fallen short of you,' the priest said sadly.

'Nonsense.' She drew her knees up to her chest. Then she removed the owl pin from her shoulder. 'I want you to keep this.'

'You need it for your dress.'

'I shall knot it.' She looked thoughtful. 'I had in my mind somewhere to come to you but I did not want to colour you the same as my own cloth.'

'You should have come straight to me.'

'What should we have done? What should your Joshua have done? I have nothing, not even Uric's stone for I threw it into the wood. You have

156

nothing. Two children run away and in the later morn two children torn apart by dogs. You say we are *barbarian* when you wax bitterly but you mistake us ... this kingdom is a smithed necklace of worth and order, every village, every farmstead will look up from the plough to a cry from Rendlesham. I cannot even sail a boat for I never had chance, and I know that you cannot. So you see I saved you too.'

'I have failed to save you.'

'No.' She regarded him at length saying nothing.

Julian closed and opened his palm around the brooch she had given him.

'I shall be safe in your keeping,' she said eventually, closing his palm finally on the gift.

'It is an idle toy,' the priest told her, 'it is to God that we must entrust you.'

'It is not an idle toy,' Leoba cried angrily, 'it is the only thing I have.'

'I am unworthy of it.'

'That is for me to decide.' She kicked out her bare feet so that both her legs were fully extended. 'If I lift up this dress now he will have to look,' she said randomly, talking of the soldier who once again was blankly staring. 'He might piss on me as if I was a festering cut but he will have to look. It is the wound of the Goddess.' She made a motion as if to pull up her skirt.

The guard leered defiantly at her. 'It is of similar savour to me as sour ham ... *cunt*.' His voice was deep and the last word reverberated around the great oak piles of the house.

'Ha, you say,' Leoba shouted at him, 'you be so lucky as to have one, twig prick. The only way you can be fucked is in the arse and I'll get a man to do it for you.'

Julian was obliged to forestall the soldier by jumping to his feet because it was all but certain he would have struck her with the round end of his spear. The soldier retreated to a corner saying for Julian to bridle his whore or he would rip out her tongue.

'Leoba,' Julian began, seeing the hot cinder of her eye dwindle, 'do you remember that time at the river when I dunked you under and the water was so cold it took away your breath?'

'Of course I remember,' she answered. 'It gave me a headache.'

'You know that I am a fallen priest?'

'Fallen how?'

'In terrible sin with my god so that I deserve the gaol of everlasting fire.'

'That is a dreaded punishment. Makes a blood hawking seem like a midsummer wedding.'

'We are all fallen and there is much argument about what this means but I have fallen badly.'

'I have offered you the fruit and you have taken it?'

'You remember the story?'

'Yes I remember it: everything is bad because the first woman gave ear to a talking snake. I do not think it good that men shall think it all a woman's fault.' She glanced at the guard who was making short thrusting movements with his spear. 'I would have strangled that snake,' she added, smiling and then kicking her legs together, 'but still I would have offered you the fruit.'

She drew her legs into her chest and clasped her hands about her knees. 'I like talking with you,' she told him. 'I never really talked with a man before, not proper talk. I am both glad that Uric sent me to love you and glad that I was able to do it.'

'I too am glad which is why the rolls of confession sit idle in my belongings. It has taken till now to know I could amend my life with marriage but only to you Leoba.'

'We are married in every way that is important.'

'Not in the eyes of God.'

'Then let him look away from us.'

'He shall not my love.'

'I like a wedding. Now is best, when stars of hawthorn dress the Maiden's hair.'

'If I had only asked you.'

'Uric would have spiked us.'

'What could he have done?'

'He has no fencing.'

'You talk of him as if he lives.'

She shivered. 'I think maybe he does. And would you have married a witch?'

'I am sorry for that,' Julian said, crestfallen. 'I thought the Lady Ealhhild had corrupted me. I tried to exorcise a succubus but it was myself I struggled with. Or perhaps I wrestled with God as Father Jacob did with the angel. I still do not know. I am not the person I imagined. The call of God was not as I had imagined it. I know only that the battle is over. Whether I have won or lost I know not.'

He took her hand and they sat for a while in silence. At one point the guard took a knife from his belt and threw it into the wooden floor. The blade quivered and then was still. The guard pulled it from the plank and replaced it in his belt.

'Officer, might I beg a bit of bread and water?'

The soldier stared suspiciously at Julian, presumably considering whether to grant his request, before knocking on the door and lifting the latch. Sunshine fell into the room like water. He made only a gesture to his mouth. Then the gloom of before flushed out the light. The single taper burned in its dish of smoky fat and the scent of it was once more noticeable.

'I shall give you this cross,' Julian said, taking it from his own neck and putting it over Leoba's head as though it were a garland. 'I shall use the cypress cross from my belongings. This trunk shall serve as the holy table and this light though it be pitiful shall be transfigured. I shall sit on this chair and you must kneel here. We shall use this folded wolf-skin. Though I myself am in sin I remain still a priest. When I call the Christ to supper he shall descend because it is for you he descends and not for me.'

'He will be here in this room?'

'He shall.'

The soldier was beginning to look uncomfortable.

'I am afraid.'

'Do not be. He will accept your fealty. A lordly ring-giver you would call him.'

'The Lord was hung on a tree for us but it only seemed as if he died.'

'No he died and then was raised up to eternal life which means forever.'

'On and on forever?'

'It is toward this candle you must turn. The Lord tells us the kingdom is not of this world. Perhaps heaven is above the dome we call the sky. Perhaps God strides across the top of it like footfalls on the beams of this house. The sun and the moon chase each other, romping like children around the earth. They are impelled by the love of the Lord for his creation. For it is love that first moves everything. You might be a spark jumping from the flint or a seed blown by the breath of angels. You shall know everything that has been, and is, and will be. You play in the mind of God. Think on it Leoba. How can it not be an utterly unthievable treasure?'

'I see another world as a gentle valley and I am dancing steps with the sun among the sweet blooms of the hawthorn tree and a cool air kisses me and I know it is not this fearful world because I am shorn of fear and I skip and I come to a house that I know and my father who I do not even remember comes out to meet me and my mother too and all the worry of her face has gone and they take me into the house as if I was only a little girl playing games in the wood …'

'Our dream is of safety and the Lord Jesus can deliver us.'

'What must I do?'

'Fulfil the sacrament. It is threefold and perfect as the Father, Son and Holy Spirit. It is contrition, confession, and satisfaction. The first means sorrow together with change of life for better, the second is to tell me of your sins in full, leaving none in the darker wooden boxes of your mind, and thirdly to do the goodly acts that I shall give and any that are prompted by your own heart. The rite at the river, which we did only in fun, must stand in deadly earnest for I performed it with a prayerful heart. Let it throw off the old Eve.'

'She is thrown off,' Leoba said strangely.

'The cross I drew across your brow is a visible sign to the angel at the gate.'

'I know not where to begin.'

'Can you remember the ten laws given in the story of the desert?'

'King Moses,' the woman murmured. 'His people found it hard to follow him.'

Julian listed for her the ten laws of the tablets.

'I have done them all,' the woman cried, hopelessly. 'I have done the worst. I have killed a man and he was an evil man and I cannot be sorry for it. Indeed I am glad of it.'

'You must ask God to fill your heart with sorrow for what you have done.'

'I shall not,' the woman said obstinately. 'Should I be sorry for loving *you* because I am not. I am *not*.' The last word she shouted and her eyes were full of defiance.

'Leoba, Leoba,' Julian said, leaning forward in the chair and taking her hand. 'I do not say that it is easy, I say only that you must see your sins as God sees them.'

'He is a god of stone. He takes a heart and wrings it of blood.'

'You are to be perfect Leoba. There is no human bargain.'

'I am sorry for all my life but those two things,' Leoba whispered through her tears.

Julian kept his position in profile to the woman, as was the sacrament, for he dare not look at her. The pain of her confession was to him as when a physician schooled in the art of surgery goes trepanning into the bone of the head; for he himself was the sinful woman rather than she and he felt himself entirely abject at her feet. His soul cried that it was she who confessed him though he knew this could not possibly be.

'You are to be perfect Leoba. There is no human bargain,' he said again.

The woman sighed and looked at her hands.

'Pray now child.'

'What should I pray?'

'Pray that you may forgive your enemy and stay pure unto marriage.'

The priest dropped his head and the woman did likewise. When eventually she lifted her head and was about to speak Julian stayed her with a gesture of benediction. He then recited the eight beatitudes but not in Latin, in her own tongue, such that she was able to understand them.

'I wish you to forgive Uric for whatever he did to you not for his sake but for yours. If you can do this you may see it was wrong to do as you did even at the same time the Lord may have used you as an instrument of his justice. The Lord gave no time for Uric to come to penance but he died him in mortal sin and it is as certain he is in the fire as these boards are under our feet. God has given *us* time Leoba ...'

'I am sad as after festival I stabbed him but he *hurt* me,' she insisted. 'He is a monster.'

Julian nodded and said in a gentle tone: 'I wish to cut you from him and cast you with a good wind toward the shore of heaven. I wish you to repeat the prayer I have taught you over and over. You cannot say it overmuch. All night I wish you to repeat it until your very heart is saying it. I absolve you from your sins in the name of the Father, and of the Son, and of the Holy Spirit.' He made the sign of the cross in front of her and bade her do the same.

'I should have laid stones on him to stop him getting up.'

'He will not get up.'

'He wants to kill us.'

'He cannot harm us; leave feuding to the Lord; he shall repay.'

'If the Lord Jesus had been raped and feared to death by Uric would he have killed him?'

'You have your answer in the Cross.'

'How then should Uric be stopped?'

161

'Perhaps by a woman's hand.'

Leoba shook her head. 'It is difficult,' she said, looking up at him with a smile. Her eyes were like grey pearls set in an iridescent shell.

There was a rapping at the door, the sound of a cudgel against it, and the soldier who had been listening without much interest was stirred into life. Again the lift of the latch, the door opening, and sunshine falling over the threshold. It was not the second soldier though, who entered the gloomy guest hall: it was a boy around ten years old whose hair would have been lost among the feathers of a swan. It was the Queen's familiar and on his shoulder rode the baby princess. Across his other shoulder was strung a hemp-weave sack and a water bag.

'I have been sent with bread and with a skin of water and with a paste for the woman's nose,' the boy said tonelessly.

Leoba unexpectedly let out a wail which seemed to Julian as though it voiced the agony of her soul. It was like an exorcism and she beat her head against the boards in violent sobbing which to him was beyond endurance. In his arms she did not fold but struggled like a terrified hind. She broke free, springing for the open door, only to have her legs scythed from under her by the soldier's spear. He picked her up roughly and threw her back into the room saying at the same time that she should have been locked in the gaol-house along with the other rubbish.

As he comforted Leoba, Julian said calmly: 'Lay the bread and water on that trunk ... yes that is right, the one with the candle. Is there not a woman to bring the salve?'

'No,' the boy, who seemed unimpressed by the short commotion, answered, 'Finn asked me to bring it. I have some learning in the plants. My grandmother was a skilled leech woman.'

'Yes I remember,' said Julian. 'Why carry the baby here?'

'I have charge of her,' the boy replied simply, bringing the baby closer. 'She is happy except for the grinding of her gums. Listen. She gnaws like a mouse on her knuckles.'

There was a muffled snuffling like a runt struggling under the healthy portion of the farrow.

'She is nine moons and she will not sit up. Her neck is a stem of grass with no wood in it.'

'She is blighted,' Leoba cried. 'She is a cankered bud. What can she ever have of life?'

'I don't know,' the boy answered. 'Some say she should be drowned in a sack and if I told the Queen it would be the end for them. I have

162

taken Swanhild to the wood and she has seen the oak king wrapped all in green and I have dipped her in a water barrel when she was hot and she was quieted. What have you had of life that you know to be better?'

Leoba was silent and Julian merely looked at the boy, struck by his precocious reasoning.

'Shall I apply the paste to your nose?' the boy offered. 'It will make the soreness less.'

Leoba nodded and looked away.

'Why bother?' It was the sonorous tone of the guard.

'Finn sent me,' the boy answered looking over his shoulder; 'and I shall apply it.'

Julian marvelled at the boy's strangeness of manner. He was then taken aback as Swanhild was deposited in his arms. He felt her nuzzle at his neck and, a moment later, he had to rescue her as she swung herself backward like an eel caught by the tail.

The boy took a small leather bag and began dabbing ointment from it onto Leoba's nose.

'You have a soft way,' Leoba told him. 'Like a girl.'

'I am not a girl.'

'No, I see that you are not,' Leoba said. 'It was not an insult.'

'Your nose will be crooked when it mends.'

'It is not the first time it has been broke,' Leoba said. 'Perhaps it will straighten.'

'Let's hope so,' the boy said, gazing at her with curious green eyes.

'A girl will dive into those one day,' Leoba remarked sadly. 'Where do you hail from?'

'Wulfingstow in the hundreds of the Earl.'

'The baby has been sick on my shoulder,' Julian complained with disgust. 'A stink of unholy goat's milk.' He took up a cloth from a nearby chair and rubbed the mess from his shoulder.

'I should not jumble her about if you don't want her to be sick,' the boy advised, dabbing ointment around Leoba's nose. 'Is it helping?'

Leoba nodded. 'It tingles now instead of throbbing.'

'Good,' said the boy, standing up and stretching out his arms to receive the baby. 'People say you are a murderess.'

Leoba remained sitting on the floor. 'I am.'

'Why did you do it?'

'You shall find out when I face the King's justice, if you are there.'

The boy nodded as he tucked the bag of ointment into the sack he was carrying. 'Goodbye,' he said, going to the door with the face of baby Swanhild leering over his shoulder. The round shape of her face was like the cup of a mushroom with four specks of dirt for nose, eyes and mouth.

'She accuses me,' Leoba said sorrowfully.

'Why?' the boy said, turning briefly to face her. 'It is not she you have murdered.'

'No it is not,' Leoba said faintly. 'Thank you for the healing.'

'Nasty sprites can torture a wound,' the boy told her; 'they cannot stand these herbs.'

Once again they were alone, except for the watchful officer, in the room which, despite its handsome furnishings, was dismal as the inside of a plain shuttered box.

'I have kept something back,' Leoba murmured as Julian drew close to her. She had motioned that he should do so. 'Something I have not told you.'

'What is it?' Julian mouthed, realising instinctively the gravity of it.

'If you are plotting I shall beat it out of you,' the soldier warned.

'There is no plot, officer,' Julian said quickly. 'It is the way of my worship, to which this woman is agreed, and which I have by right of the King freedom to speak, at least until the Queen persuades him otherwise. This woman must tell me all the wrongs she has committed.'

'Are you young enough to be there at the end of it?'

'Very good officer,' said Julian. 'As I say they are a woman's wrongs, slight enough in their way, but difficult for her to say out loud, especially in the hearing of a man such as yourself.'

The soldier smirked. 'A whore become ashamed. You have worked quite a spell.'

'Have we leave for her to whisper or not?'

The soldier tapped his spear against the floor making them wait for an answer. Then he shrugged. 'She is as good as dead.'

'I thank you for it.'

'There is no help for me,' the woman said when her confession was finished.

'It is fearful Leoba there is no denying it,' Julian whispered. 'It was your own hatred he exploited. It was a scar that he reopened but the casual *malice* was your own.'

'It was not done lightly,' Leoba hissed. 'It was not.'

'It was done for payment Leoba; for the stone.'

'I have thrown it.'

'A blood stone Leoba, a blood stone.'

'I have *thrown* it,' the woman insisted, turning away and covering her face with an arm.

'Your sorrow already shouts to heaven. Do not despair, God will forgive.'

'He will not.' Leoba faltered and then sighed. She looked at him with tear-streaked cheeks. 'How can such a thing be forgiven?'

'The greater the trespass the more love it will seed when forgiven. There is audacious love in even thinking God shall forgive this sin.'

'What is the wrong?' the soldier barked.

'As I told you a small womanly matter.'

Leoba was silent, her head hung shamefully to the side.

'The Lord calls you to supper Leoba are you ready?'

'I like a bit of supper that is a fact,' she said mournfully.

'You have made me smile Leoba.'

'May you love a woman who does such things?'

'I do love her.'

'I am to face the King's justice this eve or had you forgotten?'

'I had not and there is great fear in my mind about it.'

'If I think on it overmuch I should freeze,' Leoba said.

'Then think not on it. We have time. It is not yet midday.'

'Will they hang me?'

Julian said nothing. Instead he began busying about the small preparations for the mass using the wooden trunk with the tallow as a humble altar. He motioned for her to kneel beside it and then he himself knelt and made a benediction. On the altar was the taper dish, the skin of water, the hard lump of bread, a tiny icon of the Incarnation, and the cypress cross which was the length of a child's forearm.

He became distant like the mast of a ship that she viewed from the shore as he turned and stretched out his arms reciting the language understood by his god but not by her and then it seemed to her that she were with him in the ship and that he was no longer the mast of it but the figurehead. The night was unfriendly and they followed a single star across the chasm of the sea. The motion of the ship was gentle, like the rocking of a babe in a blanket, and the Latin chimes were a calm to the wild seas of her mind. She found herself rocking softly on her knees in the back of a ship that set its own course and took her with it.

He told her a telling in the Angle tongue, turning to face her, and it was about the woman at the Lord's tomb when he was raised from the dead. In his body he was raised up because she found the tomb empty. Leoba liked the story because it was a woman that found him first after he was dead. The Lord had come back not as the Lord of the Wood to turn the season and plough the earth but to leave the Lady as if the bread she gave was of little matter. All were to leave for another world where life meant something other than the grinding of flour. Yet how should they live without it? She struggled to understand.

The other worlds she knew of were nightmarish places of tortured ghosts, of an ochre other than that of men, and yet mannish also in the nature of their strange and evil delights. These worlds were enfolded with the world in which she lived, as she caught sight of elves across a misty distance, and this world was a hot-blooded world of violence. She listened to the words that rose and fell like a wave and all at once a lifting breeze seemed to take possession of her. The Lord had not appeared as she had trembled. He was somehow bread and also water. She became mesmerised by the flame that lit the cypress cross and cast its shadow on the wall.

'The god did not appear,' said the soldier, gruffly.

'On the contrary,' Julian answered.

'Tomfoolery.'

'He who has eyes to see let him see.'

'What sort of god has a beggar's loaf as his spirit guide?'

'Indeed a roughly-hewn penis is far more mystical.'

'It is for the crop; for the child in a woman's belly.'

'A god of fornication; something we are all quite capable of without assistance.'

'A god of power; not a god of milk and sippets.'

'I am undone,' Julian said, waving the soldier away. 'Your clever argument defeats me.'

The soldier looked pleased. 'You believe your god will save her from the King's justice?'

'It is not the King's justice that concerns me.'

'You do not care?'

'You are a clod of earth.'

'How so?'

'What the King decides is already known by God.'

'He is a weaver of fate.'

'Not exactly for he does not decide it for his creature.'

166

'Yet he knows.'

'Yet he knows.'

'He decides it then.'

'Does the watcher of a combat determine its outcome?'

'Such a man does not know the outcome.'

'You are brighter than you look at least,' Julian admitted. 'Ah, she wakes ...' Leoba lifted her head and stretched her neck. Then she flattened her hands against the small of her back and stretched her spine, much like a wintered bear when the colour of the year has crept stealthily into its lair. 'We should be married,' she said, standing up and turning to Julian. 'According to the law of the Christ.'

The priest dropped the cypress cross he had gathered like an infant to his breast. It clattered against the floor. He stooped to retrieve it and the light of his eye which had been all but moribund was moistened with astonishment. 'I had not thought of it Leoba,' he stammered.

'Why should you? I was not a Christian.'

'You accept that you are now?'

'I have eaten and drunk of the Lord. I have known him like the woman in the *gospel*.'

Julian felt about as able to make an intelligent remark as one of Leoba's cows.

'This is the word Kentish folk are using is it not?'

He nodded. 'It is the word they use.' A flower of hope had opened in his mind. 'How shall I serve as both priest and bridegroom?'

'Was the Lord not a priest and also the bridegroom?'

'The metaphorical and the material are inextricably mixed,' the priest murmured.

'Speak plainly,' the woman demanded.

'Bishop Augustine was right,' Julian said, becoming animated, 'it was not my way to look only from the peaks of the scriptorium. It was my way to read from the book of life itself, which is the book of Christ himself. It is a book like the Faith, a book of bloody yet spectacular things.'

'Speak plainly,' the woman insisted, laughing, as Julian leapt to take her in his arms. 'Julian!' she protested. 'I am bruised.'

'And I also,' he said to her excitedly. 'And I also, but we live.'

'For the moment,' the soldier sneered.

In shock they both looked at him because they had quite forgotten he was there.

167

Julian sent for Heoden to be a Christian witness. The poet had not condemned Leoba. At least not in Julian's hearing. When Heoden arrived he was visibly amazed at what the couple proposed. He went out and collected a swag of daisies for Leoba's hair. A small crowd gathered at the open door. Heoden had suggested to the soldier, whose face was filled with astonishment, that sunshine be the companion of a wedding and not a shuttered room. At the end of the strange ritual in which Julian modified the blessings appropriately the poet wished them well but warned Julian to keep away from the Kentish warrior thanes who talked in tones of great bitterness.

Not long after this the couple were separated because the Queen wished to speak with Leoba alone. Wandering away from the buildings Julian followed a parabola of hill which had been pastured and hedged with hawthorn. Lambs bleated among the ewes, kicking up their heels like puppets on invisible strings, and it was a honeyed pain to watch them. Abruptly he felt he had stumbled against the stones of a mountainside. He looked above to where the bloody track led on and he saw a woman shouldering a cross against the earth's sharp edge. 'What is it you want from me?' he cried aloud, knowing that whatever the destiny of ordinary men it was only a saint who could trail the Lord beyond that ridge. It was to gain dispensation, not for their own salvation which was assured, but for that of humbler souls that the saints were called. It pleased him to imagine that, by her own effort and that of the saints, an oxenmaid might find herself among the cherished clay. Yet for a soul to be good, grace must empower her, and the implication *was* she should be in receipt of it only if she were already predestined for heaven, in order, so the logic followed, that she should attain it.

Why so Jacob and not Esau? As Jacob had loved Rachel but not Leah. As he himself loved Leoba but not another. It was burning the letters of the Apostle even to question it. It was a miserable state to be unloved of God as it was to be rejected by any whom one loved. Was not this worldly rejection a punishment that might last a lifetime? Julian became lost in his own meditations. How much greater the rejection from the sole source of one's existence!

In this the Lord blew hot as a desert wind which brought a plague of locusts. He was the unmoved object of affection. He might cool the brow of a sinful man with a mystical balm but only if he were a favoured production. An unloved man was helpless against the peg and wire of evil. Not for the first time the heretical shade of Pelagius took Julian's hand over the threshold of the *inferno*. It was not for a living man to question his final home. Only to slump to his knees and pray. Not think on that God knew already what that man would ask of him and whether or not he would answer. So Father Lawrence in Kent, fearing for Julian, had counselled.

Leoba from the very beginning had been designed for heaven. If she was to be gathered from this temporal life then Julian was as sure as he could be that it was for eventual translation to the barns of *paradise*. His own dimly perceived steps would lead on through the nooses of the scaffold. He felt her hand in his as he strode across the field and the breeze blew out his lungs and the sheep-cropped grass of the field was starred with tiny flowers. The blooming hawthorn of the boundary was lovely beyond all description. The river threaded a course across the verdant dish of the valley feeding deeply into the Anglian heartland. He paused to look on it and it steadied for a moment the maelstrom of his feeling. 'If marriage means anything at all it means this,' he said to himself. 'It is for this that a man leaves his father and his mother and clings to his wife. It is to show us that even after the *Fall* we are before it.'

Chapter
23

The King's guard were arrayed around the walls and as a precaution the Kentish weaponry had been laid aside. The high doors at the western end had been flung wide so that the sun put hands on the King's shoulder and seemingly crowned him as a god. The eastern door also was open to the lee of the light but the lower space was plugged with a wide-eyed public. Tawny sunlight fell over the throne of oak, made a stage of the area in front of it, and inflamed the intricate carving decorating every pillar, arch and beam.

There was a sound like a startling wind as Leoba was stiff-armed into the hall. 'She is a beast!' a man shouted from the back. 'Quarter her!' another cried. There was a rising hubbub as though a wind was whipping up a sea and nasty words sprayed about the hall like spindrift.

'Silence!' It was the King. 'Bring her here.'

Threatening to break apart like a fluff of dandelion, Leoba was shoved forward. 'Look at me,' Radwald demanded but as was obvious she was unable to. Instead she fell to her knees.

Father Julian made as if to go to her from where he sat, which was next to a row of oxenmaids, only to be told to sit down. There was absolute quiet except for a muffled choking. Radwald told her in an emotionless voice: 'You will find the strength to face whatever may pass.'

Leoba then lifted her face from the mask of her quivering hands and looked at him with streaming eyes. 'Father!' she implored. A wave-like tremor fluttered through the hall.

'Why call me this?' Radwald demanded. 'You are not my child.' He asked for her name.

'Her name is Leoba,' Angletheow stated, after clearing his throat, and rising to his feet. 'She has care of the oxen.'

'These Kentish men have a grievance,' the King declared. 'It is for me to see it is answered. Lord Hengest are you agreed?'

The towering hill of Kent stood to represent his kinsmen. 'We are in the main agreed,' he said in a thunderous voice. A cloud must have obscured the sun as he spoke for the room was darkened as if someone had shut all the doors. 'We need the good Lady's word that she will not use enchantments of any kind.'

'Queen Ealhhild?' the King inquired.

'I am unaided except by my own wit,' the Queen answered and stood up. There was an appreciative murmur from the crowd. She was resplendent in a gown the colour of rich soil, which was drawn in at the waist by a striking bright yellow sash, and her hair was intricately braided so that the elegant line of her neck was plain to all. At that instant a mellow light was suddenly aureate around her so that it seemed she stepped out of the evening sun.

'This is ridiculous,' cried one of the Kentish thanes; 'the idiots think they see a goddess. How are we to be fairly heard?'

'The decision is mine,' the King said firmly.

'Is she not your wife?'

'Lord Breca ... you are not suggesting what I think you are suggesting?'

'And what is that?' the Kentish thane said unpleasantly.

'That I am ruled by my wife.'

A tense silence reigned throughout the hall.

'I had come to regard your kinsman as a friend,' the King resumed grimly. 'I feel the loss of him myself. Further I am most aware of the wrong that has been done to Kent and of my fealty to the Lord Athelbert. Whatever indulgence I may grant my wife I can ease your mind that if this woman deserves to die then she *shall* die.'

The Kentish thanes seemed satisfied with this. 'The matter of the Queen's oath, Lord Radwald?' Hengest persisted.

'I swear by the Great Mother who is the source of all we see and by the lives of my children that I am unaided except by *sense* in this combat.' The Queen threw back her head and fixed the Men of Kent with an eye that dared them to doubt her.

'We are then happy with the rules of this combat,' Hengest declared. The thickening light seemed to encase him as if a great bear might be trapped in amber.

'*Woman*,' the King stormed. 'Stand up!'

171

This absolute command appeared to give the woman the strength she needed to obey it. She hunched her shoulders and bowed her head as though she wished to be as small as possible yet still remain standing.

'What is your name?'

'Leoba,' the woman said, barely audibly.

'Speak up!'

She cleared her throat. 'Leoba.'

'What is your duty?'

'Ah hem,' the woman coughed. 'I am a maid of the oxen.'

'Are you a free woman?'

'I am not.'

'To whom do you belong?'

'To you Lord Radwald.'

'It is said that yesterday night you had a tryst in the wood with the Kentish Ambassador called Uric and that during this tryst you killed him. Do you accept this?'

Leoba nodded. 'I stabbed him as he lay on me.' Then there was a kindling of defiance: 'He was *hurting* me,' she cried. The King stayed her with a gentle gesture.

There was impatient shuffling from the bench of the Kentish thanes and some huffs of amazement from the audience.

'It is also said that after you killed him you cut off his head using his own sword and brought it back with you to your quarters. Do you accept this?'

'I do.'

Shouts of utter disbelief. 'Wanton bitch!' The words were hurled from the Kentish bench.

'Silence!'

A pause as if the sun had stopped revolving around the earth.

'What has happened to the body and further its head?' the King then inquired.

Angletheow rose to speak. 'I am pleased to say that they have been reunited and await burial in Kent since this is the wish of his kinsmen who shall ship on the morrow. I need hardly add that a whole garden has been needed in its wrapping and that much of its flesh is devoured. Some animal, if indeed it was not this woman, attempted to drag it from its resting place but perhaps finding it too weighty feasted where it lay. A fine end for a treasured guest whose only crime seems to have been the taste he acquired for this snake-eyed harlot.'

The Earl sat down emphatically and seemed pleased with the highly charged effect of his words. It was a forlorn crime and the collective stomach sank visibly under the weight of it.

Queen Ealhhild did not stand to answer for Leoba immediately. She sat on for a time brushing at the nap of her skirt as if she were idly waiting for her nurse to bring her something. When the King softly inquired if she might stand to speak she ignored him and delayed her standing until the shared nerves of the hall had been racked almost to snapping.

'Has the Queen been struck dumb by the horror of what we have heard?' It was the voice of Lord Breca and his words seemed to ring around the roof beams.

'No she has not,' the Queen said quietly and then stood up. There was a gasp from the crowd. The phrase *'for godsake'* was heard and it came from the Kentish thanes. Lady Ealhhild moved gracefully to the middle floor and once again the sun followed as if it were hers to command.

'My heroic brother is right,' she began, helplessly, with an open gesture of her hands toward all. 'The woman denies nothing … an uncapped man lies wrapped in a spiced blanket when only last night he regaled us with stories and jokes right here in this hall … an esteemed guest dealt with most dishonourably to ridiculously understate it but …' the Queen paused for a few moments. '… for the sake of avoiding a feud with Kent should this lowly woman be refused her side?' She shook her head in answer. She strode over to the Kentish thanes and faced them down. 'No,' she cried. 'She should *not!*' The thane Breca had to be restrained by his kinsmen. Hengest's powerful forearm reached across his lifted chest and forced him back. Earl Angletheow had stood but sat down quickly once the spark was put out. The Queen for her part had relinquished ground and once more took the middle floor.

'I shall show that this woman, whom the whole world seems intent on hating, killed this man not in the manner of some cold-eyed lizard but out of simple and entirely understandable fear for her life. He butted her, he raped her, and paid the price.' The Lady turned toward the King. 'My brother implies the sale of this woman's body to the man now dead. I wish to make clear as the pool of a water elf that this *sale* was not as this woman understood it. In short the tastes of this thane were far more severe than she expected … I ask you all to look on her face.'

At this Leoba lifted her head briefly and looked up with tearful eyes, the narrow pupils of which were like rocks cropping in a calm and melancholy sea.

The Earl shrugged his broad shoulders. 'Any man might have done it.'

The Queen smiled. 'I think in all likelihood not.'

'I say only that another may have done it.'

'Suggestion is not likelihood brother.'

Angletheow shrugged again.

The Queen paused and ran her eye around the room. 'Leoba, come over here.'

Hesitantly she stood and shuffled over to where the Queen waited. There was a grimace on her face as if her bowels were being wound onto a bobbin. 'Now if your fellow maids might shield your breast I would ask you Leoba to uncover your back for all to see.'

'You do not have to do it,' the King told her. 'Say and I shall prevent it.'

'A whore lets slip her clothes, so what?'

'Ha!' the Lady Ealhhild cried. 'So the youthful Godric says!' But already there were sounds of astonishment elicited by the showing of the woman's back. 'Who gave you this scar Leoba? It is as fearful as if a snake rooted under your skin from shoulder to tail.'

Leoba cleared her throat. 'He did.'

'Who is *he* Leoba?'

'The Kentish thane called Uric.'

'Woman,' the King commanded, 'turn so that I may properly see.' In response the three maids shuffled around with Leoba to assist in hiding her nakedness from the rest. She had shuffled out of her inner linen and there remained only her grey dress fallen to the waist. 'A battle wound indeed,' the King grunted. 'Please cover yourself.'

'I now ask you to tell all in what manner this occurred.'

'Who shall I tell Lady Ealhhild?' Leoba stammered, fumbling now at the shoulder of her dress. It had taken her much effort to pull the inner garment over her head. 'She has no brooch Lady Ealhhild,' one of the maids whispered. This maid whose name was Modthryth was as thin as a willow branch with eyes the colour of faded woad. 'Then help her tie it or pin it as it was before,' the Queen said impatiently. 'I shall gift you a brooch, Leoba, when this is over.'

'How *touching*,' a voice sneered from the row of Kentish thanes.

'Tell all of us.'

'The lord sliced me with a dagger as he lusted,' the woman said.

'Lusted?'

'When he was inside me as a bitch and hound he sliced me with a dagger.'

'Nobody heard you cry out?'

'He held his hand across my mouth so that the noise of it was strangled.'

'Then what?'

'He told me to quiet or he would push the knife in deeper.'

'And did you?'

'I bit down on a folded skin – it was a sheepskin – until he stopped.'

'Quite something in the matter of 'taste' would you not say brother?'

The Earl merely looked at his boots.

'I thought I had fallen apart like an ox when it is hacked away from its backbone,' Leoba whispered as if to herself.

'Like an ox away from its backbone,' the Queen repeated loudly. 'Yes indeed, for the actions of this man in *love* had all the delicacy of a butcher.'

'Now she insults the honourable dead,' Hengest protested, pointing a menacing finger that in its sweep took in the King on his throne as well as the rest of the enormous room.

'*Honourable*,' the Queen said with a grimace. 'A curious word to use Lord Hengest.'

'You have not shown Uric did this to her; she is a saleable wench and it is a dangerous market.'

'She is not in general a 'saleable wench'. Any cattlemaid will confirm it.'

'The favour of kith and kin! It seems a dumb show of this stands for the law in Anglia,' retorted the giant thane and his determined expression was of one who knows himself to speak the undeniable truth. 'You will call also an oxenmaid to confirm the evidence of the scar I suppose? Or that traitorous priest who turns himself pimp for the good of the church?'

'I would ask the Kentish poet Heoden to stand,' the Queen then said and the effect of this was little short of astounding. If a curious wind had been wrapped around the gables of the hall it would have been dragged into a commonality of lungs.

'Sit down fool,' Hengest said angrily, grabbing the singer by the arm.

'This is clear of shameful and your songs shall not save you,' warned Breca.

'Sit down Heoden,' shouted Godric, but the poet wrested himself free of Hengest's grip and, drawing himself up to his full height, which was considerably above that of an average man, indeed he was as lean and stretched as any string on his lyre, he stepped forward. His face, which was bony and angular, was as set and stiff as well-beaten egg white.

'I thank you thane for your higher cast of honour,' the Queen said courteously, but the poet did not immediately answer. Then he frowned. 'I am not a courageous man.'

The Lady Ealhhild smiled warmly. 'How long had you known Ambassador Uric?'

'I met him at the halls of Canterbury when I came there to sing.' The poet stretched his chin outward and upward as if a collar restricted him.

'Where had you come from and how long ago was that?' the Queen inquired pleasantly.

'From Constantinople several summers ago.'

'The Rome of the Sunrise,' the Queen said, presumably to inform the wider herd. She nodded as if she were impressed. 'And is this how you add spice to our northern songs?'

'I try to learn from all singers that I meet,' the poet said modestly.

'You have learned well,' the Queen acknowledged. 'But you are Kentish born?'

'I am, from the south near the short but difficult crossing to Francia.'

'Would you say you knew the Ambassador well?'

'Very well,' the poet answered.

'He was in the habit of sharing confidences?'

'Yes.'

'Ones that he may not have shared with others?'

'I do not know.'

'What sort of things did he share?'

'All sorts but he took delight in shocking me.'

'Shocking you?'

'Yes.'

'*Why* do you think?'

The poet frowned again. 'I think he wished to show that the monsters in the songs are always from among men and that there are reasons why they do what they do.'

'He did not believe in other kinds?'

'No, he did not.'

'Do you?'

'I know not, that is I am unsure.'

'So the nightwalker *Grendel* for example was a hero to him?'

'Not hero no,' the poet answered, shaking his head. 'I think he was

176

aroused by the idea of a lunatic who ate the flesh of men. He said he understood the lonely bliss of it.'

'Would you say that *you* understood *him*?'

'No I did not.'

'Were you afraid of him? It is alright you do not need answer.' The Queen paused thoughtfully. 'What, would you say were his feelings toward women?'

'He thought nothing of them.'

'He did not like them?'

'He liked few men also but hid it well.'

'He was a lone wolf?'

'In his soul but outwardly not, as you yourself have seen. He delighted in a feast and the drinking of ale with hearth companions. At least as I say, outwardly.'

'Uric was the best of men,' Breca shouted. 'The stinking poet lies!'

The Queen ignored him. 'So Uric delighted in taking people in?'

'He was a mover among the courts and an excellent one.'

'When did he tell you of this woman?'

'Around harvest month not long after we arrived in Anglia.'

'What did he say of her?'

'He said he had found an ignorant shag sack who pleased him.'

'Why did she please him?'

'He said she liked to be hurt.'

'Did this shock you?'

'Not this no, for I have come across men who wished to be hurt and women also. It is like a herb to them and within reason seems to me to be their own interest.'

'What then did shock you?'

'The millstones in his head were always grinding a doom for others.'

'What do you mean?'

'I mean he joyed in preparing bear pits and watching people fall into them. He once suggested mischief as the gravy that made life edible.'

'Why do you think he confided in you?'

'I know not, although he once said there was something in me that he could not get at.' The poet shook his head. 'I know not what he meant.'

'Perhaps it was your feeling for the age of heroes. Such men must have irritated him like a horsehair shirt?'

'Heroes did not exist for him,' the poet said almost wistfully. 'He said the ends they sought were always for themselves. Empty glory he called it.'

'Do you agree?'

'I do not agree that because an intention is found to be mixed it is therefore worthless,' the poet stated and then coughed as if he were embarrassed to state it thus. 'If the outcome for another is good it is good, if bad then it is bad; for myself that is how I judge.'

'Quite,' said the Queen. 'Did he cut this oxen woman from her neck to her arse?'

'He told me of it.'

Noises of disgust and mockery were hurled from the Kentish bench.

'Will you then tell *us*?'

The poet sighed. 'He said he had unfastened her while fucking her and that it had been a bore to bind her up.'

'Bind her up?'

'Yes.'

'How did she survive this wound?'

'I know not what she did.'

There were sounds of disbelief from around the hall. 'It is true,' a voice cried out, 'a monster has been among us and his fastness is in Kent!' The King demanded silence and bade the Kentish thanes cool themselves.

The Earl waited for his sister to settle herself before slowly standing. He stroked thoughtfully at his beard before crossing the floor. He was as tall as the poet, who stood seemingly unafraid before him, but in build the Earl was almost ludicrously wider. 'Why wait until now to betray your kinsmen?'

'I speak only the truth,' Heoden answered, but the remark had caused a blench. It lingered in the form of a slight twitch to the poet's eyelid.

'Ah the truth,' the Earl said, nodding. 'Something a shaper of entertainments knows all about.'

The poet's teeth seemed clenched. He glanced briefly at Leoba who had been allowed to sit down. She was sitting on a three-legged stool in despondent aspect with her hands crossed loosely on her lap.

'You say that Counsellor Uric confided you of this wounding?'

Heoden nodded warily.

'Yet you did nothing?'

'What is it that I should have done?'

'Told your kinsmen, told me, told anybody, made up a tale about it ...'

'Your barbed remarks do you no honour.'

'Your erratic sense of right and wrong also does you little.'

The poet made no answer; instead he merely rolled his eyes.

'You imagined Anglian law did not protect such a lowly creature?'

The poet nodded. 'I know the law is pressured according to custom and politics.'

'Did you not think yourself of confronting Uric?'

The singer laughed derisively. 'Uric was never 'confronted' as you put it by anybody that I ever saw, except that is for Athelbert the King. He was a leading hunting dog for the Kentish hall, vicious beyond the ken of a sane man. To face him would not be a light breakfast even for my kinsman there, the Lord Hengest.'

All eyes looked at the great warrior of Kent who despite remaining steeled in his expression did not contradict what the poet had said.

The singer pursed his lips. 'I am no warrior I only tell of them,' he said finally. 'To deal with Uric I should have had to quit him as he slept, just like this poor woman here, because to wound him ... well like the unarmed man against the worried boar, death follows swift on.'

'How long are we to listen to this horse crap?' the warrior Breca called out. 'Hengest,' he implored. 'How *long* my kinsman?'

'You were a witness to this morning's pretty rite were you not?'

'What do you mean?'

'I mean lord wordsmith at the wedding of this woman.'

'I was.'

'You have sympathy then for the woman and the Roman priest?'

'Not pity if that is what is meant.'

'Why then?'

'I was pleased that one of Uric's schemes had flowered unexpectedly.'

'Explain.'

'He planted poison nettles but husbanded eglantine.'

The Earl shrugged the large fell of muscle and bone that formed the massive of his upper back and shoulders and accompanied the shrug with a strange harrumphing noise which was like the call of a giant elephant strolling the shores of Asia. 'Why is it a poet cannot call a beam a beam?'

'Habit,' the other answered dryly.

'You mean something beautiful sprang from something rank?'

'Yes.'

'Go on.'

The poet sighed audibly enough for all to hear. 'Uric wished to foul the priest. Father Julian, excuse me, but you were an easy mark.'

179

'Why?'

'He said he had become an embarrassment to the Faith and our mission. He said he wished to foul him and then quit him in mortal sin. He enjoyed seeing Father Julian trailing after a whore like a lust-ruined whelp.'

The Earl looked quizzical. 'Mortal sin?'

'It deserves punishment in flames under the earth.'

'How pleasant,' Angletheow remarked, looking to the wider audience; 'and these Romans call *us* barbarians.'

Heoden looked into the air above the Earl's head.

'Has he not been fouled?' Angletheow inquired.

'Not to my way of looking.'

'You are a Christian man from Kent are you not?'

'I am a man from Kent.'

'You are resistant to change then as a rock in the tide, like us poor folk here at hall, clinging to the old ways, the old service to the Lord and Lady of the World?'

'I cling to no god.'

'The Goddess, then.'

'Perhaps,' Heoden said, nodding. Then he added strangely: 'A goddess might be glimpsed but it is no more than a womanly quality.'

'Who then made this world?'

'I know not; perhaps it made itself.'

Loud laughter rang around every part of the hall.

'Be careful poet,' the Earl said when the laughter had died down; 'a singer really is 'shorn from a different sheep' as the saying goes. You are in some sort of sordid alliance with the priest and his wench. It is clear no love was lost between you and the Ambassador.'

Heoden was visibly agitated and his voice shook. 'Those words are unworthy of you.'

'I take them back,' the Earl said quietly. 'I have no wish to insult such a fine singer.'

King Radwald then stood up from the gilded throne and stepped forward into the clearer torchlight. His opulent tunic was the colour of haematite and his leggings a soft grey like the breast of a wood dove. His long cloak which was of the same optimistic grey was fastened by a chain of golden rings. His shoes were of soft comfortable leather and the laces bound his leggings neatly to the knee. His belt buckle was an intricate showing in gold. He wore a leather breastplate of such work as to flatter

180

a Roman governor. In the middle of it was a wolf's head which seemed like a living skin at the Lupercal. When he spoke, though it was only to call his brother Eni and his brother by marriage, Lord Aelfwine, to confer and give him salted meat for his thought, it was like the ominous thunder of a god. After considerable deliberation with his closest thanes the King said simply: 'She has nothing to answer.'

A woman might step from her house and feel the touch of a storm god brush against her skin. There was a squall of curses from the Kentish bench. A soldier who barred the way was thrown over and had his face stamped on for good measure. It took more than one to restrain the wild Kentish stallion who was amok in the hall. The bench he had lately been sitting on was slung at the crowd. Angletheow, Aelfwine, and Eni rushed in defence of the King who strode forward to meet the fury. The Queen stood protectively in front of the oxenmaids. Few appeared to notice the strange round-shouldered man who was the priest get up in tears and hug the stunned and happy woman.

The King stormed back at the thanes of Canterbury: 'This is the decision of the trial by word and none shall overcome it.'

A hail of Kentish curses answered him.

'This is how you deal with the guests of your hall!' Hengest raged, and it seemed that blood had tinged his eye. 'A woman not worth a light and yet more to you than the goodwill of Kent.'

'Needs be you shall kill us!' yelled the truculent thane Breca. In contrast to his kinsmen the Lord Godric had fallen into a sullen and hate-filled silence.

'No killing is necessary,' the King insisted. 'All that we require is that you respect our law and on the morrow ship with your unfortunate kinsman back to Canterbury where you are free to treat him with such rites as you see fit.'

'But I *require* a killing,' Hengest retorted in a voice that had quenched in a moment from fire to rime-covered ashes. 'In the name of Athelbert proud king and Christian sovereign of all these lands, I challenge the Angles of the Sunrise to single combat. This is what I demand on the morrow before we leave with the white stallion of Kent held high.'

The benches were in uproar.

'Should I win tomorrow,' Hengest cried, when his challenge had been met by the Anglian champion, Lord Angletheow himself, for all the hall and those crowded in at the doors to hear, 'Kent shall require the life of this shameless woman; for a woman's soul is a stagnant well and foul is the water that is drunk from it. I task the Lord in heaven to oversee my trial and be strong for me; for he is the true Lord and his power is mighty; he brought his people out of the land of pharaoh where the sun is unwomanly and fearsome hot and he brought them to a good land, to a land of good soil and good fielding where cattle and sheep increase and the corn grows high as a head. This he has done also for us ...' The thane paused to wipe his mouth with the spade of his hand, and then emotionally he continued: 'We, the Jutish, the Geatish, the Frisian, the Saxon, yea the Anglian kin also, have we not been brought out of slavery to devils and across the desert of the sea to a good land?'

'And what *thane* makes you lay this feat at the door of your Roman god?' It was the Lady who had spoken. She had stepped forward from the bench of the oxenmaids and now stood shoulder to shoulder with her noble kin.

'Kent prospers in alliance with all good Christ-folk. We are one kin in Christ.'

'Forgive me,' the King said with a wry smile, 'does Counsellor Uric walk again?'

'You are enslaved to foreign kings who hide behind this Christ,' the Queen remarked.

'Does not Anglia prosper?' It was the King who had spoken.

'For the present,' the warrior of Kent answered; 'he gives you time to accept him.'

'What if we do not?'

'You cannot endure alone; you have many enemies.'

'It is a strange offer you make us,' the Lady Ealhhild noted, 'this gift of friendship bundled up in threats. Francia is an iron fist in a mitten of homespun.'

'Common purpose, common feeling and identity bring an end to feud, but you refuse this, you insult us and insist on warring against us.'

'We wish only to decide things for ourselves according to our ways as we have always done,' the Queen said angrily. 'If our girls at rising time wish to dance naked through the woodland halls and we decide that it is not unseemly at festival for them to do so then they shall dance and no woman-hating priest or king is going to tell us that it is shameful and forbid us with laws we do not recognise.'

'Then tomorrow shall trial the true Lord against your devils,' the Kentish warrior said grimly. 'And overturn this wrongful verdict.'

'It is the dragon who tends you all!' a voice cried of a sudden and all turned to look in its direction. A tall gangly youth had pushed between the press. His hair was a reddish brown the colour of the poison conker when it falls from its green spiky shell and his stature like that of a heron but no beak did he have for a nose, rather it was perfectly proportioned, like the rest of his handsome face. 'The Christ walked on this land and we built a proud city in honour of him but then we turned from God and we were wicked and he gave us up to Satan whose cruelty was let slip on us and it was you the godless *Saxons*, so many heads of Satan, and you killed us and enslaved us and the walls of the city fell …'

'*Daniel*,' Lord Angletheow shouted. 'Shut up and step back!'

'You know this fool?' the King said in bewilderment, as were all the royal onlookers who had been momentarily stunned it seemed by the outburst from this youth, who looked nothing more than a favoured slave. 'Tell him if he speaks again his tongue will be bitten from his head.'

But the youth mumbling and in tears had already fallen back into the crowd, his arm pulled insistently by a boy with hair as fair as a washed fleece. People looked quizzically at one another as much as to say, 'What a strange occurrence!' But the youth's outburst had not been lost it would appear on the mighty warrior of Kent.

'You speak wisely *islander*, for you are a foreigner are you not? You say the devil drove us; is it not the will of God? Was it not as much *our* fate? You see God's dealings with yourself alone but he deals with all of us kin and foreigners alike. If we have now a homeland and you have not it cannot be against God's will. It cannot.' Hengest searched after him with eyes that were hot with feeling; but the youth had vanished. 'Come back to your God,' the thane shouted. 'You will find him alive and well in Kent!'

'You are all *fools*,' the Queen cried; 'an idiot boy tells a golden story of final ruin but he was a Roman *slave* and now he is the slave of another. What of it? He has been freed but no matter. He might have been sold and shipped away but as I say a thankless slave is no matter. You, thane of Athelbert, are likewise a Roman slave. You speak of the *man who died* as if it were more than a common gift; as if you had forgotten the Lord of the Wood. The Rome of old reached far and it reached wide but they never ruled us. Safe in our forests we were and when they came crawling we hammered them with an iron hand and we hammered them until they fell back with the curses and taunts of our women in their ears. They marched over every soul in their hateful path and trod them into dust but never us. *Never* did they trample us. And they shall not trample us now. What should your witnessing grandfathers think of you? Look at that *priest …*'

All followed the line of her pointing finger and saw the shabby figure who still embraced the woman whom the law had saved.

'He looks a sight for pity but he has all the power of a newborn order behind him. Yes, yes,' the Queen continued, nodding her head, 'a few of you laugh at what I say; you are blind *fools*. This is a trespass we have not faced before; it is slimy as a pond eel; it has gleaming eyes that promise us gold here at home and after death. It has a tongue that seems to be sweet but is forked as a worm's. It will not meet us manfully on the field because it comes always in peace, speaking of fellowship, and of brotherhood, and of an end to feud. Who does not wish an end to feud? The importance is what is its *price* and does the promise have weight? I say the price is too high; the weight that of a feather. One empire is raised only to clash with another. The safety it claims to bring is false. More still you are safe like a sparrow in a cage while the hawk flies free on the wind. I say it is time for the Angle kin to choose *freedom* from Kent and from Francia and from the Roman high priest. If we stay in service to the Lady of the World she will protect us as she has always done.'

She fell silent unusually overcome it seemed by the heartfelt charge that gave her words power. There were cheers from the assembled kin for the Lady was well loved and respected.

'My combat is not with words but with fist and spear,' Hengest told her flatly. 'On the morrow Lord Angletheow. On the morrow.'

Chapter
24

Away the crowd went to sit at supper, to unplug firkins of ale, to lay in moments of excitement with one another, and do all the things that were customary while the first star shone above them. A few streaks of blood were left beneath a looming plate of cloud. Crawling over the hollows and darkening slopes the small festival fires were like glow-worms in the Maiden's palm.

Shepherds had driven the animals in from pasture and the pigs had been rounded up from the woodland range. These toilers of the royal hundreds flocked themselves to the fires, to warmth from the chilly dusk, to hunks of bread and cheese and salted meat, to clay beakers of ale, and to gossip that bubbled away like a boiling pan of gruel.

Through this atmosphere of roaring lights Father Julian picked his way, hunched and bent as if a bundle of sticks were on his back, and his mind was in some way similar to the night spread out before him: blackness, dotted with flashes of feeling and of memory, and a sense of foreboding, which breathed like a dragon in the darkness. Leoba had been freed only to be pegged again like a leveret to a snare. She had been sent to the gaol-house to stew away the night. Julian had insisted on accompanying her. The gaoler was a slow-witted ape and brutal. He had a tattoo of a spearing boar under each eye. Thankfully it appeared that since the Queen had taken up her cause the attitude of the people toward Leoba had altered. She had become an embodiment of tribal feeling. Father Julian saw the way of it. The Anglian nobility cared nothing for the life of a cattlemaid. They had not been long in the gaol-house when a servant had come to them, directed by the thanes of Kent. Lord Hengest had requested that his priest confess him.

'Hengest will be stoking his rage for tomorrow,' Julian had assured a stricken Leoba; 'he will not waste it on me. They are Christian men and they will respect this cross if they respect not me. He tapped the cypress cross tucked in his belt. More than this if Lord Hengest wishes me to confess him before his trial he will hardly want to blacken his soul once more with the sin of my blood.' She had not immediately understood. 'His wrongs shall be wiped clean by Christ through me, as your own sins were, and if he should fall tomorrow he may be taken into paradise. In harming me he risks falling into darkness.'

At the edge of a bower he suddenly noticed a fornicating couple; like two shameless creatures of the forest they were and but for the human addition of a blanket might have been two rutting hares; the larger of the hares made an unmistakable grunt of release and then the two lay still; more now like a pair of senseless logs than animals of living blood; but animals they were as Julian stepped on a brittle twig and the snap brought the gormless man to his feet. As the man pulled up his trousers he fell over and Julian heard the silly giggle of the woman. Then the pair were up and away taking with them the blanket and the candles that had made an unholy cross of their woodland couch.

There were small drifts of fire-beetles in the air and on the vegetation. The supernatural rode high under a nubile moon, which coyly drew scarves of cloud across her face, the way a high priestess of Isis might have toyed with the veils of her concupiscence. Something deeper in the wood called him to perdition and he kept to the margin. The gaol-house was a tiresome distance from the noble buildings.

The core of the feast lay in the King's hall and on the slopes that fell gently away from it and this was where the majority of revellers were to be found. Father Julian became fully conscious of these floating convivial sounds as moments before at the edge of the strange bower he had become abruptly aware of the fine shower of fire-beetles. He discovered the guest hall dark and seemingly empty. Once inside his immediate impression was of a cold and bitter darkness which in its feeling made the chilly woodland night seem pleasant. And following hard on that feeling was the knowledge that he was not alone in the room but that the Men of Kent were there all three and watching him like wolves in the shadows.

'Why have you no light?' the priest said loudly. 'Are you sleeping?' In the darkness he was fumbling to the corner where he knew his bed to be, for it had occurred to him he might collect his icon of the Madonna and the rolls of his own confession.

186

'It seems a long time does it not since that woman first said for you to make of her a pallet?' It was the unmistakably gruff voice of Hengest. 'Have you returned Father, like a murderer to the scene of his crime?'

'Why have you no light?' the priest said again.

'Night has fallen on this land and far be it for we to lift it.'

'You are stoking an icy rage.'

'Have you not found that frost burns better than fire?'

'It may, it may,' Julian agreed. He hit his shoulder on one of the house posts. 'I do not wish to disturb you in your preparations however they may be.'

'Warriors have been known to eat the flyblown mushroom.' The timbre of the voice was as cold and tight as a drumbeat in the snow. 'Such are cut down in their recklessness if a fighter like an icicle stands firm.'

There seemed to be a mood of grave agreement in the room but the Lords Breca and Godric said nothing. Julian had not been sure even exactly where they were but had assumed them to be resting and as his eyes accustomed themselves to the different quality of this enclosed darkness he discerned them.

'What pray are you rooting for like a pig in a beechland must?'

'Trifles of my trade,' Julian answered, throwing over the woollens and skins. 'I almost have them.'

'And what exactly is that?' The voice once again was like the echo of a funeral drum.

'What?'

'Your *trade*.'

'You are amusing, Lord Hengest, but I assume you wish me to confess you anon.'

'I have confessed myself already with no need for you.'

'Without a priest,' Father Julian said sharply; 'you are sure you have not addled your mind with mushroom?'

'God knows what he knows; he knows my heart already, what little there is of good and the plenty that the crow also knows.'

'You balk at the law of our Father in Rome?'

Julian was only half-listening because he had in his arms his confessional roll and the cloth of his covenant but the tiny icon, in size not much bigger than an oak leaf, was not in its usual place of keeping under the folded sheepskin he used for a pillow; he remembered replacing it there before Leoba was escorted away for her audience with the Queen. He liked the Madonna there under his head for he felt comforted by her in the often savage gloom; it was as if he rested his head on the bosom of the world.

'Many are the Christians that dissent from it.'

'Yes they are heretics and blasphemers swollen with the hubris of the tree of knowledge; they shall be called to account by Saint Peter himself.'

'You know the story of the *prideful tower*, Father?' For a moment this bodiless voice had warmed a tick in its conversational tone, as if it had raked a single ember from the ashes of its own cremation.

'You have an expression 'do not teach your grandmother to suck eggs' I believe?'

'Fair play to you Father, but do you not think when the Lord smote that tower and sent the folk babbling into the darkness, leaving us in the world where there is much talk but small meaning, that he still understands us all, every one?'

'Of course.'

'You find it hard to imagine the language of angels as *our* language.'

'Each may imagine it as he wishes as none of us know,' Julian answered; 'but I am here to tell you clearly that if you are not shrived by me you are not in penance properly before God; this apostolic power comes not from Rome but from Christ himself; I charge you Lord Hengest to pay your attentions closely to the new teaching and not become too distracted by the old.'

'I have your picture of the Lady Maria.' Again the disembodied voice was an abrupt falling of sleet.

'You have the icon?'

Hengest had his bed furthest from the door. His shadowy bulk was like a great hill dimly covered in snow.

'It is the old Mother you worship *Roman* and you are too puffed up to know.'

'You understand nothing,' Julian retorted. 'I charge you; please give me the icon. If you want confession then fall now to your knees and I shall attend you.'

'Take it!'

The words snapped like a branch under the weight of too much snow. There was the tiniest sound of a small object landing on a rug and Father Julian grovelled about with patting hands in a desperate search for it.

'It is an ancient goddess who commands your allegiance,' Hengest said crisply and at the sound of his words a hunter in a forest of bare trees might have lifted his head to watch for a startled bird. 'See how you fall at her feet.'

'You have learned nothing,' Julian answered; 'a bear may as soon be taught to appreciate the reaching of man's spirit in art.'

'You talk well Father, as always; but your lips are glued to your mother's fanny.'

'My mother is dead,' the priest said distractedly, for his inquiring fingers were unable to put themselves on the icon. A roar of laughter rushed around the room like the sea slapping against the steepness of a cliff. Then a long pause as if the sea had been stilled.

In a blink of miracle Father Julian laid hands on the sacred icon. 'I shall come back to you Lord Hengest and offer you salvation and the holy viaticum before your trial of arms.'

'I shall kill all goddesses for you,' the warrior answered.

Chapter

25

The night as before was creepy but after the dankness and fastened cruelty of that Kentish tomb it was as soft and sweet smelling to Father Julian as a newborn baby's scalp. The celebrations went on heedlessly as before. His attention wandered for a moment toward the royal hall where the feasting was loudest and it was like a kernel of fire in the heartland of a proud and ignorant kingdom. He was again at the margin of the wood with its strange whispers and moans. His only thought was of Leoba and that they should pass the night in such a lonely place as the gaol-house in its dismal setting of tortured birch.

He had once seen from a window a songbird captured by a monastery cat. The witless bird pecked about the yard gathering into its beak a few seeds or crumbs of bread more like an innocent one year old than a wild and wary creature; but a cat as thin as a strip of leather was hunting it, motionless against the wall as a caryatid. When Atropus clipped the thread of that bird it was not expecting it. In the flash of a whip the cat had it, smashing the reedy bones of its wing with a practised paw, and Julian had watched the sadistic pleasure of the cat as it let the injured bird limp away before finally taking off its head in an exquisite mouthful of blood and feathers. There would be no more songs from that tiny beak. He had wondered at the creation of such a world and it had continued to trouble him that night as he studied the testament.

A single cry was heard before the sound was muffled out of existence. Father Julian knew only he had been assaulted and some kind of sacking scratched against his face. His nose had been squashed almost to breaking but the sack smelt intensely of malt. A powerful fist had twisted any slackness against his neck. He tried to yell but his cries were extinguished like a suffocated flame. He tried to stand his ground but a torrent swept him along. His feet scraped against the woodland floor. His mind whirled as if Charybdis herself had captured him. Devils were dragging him on a cross of fiendish frame. His arms were locked and wrenched at the shoulder. On these devils dragged him to the very gates of the inferno. Pain he found there such as he could never have imagined. Darkness such that it seemed there would never again be a light.

It became apparent to him then that the human frame had not been designed to withstand such torture. He was unable to move because they had tied him to the tree tightly and his face was mashed against the bark, which was smooth and feminine, not that of the common oak. His outstretched arms were lashed to a pole of sapling and the agony at his shoulders was as if delighting devils had kindled a fire under the pits of his arms. His tunic and undershirt had been stripped from him and he knew not exactly what had happened except they had hacked into his back and at first he had not even felt anything, and this was the way of it, but then he felt the streams of blood run down like upset wine and a gruff voice that he recognised as that of Hengest shout in his ear: 'Use these *wings* to fly to heaven Father!'

He arraigned the Lord, shouting voicelessly into the sky that he was a merciless God, that he should send a soul to the inferno for things he could not help; for things the Lord already knew he could not help; for wrongful decisions that angels already knew would be taken; for being pawn to his own inherited circumstances; for being human. The Lord had made a cracked pot and the fault lay with the potter. The Lord had mended a few with the clay of his only son and the rest were to be cast to the ground in anger; let the serpent take the pieces.

He could not catch sufficient breath to raise a whisper. With one last effort he twisted back his head and among the shadow of leaves he saw an angel with a raven's wings; and this creature, whether of God or of the Devil, regarded him with a leer of fascinated interest. A harpy had come to feast on his remains. They had torn away his hood so that he should know them in the moments of his agony; but already he had known it was his companions from Kent. Even this small event felt to him inevitable for without it he would not have seen this apparition. It was the one thing he would not give that the Lord seemingly demanded of him. He knew he must leave Leoba and he thought of her languishing in the prison. And though it felt to Julian like the bones of his legs were broken he knew that they were not. The Lord had touched him in the thigh for the last time and like an oppressive cloud that is lifted by the sun he saw the angel of black with outstretched wings take into the air and it seemed as though the tree, in this penultimate moment on earth, had blessed another death, with a nocturnal shower of leaves.

Chapter
26

Leoba woke with a start, as if a cold fish had been touched against her cheek. The gaol was still dark but the sound of birdsong spoke of first light. She cursed herself for falling asleep and then an iron band tightened around her heart. Julian was not yet back. The snores of the gaoler rattled around the room which was like a gloomy version of her own shelter. 'Some guard they leave me with,' she said to herself. 'My throat could be cut and those thanes set sail already for Kent.' Her shoulders ached from where her arms had had been pulled in tying her. There was only one other captive, a young man whose head was slumped to the side as if he were dead rather than asleep. Leoba knew him for a chattel who had stolen a silver cup from the King's hall. Last night he had cursed the gaoler who had answered with a blow of his cudgel. The youth's face was smeared with blood from where the cudgel had caught him above the eye. She told herself that the telling of the wrongs had taken most of the night. She could believe the giant thane had many to tell of. As she herself had. There might be more to the rite for a warrior than for a serving woman. This seemed to her to make sense. Perhaps Julian had stayed with Hengest as the custom might be. She pulled her knees up to her chest. And much as she wondered and worried about Julian she could not help fearing the arrival of the sun. It seemed her light was already at the threshold. If Lord Angletheow were to lose then a cattlemaid's life would be measured in the time it took to eat a breakfast. The rightness of her act in killing Uric was still obvious to her. She could not yet regret it as Julian persisted she should. The Christ's demands went against all common sense. There was a part of her that understood, if dimly like the grainy shadow of the room, but in feeling she was still opposed. The rightness she felt told her that the trial of arms would go in her favour. The Earl was a mighty warrior and the Goddess would give him the necessary strength. All at once she was very aware of the small cross of wood that Julian had given her. It seemed to have a sleepy weight against her breast even though she knew it was light as a leaf.

Her throat was dry as the dust from a threshing. The remembrance of a dream then came to her. In the night she had been visited by the owl she knew to be her spirit guide. She found herself at the river where the women went to wash the clothes. She had stepped out of her dress to bathe and she washed with solemn ceremony, scooping up handfuls of the shining moon. It was the white and heatless moon she smoothed from her limbs and which collected in a puddle at her feet. She was like to an elf and made from a strange and delicate light. On a nearby branch she had seen the owl and of course it knew her by name. '*Leeeobaa*,' it called to her; '*Leeeobaa, Leeeobaa*!'

'If only I could see with those big yellow eyes of yours,' she said to it. 'If only I could tear the folk who have hurt me with that cruel knife of yours.'

The owl blinked at her as if in answer. There was a pale light like butter that fell on them both and looking over her shoulder Leoba saw that the moon had thrown off the black sheets of her bed and stepped into the fragrant night again. She put out her hand tentatively and touched the bird's proud feathers.

'How beautiful you are,' she whispered, 'to look after someone so ugly as me.'

'Leeeobaa,' the owl said again.

'I like the way you say my name.' Leoba smiled. 'Why have you come?'

The bird put out its wings and retched, bringing up a barely swallowed meal.

'That is *disgusting*,' Leoba cried in wonderment. 'You bring me your dinner!'

Somehow she knew what she must do as she had somehow known to put out her hands. She had closed her palms but now she opened them to reveal a sticky mess. The warm meal of bone and fur and black blood glistened under the moon. 'Thank you,' she said to the generous bird, which then was gone into the darkness of the wood. It seemed she rode on its back seeing the shadows of the trees and the ground below.

Using the wetness of her body she made an ointment of the gift. She applied it even to the dripping lids of her eyes and the fractured bone of

194

her nose. She felt less heavy and saw the down on her arms become like the fluff of a baby bird. Soon her skin was a thicket of glorious feathers. Her nose hooked and her feet drew in and her toes became murderous talons. She found that she was able to turn her head right around and look directly behind her. When she tried to speak, her own name issued from her lips.

A lifting wind blew through the hollows of her bones and carried her. She flew high above the trees and brushed the nymph-like moon with a feather. She felt sure Julian's love for her in that dark wood would be a beacon of fire to the sharpness of her eye. She felt sure that love would guide her directly though the object of her love be dead and in the Hidden Place. She saw the firelight of Rendlesham and the people making merry. She sat on the gables with an egg yolk eye and watched the festivals of love. She saw the Men of Kent sleepless on their pallets, the King and his liegemen in good spirits, and the Queen tipping out the mead with an impassive face which might have been carved from milk-coloured marble. Fear was a broken comb through her feathers. Fine though the night was for hunting she did not find him.

She wriggled desperately against the ropes that bound her but the gaoler knew his trade. Try as she might she could not free her hands. It felt like she was carrying the post on her back. She seemed to bear the weight of it. Something had happened to Julian she was certain but the post held her as tightly as her own fate. She whimpered, like an animal caught in a trap, and struggled for the longest time but eventually she had no choice but to give up as the gaoler woke with an almighty snore and stared at her with blank and bleary eyes.

Chapter
27

The nobles had caroused the night away in spite of, or perhaps because of, the fateful contest. It was, after all, the time of the midsummer festivals. Heoden had sung the tale of *Sigemund the Dragon Slayer* to great acclaim. It had annoyed Imma that he had not been given leave to hear it. He had noted that the poet stayed close by the Anglian thanes. As well he might. Imma was more than perceptive enough to see that Heoden, whom he liked very much, could hardly now return to Kent. It pleased Imma that the poet would be staying among them. And then he had been ordered out of the hall with the other children as if he *were* only a child. Imma had then gone looking for Daniel. Since his outburst at the trial of wordcraft he had not been seen. Eventually Imma had discovered him at the hall of the Earl sitting on his own in the dark. He found him morose and stubbornly silent. Imma asked him several times if he intended to view the battle but received no answer. After sitting with him on the pallet for a time Imma had left him. He found Nurse Gudrun and the wet-nurse struggling to set Swanhild comfortably for a feed. The baby wailed loudly and thrashed about like a fawn in a briar. The royal children were kept awake, and Imma also who for once was unable to calm the sobbing princess. The cries of the baby had rung around the nursery hall until the night had been scared away and it was almost morning. At least this was what Nurse Gudrun had suggested. At first light when it was time for everybody to get up Swanhild had fallen asleep.

On learning at breakfast that the Lady was not to attend the trial, Imma had asked if he might go down to the battle. 'Of course,' the Queen had said; 'all shall be there except for me. May your good feelings go to my brother along with those of both close and wider kin.'

Imma had joined the expectant crowd gathered outside the King's hall where the Earl was readying for battle. A strange light was thrown on Angletheow's helmet when he appeared with his shield and spear in hand. He walked with a terrible gravity of glance which was as grey as the witnessing sky. People banded together behind him so that in no time the warrior had a large cloak of support. The King walked at Angletheow's right-hand and Lord Eni and the Earl's brother Aelfwine to his left. His manservant Finn and the King's son of nine winters, Lord Ragenhere were behind. Nobility, whom Imma did not know, except they were from the North Folk, and were in Rendlesham for the festivals, followed.

The Lady Ealhhild had come out and was standing on her porch. She wore a gown as red as a holly berry and the bleached sleeves of her shift were strikingly beautiful in difference. Her flaxen hair was braided with nimble skill and a few tresses had been allowed to tumble down the back of her neck. Imma could not stop staring at her and for a short time had all but forgotten the Earl who was to fight that day. She wore fine shoulder brooches of garnet and silver. Across the small distance separating the Queen from her people, a gentle drizzle had drawn a veil so that it was like seeing her through a fine mist as though she were some fountain goddess.

'I shall supper with you this night in the mead hall,' Earl Angletheow called from the beginning of the wooden causeway that led to the Queen's house.

'A woman shall await you in your bed in whatever form you desire her,' the Lady Ealhhild returned somewhat strangely and then spun on her heel.

Imma understood it was not the time to be soft or tearful. Then he jumped as the heavy doors of the guest hall were thrown aside with an ominous clatter and into the rain stepped the warrior of Kent with a stamp on the wooden porch that was heavy as a landslide. And behind him the two other warriors whom Imma knew: the thanes Godric and Breca.

In the field of trial the pasture threw shoots of green through the brown earth. The herd crowded through the willow gate. A silken rain blew in whispering gusts. The people formed an ever thickening circle around the middle of the field and they were held back by soldiers who by crossing spears made a suitable fencing. The ring was broken on opposing sides and in the gap of one stood Lord Angletheow with the Anglian thanes and in the gap of the other the Kentish champion and his warrior seconds.

Imma found himself pushed out of the way by the enthusiastic crowd. He solved this by yelling he was to report to the Queen and so must have a proper view. People knew him for the Lady's peculiar favourite and shoved him through. His heart raced for Lord Angletheow when he saw the giant Kentish warrior prepare for the beginning. He was shouting to his god and shook his spear and shield at the sky. It was like the bellow of an angry bull. The warrior was a mighty bull on its hind legs and like the horn of a bull was his spear and like the flank of a bull was his shield. His chest in its plate of leather was broad enough to run down any man. Imma took hope from the aspect of the Earl who flashed his own spear to the sky and called for Lord Ing to send him the fighting strength of a wild boar. Imma had thought Lord Angletheow the biggest man in the kingdom until he had first set eyes on this Kentish warrior feasting in the hall. Each had a helmet of polished make and the beaten tin and silver of them outshone the muted sky.

The King gave no ceremonial start. The Kentish thane charged eagerly and Lord Angletheow stepped forward immediately to fight him. The ground reeled under their stamping hooves. The clash of the linden shields was like their broad skulls cracking together. A part of Imma was reluctant to watch then but a far greater part was compelled to stay. He could not abandon the Earl but he was filled with a desperate fear for him.

The crowd gasped at the astonishing display. In the ringing of a thousand hammers they could not have imagined such fury. It seemed several times as if Lord Angletheow must collapse under the formidable shield of Kent. This linden bore a cross stitched in red leather and it had a golden boss. On the arm of the wild man of Kent it was clubbing mace of anger.

The field was slippery. There was a moment when the dragon that decorated the Earl's shield captured the spear of Kent and held it in its mouth. The point had passed through the leather and embedded itself in the wood. For several heartbeats the warriors rocked like children on a see-saw. Then with a smash that sounded like a felled tree the Kentish thane let go of his lance and brought the full weight of his shield down on the Earl's head. Imma shouted, 'No!' But although Lord Angletheow had staggered he had not gone down. The battered thane had much to thank his well-made helmet for.

The two then broke apart seemingly to reconsider their attack. The thane from Kent had surrendered his spear but now Angletheow's shield

198

was effectively useless and he threw it into the mud. Drawing his battle knife the Earl thrust at his enemy with both short horn and long and under this charge the Kentish warrior fell back walled by his shield and at the same time fumbling for his own dagger. Imma glanced over at the King. The nobles were set as a row of grim statues. Only the crowd roared and yelled for the Anglian lord to rip the guts from Kent.

A kindly light appeared in the sky and through the drizzle there was a rainbow. The Sun Goddess was coming to help Lord Angletheow. Imma looked up and thanked her. Though she would not dirty her hair in the mud of a battle, she could blind with a look. Imma prayed for this. Let her spear fingers of light into the Kentish warrior's eyes. Imma hated him. He hated all of Kent, though he had never been there, and he could not remember ever hating so much. It seemed to fill his chest so it would burst. Only stabbing or stamping in a frenzy could let it out. In his mind he plunged a knife into the ribs of Kent as he had done to the wild boar.

There was much blood now from a wound on Hengest's thigh. In the blood that dripped the crowd scented victory. They bayed like wolves in the crystal forest for it. But Hengest battled on, if anything becoming more ferocious, as though he knew that if he were to win he must win quickly. The air sang with battle sounds; the curses and grunts of desperate effort. The crowd shouted their hero onward with a chilling hatred.

Imma noticed a woman to his left, perhaps one of the northern kin, for she was unfamiliar to him, who appeared utterly absorbed in the encounter. Her eyes shone with what Imma could only assume was joy because it did not seem to be fear or hatred and from moment to moment she would dart out a little tongue and caress her lips.

Lord Angletheow pressed home his advantage. It had become apparent that the wound was sapping the Kentish thane's strength. The Anglian fell onto the retreating shield of Kent like a slide of giant boulders. The time was coming for the mighty Hengest. The crowd sensed it and Imma could sense it. There was a twittering among them like a pack of blooded hunting dogs. The timbers of grey cloud had fallen back and a fragile blue had replaced them. Still the flimsy rain fell in mysterious veils.

Then a crisis for the Kentish champion as his dagger was separated from his grip by a vicious stabbing to the upper arm and Imma saw the Earl twist the spear in and home. Hengest freed himself only at the cost of a lump of gruesome flesh. But hard upon this was a strangeness. In a desperate instant Earl Angletheow slipped on the treacherous grass and went down almost on one knee. The wounded Hengest scythed forward suddenly with the edge of his shield and caught the Anglian a staggering blow to the neck. The Earl fell. Stumbling on, the warrior of Kent tore the divine helmet of Ing from Lord Angletheow's head and threw it away like a piece of rubbish. Stamping in fury he smashed the bones of the Earl's face into a bloody pulp. The crowd watched silently and grimly. Imma felt sick. Each blow was for Kentish honour; with each and every one Lord Hengest's pride and that of his kinsmen was the better restored. It seemed the Earl's neck had broken. Before that he had carried only the lightest of wounds for all the onslaught. It was like a game of skill in which luck will have its part. They had all but won and then somehow they had lost.

'*I have come through*!' the Kentish warrior roared. 'My Lord for you I have come through!' He then collapsed beside the man he had killed. Imma had the oddest feeling. It was as though he had been lifted high above the field and was watching from an increasing distance. The folk were blowing about like pollen on a shield of green.

Things were happening. The Kentish thanes were attending to the fallen Hengest and calling for some strips of cloth with which to bind him. No such cloths were forthcoming and Imma saw Lord Godric throw off his yellow tunic and rip like a maniac at his undershirt. King Radwald and his retinue stood like a henge of royal stones. These things took only moments and yet seemed permanently embroidered. Some commoners and chattels had begun to drift away while others remained rooted to the spot in obvious anguish.

'Give the Men of Kent leave!' Lord Eni cried. A collection of soldiers, craftsmen, and farmers, clearly united in bitterness, had gathered like an ominous cloud of botflies. It was entirely possible the warriors of Kent would be set on by a mob and hacked to death. The menacing crowd fell back with a disgruntled murmur.

The rainbow had faded and the rain had stayed its hand. The sky was filled with light. A wooden stretcher was brought for each of the fallen, one to carry a dead man and the other to carry a man who was perhaps dying. The King remained as still as a carving and might have been his own strange idol. Imma had seen the sacred images in the house that was their dwelling. The Queen had once told him the temple had been built and the carvings made to please the King on his return from Kent several years ago. She told him that King Radwald had placed a picture of the

Christ there. Then she had remarked that there were ways for even a feeble woman to get what she wanted. Imma had thought it odd the Queen should say this because she seemed to him anything but feeble. Regardless, the Lady had confided that she refused the King's company for a month. The picture had been thrown out. The Lady did not even appear to like the shrine itself suggesting it was wrong to seek to imprison the immortals in a house. The Queen had shrugged and said compromise was the making of a marriage. She had used the word *Roman*. Imma had only the vaguest idea what this meant. The Lady often talked to him of things he could not understand. Imma, like everybody else, was waiting for the King to do something.

There was a sudden event which interrupted the melancholy quiet that had descended over the field. Imma saw Daniel run wailing to where Lord Angletheow was being lifted onto the stretcher. He seemed to have come from nowhere. Imma saw him roughly shoved away by the Earl's brother and a couple of other thanes. Daniel then collapsed as if he too had taken a mortal wound but nobody came to assist him. In the sobbing tangle of his slim and bony limbs he seemed to Imma like a *daddy-long-legs* which had been trodden on.

Chapter
28

Leoba had watched the light grow gradually stronger. She knew they must come for her soon. She prayed again that the Goddess might give strength to Lord Angletheow's arm. She had tried to weigh the outcome but she could not decide if she were in the right or in the wrong. She had done so many things in her life, many of them wrongful, and it felt that fate might judge her on things other than the killing of Uric. She fought away thoughts of the gallows until she went almost mad. She begged leave to be allowed outside or she would foul herself and the gaoler had let her but she endured the humiliation of being watched. On returning the gaoler had not even tied her but simply stared at her with the same blank eyes. Fear had taken her spirit by the throat and she already felt the rope around her neck.

When they came she looked about her like a cornered rat but there was no help. It was the Earl's man, Finn who told her the sorry news. 'Lord Angletheow died for me,' she murmured. 'He did not die for you, you stupid wench,' Finn said angrily. 'He died for the meadow not a solitary weed.' 'Forgive me,' Leoba said, and Finn answered: 'It is not for me to forgive.' He regarded her as if sizing her up. 'You are free to go,' he said tersely. 'I do not understand,' Leoba said. 'It is plain enough,' the Earl's man answered. 'Hengest of Kent hangs by a thread and so the sense of the trial is uncertain. The King has suggested you be freed and the Kentish thanes have not objected. They have, after all, a *body-price* of much greater value.' Leoba nodded and tears filled her eyes. 'Do not cry woman,' Finn said. 'Unless it is for Lord Angletheow.'

The gaoler stood away from the door and indicated that Leoba was to leave. She glanced at the man who had been her prison companion.

'*Marry me?*' he said to her bitterly. Leoba stepped into the morning air which smelled of the recent rain.

'I should make yourself scarce for a while,' Finn advised. 'Folk are confused as to your meaning. Some blame you for this whole mess; others say the Queen took your side and must have her reasons; for my part I should have given you to Kent.' With that he left along with the three soldiers who had accompanied him. 'It is a most unsafe peace,' he cried over his shoulder.

For a short time Leoba stood uselessly in front of the gaol watching the spindly birch trees nod to one another. She wanted to lay down on the ground and cry her heart out. Life was an evil web: it entangled you and the fangs of a spider were always stalking. She dried her tears on the sleeve of her dress. 'Keep going,' she said to herself. 'You must find Julian.'

She took a roundabout route through the woods, traversing the ground rapidly with only one thought in her mind, but when she came close to the royal halls she saw that there was much movement and commotion. She hid herself behind a tree and peeped out. The Kentish thane Breca was standing in front of the guest hall with his arms folded. There was a group of people gathered at a distance. She saw Breca run forward with a curse and fell one of the people with a single blow. The group dispersed but stayed at a safer distance watching, the way a gang of crows might await the outcome of a wound. The Kentish thane cursed them all into oblivion. A number of chattels came out of the guest hall carrying many things. Then she saw the Lords Eni and Aelfwine. They stood with the thane of Kent and all three men now had their arms folded but they did not seem to be speaking. Leoba did not know what to do. Her heart was filled with great fear. It had become clear to her there was nobody to care for Julian except herself. Likewise there was nobody to care for her except for him. She touched the cross around her neck. It did not give her much in the way of comfort. On the contrary she experienced a great loneliness such as she had begun to see that Julian must have felt. The thanes of Kent were no more Christian than her own kin. She hesitated. Whether to return to her chores as if nothing had happened? Talk to her fellow maids about the season. All talk would be of the death of the Earl. She could hardly join in as merely another gossip. Julian might be lying dead in that very guest hall. Why had he not returned to her? It could not be good and again she felt that her heart was caught in a briar. She heard a flapping above her head and, looking up, she saw a wood pigeon take off from a high branch in that clumsy way they had.

She decided to return to the only thing she had known. She made her way discreetly through the woods and down the long slopes to the cattle barns. The barns were sited near the river and the lush meadows which fattened up the cows. Very few folk were about and she guessed that everybody was up at the halls. The long sweet-smelling barn was a familiar thing and she was grateful for it. The cows, as she had known they would be, were already in the meadow. She noticed a cloak hanging on a hook and she knew it belonged to Modthryth. That young woman would forget her own head. She would not mind lending it. Leoba put it around her shoulders. She heard somebody come into the barn from the other end and she ducked quickly behind a bale of straw. She waited until she was sure it was safe and then came out. 'I cannot go on like this,' she thought to herself. She must face whatever folk threw at her.

She came out of the barn and walked quite openly toward her own shelter. She found it empty and then collapsed exhausted onto her pallet. As quickly she got up again and, finding a mantle from among her paltry possessions, covered her head and went out. She pulled a corner of it across her cheek whenever she passed anybody. There were so many strangers at Rendlesham for the festivals that people barely noticed her.

She even managed to merge herself with the crowd that had gathered to watch the thanes of Kent leave for Canterbury. A small party of the nobility which included the King but not his Queen watched from the higher ground. Nobody went down to the waterside except for the slaves who loaded the small ship with many gifts. Hengest had been laid in the centre of the boat like a burial. Next to him to one side must have been the wrapped body of Uric. Leoba shuddered in the sunlight as she thought of him. From the chatter of the crowd she was able to learn that the Kentish champion had died not from the terrible wound on his leg but from another stabbing not so obvious during the battle. The thane's war shield had been laid across his chest. A summer of swallows curled across the valley in a spiralling display. They were a short distraction for the people standing on the hill. Through the veil of her mantle Leoba asked a stranger where the Roman priest might be and was shocked that his body had been found butchered and tied to a tree. He had been discovered by a young thane running his hunting dogs through the wood. Somehow she managed to further ask whereabouts he had been found. Not far from the guest hall. 'His lights are tugged clean through his back,' the man said to her tonelessly. 'A blood hawking.' It was as she had suspected in her darkest thoughts. She chewed on her lip until it was bloody. Again she did not know quite what to do or where to go. A black idea took hold of her. She might find a quiet place to let out her own life. 'The thanes say it is a foreigner's own business,' the man added, looking almost with disinterest toward the river.

The Men of Kent were slowly launched. Soon they had disappeared behind a screen of waving trees and Leoba, along with the rest of the gathering, turned away. The talk of the crowd was of the Earl and of his funeral and of concern for the kingdom. It struck Leoba most strongly that she was the only person whose thoughts were of another man's death.

A woman then came up to her and it was young Urse from the oxen sheds. Her hair was unpinned and she still had a crown of sun daisies from the festival. 'Leoba, where have you been?' she asked. 'You are freed. We knew you would be.'

'I knew not what to do,' Leoba said frankly. 'I was told that folk are hating me.'

'Some as maybe,' Urse replied, 'but not *everybody*, not your *own*.'

'Oh Urse!' Leoba cried, hugging her almost to death.

'You did right to kill that Kentish pig, noble or not, and don't let anyone tell you different.'

Urse put her arm around Leoba and together they walked with the crowd which was now heading toward the gabled hall to pay respect to Lord Angletheow. Leoba still kept her mantle as a covering. Urse told her that she and Modthryth had gone down to the gaol but had been scared off by a soldier.

'We offered to be most friendly to him if he let us see you.'

'What did he say?' Leoba asked.

'Not interested.' Urse laughed. 'Trust us to get the only man who ranks duty above his own cock. He was hideous so you should be grateful.'

Leoba hugged her again and the tears filled her eyes.

'That is Modthryth's cloak,' Urse then remarked.

'I know,' Leoba said. 'Urse do you know where Julian is?'

Urse looked at her shoes. 'He is dead.'

'I know but where?'

'You must not see him.'

'Urse I must.'

'I know where because fools have gone for a grisly sighting. He is still tied to the tree.'

'What!' Leoba cried. 'Why did they not take him down?'

Urse hesitated in answering. 'They say the good Lady said to leave him for he had died a death like his meagre Lord.'

'Urse you must help me.'

'What must I do?'

'Take me to him.'

The path that led to Father Julian's blood-hawked body began behind the guest hall and was already quite worn. The area was unfamiliar to Leoba as it was a part of the woodland frequented by the nobility. Her own stamping ground lay from the river up to the halls but not beyond them.

It did not take long to find him. He was tied to a young but spreading beech tree, the canopy of which was already dense enough to starve the undergrowth of light. With a cry she ran to him, the mantle slipping from her head, and she heard some ghoul shout, 'It is the cattlemaid!'

The body was like a rack of drying meat and the summer flies lay thickly on it. Leoba frantically swiped at them with her mantle but as soon as she stopped they resettled again. It was this, peculiarly, that for the moment she found most upsetting. She could not make the flies go away. She struggled at the ropes that held him. 'Give me a knife!' she shrieked and Urse ran forward to help her with a small blade she took from a leather bag on her belt.

'The Lady said to leave him!' somebody shouted. Already it seemed that word had spread and people had come running to see.

'She shall speak to the Lady!' Urse returned fiercely. 'It is her man. You should be helping her. What is *wrong* with you folk?'

'It is a foreigner's trouble,' somebody else called out. There were cries of 'Aye!' and 'Leave him be!'

Together the women managed to cut the body down. Leoba hugged him tightly to her breast and Urse knelt beside her. Leoba let out a wail such that the onlookers took a step back. Then all was quiet except for the sound of a thrush singing somewhere in the branches. Urse rested her head on Leoba's shoulder. People began to drift away and eventually stopped coming.

In the afternoon Urse went to the river to wash Father Julian's robe. 'It was because of me that he stopped wearing this,' Leoba whispered. 'He must have fetched it from his things.'

'I think it has been pissed on,' Urse remarked. 'It stinks awful.'

It was then Urse had noticed a small metal object at the base of the tree. It was a picture of the Lady with the baby Christ on her lap. 'He must have had it in his hand and dropped it when he died,' Urse suggested.

Leoba took it and examined it for a moment. Then she closed her palm over it.

Urse was gone a considerable time. When she returned she was carrying Julian's robe neatly folded over one arm and was shouldering a shovel with the other. Modthryth was with her and she too had a shovel.

It was nearly dusk when the women were finally ready to lay the body in the grave they had dug. Leoba had placed the picture of the Lady in his hand. Then they covered the soil with flowers from close at hand and Leoba made a little cross from two sticks, knotting them together with the rag she used to tie her hair. She thrust the cross into the soft earth at Julian's head. She tried to say the prayer he had taught but for some reason she could not properly remember it. 'Let us hope *your* heaven and *mine* are the same,' she said feelingly to him.

The three woman stood for a time over the grave as the night came on.

'Let us go,' Leoba said with a sigh. 'We have done all and can do no more.'

Chapter
29

When Imma, who had been amazed by his inclusion in the inner circle of mourners, entered the King's hall, which had become a temporary tomb, he saw at once the fallen warrior on his bier in the middle of the great room and almost at the same instant the Lady Ealhhild slumped in a chair at his side. Her arms were crossed on her lap and her head was bowed. She wore an ankle-length shift the colour of wheat. He went to her and wordlessly stood next to her. It was his honour to carry the baby princess who was as far in her mind from the world as ever and for the moment at least seemed the happier for it. The Queen lifted her head and her eyes were two wells of tears. She took his hand and pressed it gently and then bowed her head again. Imma took a place on a nearby bench together with the royal children. The eldest, Ragenhere, was clearly in shock for his uncle while the other two, Aethelthryth and Aethelric, the twins of five summers, looked merely unhappy and somewhat bewildered. Six warrior thanes who were leaders of the fyrd and were tied to Lord Angletheow by a blood that Imma could only imagine was as thick as any family tie sat to the other side of the body. The King had wearily stepped up to the mighty throne and he collapsed in it like a broken doll. Then he bent forward with his elbow propped on his knee and supported his head in his hand. Imma had never seen a king brought low and he had not imagined that it could happen. Lord Eni sat on the step of Radwald's throne in dismal aspect. The Kentish poet was also there. Imma wondered if he were composing a song of honour for Earl Angletheow. Imma shifted Swanhild to his knee and jogged her up and down. The baby giggled and a few of the mourners turned to look and smiled. There was then a commotion at the guarded door. It was Daniel crying to be let in. Imma recognised his voice and was in fear for him. Either he would be given leave or he would be killed. He saw the Queen glance up; she said these words: 'Allow him.'

Imma studied the noble warrior who in death had taken on even greater dignity. The shining helmet of Lord Ing had been placed again on the Earl's shattered head after the women had washed him and prepared him as best they could. His mortal injuries hidden he looked the very same as if he had fallen asleep on the battlefield while men raged all around him but paid him no heed. His linden lay to his chest as was the custom and his sword, which had slept throughout the contest, was placed at his side. The jewelled head of it and the bright metal helmet caught glints from the ring of tallows which surrounded him. Lord Angletheow was to be buried with his horse.

In the late day the Earl's family arrived from the Gipping. His wife, his four daughters, two sons, and a baby, together with his eldest daughter's husband. They entered the great hall accompanied by Lord Aelfwine who had been sent with a sailing crew to fetch them. A huge man whom Imma did not recognise had also come. He asked Ragenhere in a whisper who this might be and was told it was a merchant from Gipeswic. Imma looked to the wife who had arrived, remembering how kind she had been to them at the Earl's hall. She was the big-framed obvious woman he remembered and she wore a weeping dress of bleached fabric. Her eyes were bloodshot from copious tears. The Earl's daughters were beautiful and they sat down like a row of blonde goddesses. The baby had a wet-nurse and was locked on the bub. There was an ealdorman too with the fog of winter in his hair and tidy beard. This must have been the Earl's father-in-law because Imma knew that Angletheow's father had passed prior to the rising of last year.

The evening had come with a red rim above the trees like the eyelids of the women who wept when the commoners were finally admitted to the tallow-lit hall. In single file they snaked in and around the sleeping warrior and the hall was filled with a respectful murmuring like the gentle hum of a hive of bees made calm by smoke. From time to time a woman would begin a hopeless wailing and clutch her head in her hands. The wail would then be taken up by other women who similarly would beat at their heads in anguish. The fury of grief would then subside and the death song of the bees begin again. The passing was endless as though a serpent god slipped by and Imma watched in vain for the tail. All night long the snake slid through.

A chill seeped into the wood on which Imma sat but the hearth would stay cold. Even the glow of the tallows was no longer a comfort and it felt as if the Earl had been already buried and that he too had been enclosed along with him. Cheerless and friendless was the hall in spite of the throng; a giant tomb where a living body could only survive a short time before the heat was taken out of it. Imma longed to file out with the rest and know again that he was living. Then to his surprise, after yet again he had almost nodded off, he saw Aldwulf and Mother Eost. They filed around the splendid corpse in turn and then went out. Word must have reached home from the Earl's hall and the elders had come to represent the village. Imma pretended to be asleep when they came past and so he did not know whether they had seen him or not.

Later that morning the warrior was taken from the mead hall. The slow way across the fields to the burial ground took a quarter day and it seemed the whole of Anglia accompanied the well-loved lord to his final resting place. It was then that Aldwulf approached with Mother Eost and walked with him. 'You are in the Queen's service young man?' Aldwulf said.

There was a part of Imma that wanted to give him a hug but for some reason he did not. Aldwulf shook his venerable locks and smiled. He put a hand on Imma's shoulder in the way he used to. 'It is a small patch from the Earl's house to our own.'

'I ...' Imma began.

'A man should find his own path,' Aldwulf remarked; then he added with a twinkle in his eye: 'Even if he does run away and worry his family half to death.'

'I ...' Imma said again; but he hardly understood himself what he had done.

The sparkle in Aldwulf's eye was matched by that of Mother Eost who told him he had done right by the Goddess and that was the main thing. The crops were growing strong and green and it seemed the village had never been as blessed.

'So it is better I am away?' Imma suggested.

'That is not what I meant and you know it,' the old woman replied.

'Imma you must visit us, perhaps at Yuletide,' Aldwulf said, stroking thoughtfully at his beard. 'I know you must ask leave but I am sure the Queen can do without you for a couple of days.'

'I shall ask her.'

'Eanfled wants to see you.'

'And I her.'

'You have grown,' Aldwulf said; 'but what is your purpose here?'

'I wish to make a life my grandmother can be proud of.'

'I cannot fault that,' Aldwulf said; 'only the way you went about it.'

Imma did not answer. The life of the village felt small and choking to him. He had seen such things since he had been in Rendlesham. Aldwulf seemed to be trying to rope him with guilt.

'Youthful restlessness,' Aldwulf said, as if he had half-guessed what Imma had been thinking. 'You shall come home when you are ready.'

The earthen room had already been cut and the sides of it were boarded like a house. It was almost as large as a small house. A man standing in it could not see over the top. Imma had never seen a burial before and he wondered why the Earl was not to be burned. Possibly the journey of a warrior was different. Maybe a warrior needed his bones in one piece so he could come easily to a battle. The men who had not long finished preparing the tomb stood around with the wet clay smeared on their tunics and trousers. Sweat was beaded across their foreheads like dew on a cold bottle which has been brought into the sun. Behind the warrior who was borne on the shoulders of his thanes, his beloved mare was led. The horse was released of her life and the blood soaked into her dapple-grey coat. She was laid with great effort in the grave so Lord Angletheow might ride into the shadow life. The Earl was noble and his horse was fine. Imma was resigned that they must leave him but then he started to cry and used the woollen of baby Swanhild to wipe his eyes. Angletheow was committed to the room and the warrior in all his finery looked up at them. His kin were close enough to the edge that a single step would have seen them over.

The roof was lowered onto the lonely house of death. It seemed to Imma that the Sun Goddess, who in her evident joy appeared to know things of which he was unaware, gave the warrior the happy sorrow of a parting kiss before the door was closed. The soil was shovelled on, rattling on the wood at first, and then a soft splatter as earth was thrown on earth. A breeze blew up from the river and in it was a scent of the sea. It spoke of adventure and new beginnings and unexpected ways of coming home. Imma wondered whether a ghost horse might ride the waves and take the Earl for a visit to the homelands. Anything, after all, was possible.

Chapter
30

Nearly everybody was at the raising of the mound. Fifty men or more dug the earth and slung it in heaps across the grave and women in mucky dresses patted at the loose soil to make it firm. Steadily, with persistent effort, the royal monument was being built. Soon the dead warrior would have a great bald cap of mud for a helmet. Then the wild sowers of the year would husband grass and tend flowers there without need of any plough. If Lord Angletheow himself stood tall with his magnificent horse on the top of it he would be able to see forever. Imma imagined a huge crowd but like the Lady Ealhhild he wished to be alone. She had taken to her chamber.

He found Daniel at the point where the women went to wash clothes. He was standing in the water, bare to the waist, and slapping his shirt against a rock. Willow trees dangled long hair above the bank, flirting with the river. The sun poured drops of light like a libation. It was both a holy and a homespun place. Daniel glanced up to see who approached down the well-trodden path but then went on with his washing. The slap it made was loud and unnaturally insistent in the quiet wood and all the birds had been frightened away.

'What are you doing?' Imma asked him.

'Nothing.'

'You are washing.'

'My literal friend strikes again.'

'You do not want to see them make the mound?'

Daniel did not answer. He merely snapped his shirt against the rock even harder. It occurred to Imma he would spoil the shirt by treating it so but he stayed silent. He adjusted Swanhild on his shoulder.

'What is that baby doing now?' Daniel said irritably.

'She is living,' Imma answered.
'I see you have made a sling for her.'
'Yes.'
'Why don't you use it?'
'She was happier on my shoulder.'
'Oh.'
'I will leave you,' Imma said sadly, turning away. Then, looking back:
'I know what it is like to lose someone,' he said.
'You cannot lose something you never possessed.' Daniel was staring
directly at him. How strange he seemed, standing there in the glittering
river, in the middle of his pointless task, with his face all pale and twisted
like the time he had recovered from a fever.
'I don't understand.'
'You are too young to understand.'
'I thought we were friends.'
'We are friends Imma.'
'I will leave you,' the boy repeated and began to walk away; but a
shout from Daniel made him face around again. 'What?' he said.
'You should go back to your village and marry that girl you always
talk about.'
'I will.'
'No I mean you should go back now and tell her.'
'I can't I told you. She will not wed for ages.'
'Tell her how you feel.'
Imma shrugged. 'I have nothing to offer.'
'Then you are a fool. Don't ask permission. Run with her when you
are old enough.'
'And go where?' Imma said angrily. 'Now I seem older than you.'
'If she is as beautiful as you say she will be betrothed early.'
'She would tell me I had elvish laughter in my head.'
Daniel smiled. 'What's wrong with that?' It was the first time Imma
had seen him smile since the Earl had been killed.
'You are riding on the moon,' Imma told him.
'Imagine how you would feel if she married someone else.'
Imma frowned. It was true it felt awful beyond words.
'Now leave me to get on with this,' Daniel insisted, beginning over the
seemingly purposeless washing of his shirt and tunic. 'A black dog is
biting me on the neck.'
Imma settled the baby into the sling which left his arms free. It was

common practice among the womenfolk. He left Daniel fighting off the dog and wandered with Swanhild aimlessly through the wood. The bumping movement as he walked was a useful lullaby and she was no trouble. In the middle of the day he fed her with a meal paste, which she smacked around her gums, and gave her cool water to drink by encouraging her to suck the drops from his finger. She still needed the wet-nurse but now she could go long whiles on water and a little mashed food. Then he took a refreshing swig from the water-skin himself and rested his back against a tree. He was thinking long and carefully about what Daniel had said. He rested there a good measure into the day knowing he must take Swanhild back but not wanting to return.

The magical scent of the warm late afternoon was everywhere in the wood and it seemed that like the air he was nowhere and yet everywhere as he floated with it. Somehow in his roundabout ways through the woodland he had ambled into a much older part which reminded him of similar acres of the Motherwood. Some of the trees had been coppiced and bristled from their stumps with useful leafy poles and spears. There was an ancient oak with each and every limb covered in creeper and the nests of a hundred birds built into it. The various birds sang and squabbled and the nests sounded full of young. It struck Imma that the tree was like his own village of Wulfingstow: full of fun and trouble. There were jubilant mats of bluebells under the trees, filling the air with perfume. 'See all these beautiful flowers, Swanhild,' he said to the baby, looking with wonder about him; but Swanhild was asleep again. 'What a weird thing it is,' he said aloud to her anyway, 'that our lonely lots have brought us here together.'

When he returned to the river he found Daniel still there, talking happily with a couple of chattels who were collecting up washing they had dried on the bank.

'Why it is young Imma,' Daniel cried, 'the most serious boy this side of Christendom.' He was stripped to the waist as before and it was obvious the young servant women were eating up his flesh. They laughed at what Daniel had said even though it was not funny. Imma did not know what the last word Daniel had used meant exactly and he was pretty sure the girls who had laughed did not either.

'You are wasting your time,' Imma said to them curtly.

'It is the Queen's favourite,' one of the girls observed to the other. She had hair the colour of a field mouse and a pitifully stupid look.

'I need to talk to my friend,' Imma said to her.

'Go on then,' the other said.

'I will when you leave.'

'Possibly I shall see you at supper,' Daniel said to them.

'*Possibly.*' It was the girl with the mouse-brown hair. Then she giggled.

'Wet-nurse is no job for a man,' the other girl said to Imma with a laugh.

'The Queen wants me to look after Princess Swanhild that is all.'

'She is addled like a gone-off egg,' the field mouse said.

'No more addled than you,' Imma told her.

The girl made a face. 'Come on,' she said to her friend. 'Don't think much of yours.'

'Little idiots,' Daniel remarked when they had gone.

The rays of the sun came slanting almost flatly through the trees. Daniel was pulling his tunic over his head. He went and stood at the edge of the river. It was the drowsy time of afternoon when even the gnats skimming across the water seemed sluggish.

'I want to see Leda.'

Daniel turned around. 'Well let's go and see her.'

'It is a long walk and I'm not sure of the way.'

'Let us take a boat,' Daniel said excitedly. 'No let us take a *horse!*'

'I cannot ride.'

'You can ride with me.'

'What *horse?*'

'Haven't you noticed? There are horses in the field.'

'They belong to the King.'

'Well we shall only borrow.'

'*Borrow* could put a noose around our necks.'

'True,' Daniel agreed; 'but before we swing we shall know that we have been *alive.*'

'What about the baby?'

'Leave her with old Nurse Gudrun.'

'What should I say?'

'You'll think of something. That's it. It is agreed. We go first thing tomorrow. Be back by afternoon.' Then for some reason he rushed into the river and dived under fully clothed.

Imma laughed. It was good to see him happy again. 'Look,' he said to baby Swanhild, turning around so that she might see; 'it is mad Daniel.'

They strolled back together to the halls. A churl they passed stared at

Daniel's dripping hair and clothes. 'Do not worry my good man,' Daniel said to him; 'I sweat more than most.'

At supper Nurse Gudrun made it plain she disapproved of his wandering so far with the royal baby and Imma saw an opportunity. 'I have been *restless*,' Imma began but was told it was not for a servant to be restless. He tried a different tack. 'I wish to see the Earl's new burial mound.' 'Why did you not go today with everybody else?' she asked. Imma shrugged. 'I did not want to go with everybody else.' 'Why?' was the reply. He had no good reason. 'I shall ask the Queen if I may go tomorrow,' Imma said. Nurse Gudrun gave him a quizzical look. 'Well you can ask her.' And for the moment such was his favour with the Lady that when in the late evening he brought Swanhild to see her he asked and received a favourable answer. The Queen did not even inquire why he wished to go and he loved the Lady for that. She understood that sometimes people didn't always have a reason that made sense.

'Take your friend, the freed slave, for my brother was fond of him,' Lady Ealhhild suggested, bouncing Swanhild on her knee. Her face was all puffy from crying. 'Go and fetch the twins and tell Lord Ragenhere to attend me, if he is not with his father. I want my children about me.'

As he reached the threshold of her chamber she called to him from the great carved chair in which she sat and he turned around. 'It is not my brother whom you wish to see is it?'

'My lady?' His heart leapt in his chest.

'You lied to me but I am not sure why.'

His face burned with shame and the inside of his mouth dried up like a prune.

'Never go in for thievery Imma. Your face shall betray you.'

'How did you know?'

'You have asked me several things but never with such a guilty look.'

'I wish to go home.'

'Ah …' the Queen said with a smile. 'For good?'

'No Lady Ealhhild, not for good only to see someone.'

'Your uncle of course?'

'Yes, I mean …'

The Queen waved away his fumbling. 'If you were homesick why did you not say?'

He did not answer because now he didn't know why. Then he thought of something: 'I did not want to make it seem as though I was unhappy here or that I was ungrateful.'

216

'There seems to be a mote of truth in that at least,' the Queen said with a frown. 'Well you may go … walk, take a horse, take a boat, do as you wish.'

Imma ran to her and clasped his arms around her knees. She put her hand on his head and he felt Swanhild take hold of a clump of his hair. She pulled on it and he reached up and gently prised apart her tiny fist. 'Do not lie to me again Imma,' the Queen warned. 'This place is crawling with liars.'

'I am sorry I lied,' said Imma. 'I do want to visit Lord Angle but not yet.'

The Lady Ealhhild sighed deeply. 'Do not worry; there are no right feelings for such a time; indeed your sudden impulse to go home is perfectly understandable.'

Imma hesitated. Then he said: 'Nurse Gudrun says that Kent will return with an army.'

'Does she?' the Queen said with a wan smile. 'Well we shall have to see; if they do then we shall be ready for them. Tell the twins to come in.'

Imma nodded and with that he left to do her bidding. Afterwards he sat on the stoop of the nursery house and looked up at the stars. He watched the whorls of fireflies in the wood and wondered if they might be tiny souls in a dance and noted that the figures they made resembled the arrangements of the stars. When he looked into the sky his soul felt as small as a firefly. On his pallet he soon fell asleep with the gentle snoring of the royal children in his ears.

It was the time of year when the Sun Goddess only napped before she was up and giving light to the world. The horses were motionless until Imma and Daniel approached and then they ambled away and began ripping up tufts again for their breakfast. Imma stooped and wet his hands with dew so that he might freshen his face. He had not slept the entire night but had lain awake part of it listening to a nightingale. He saw a lark, wing across the field, and he wondered if it were the ghost of the nightingale in different shape. Cobwebs lay like flimsy glass across the ground. He watched as Daniel succeeded in roping one of the less-shy horses. It was a stumpy brown mare. Not the splendid horse he had imagined. 'She is a friendly beast,' Daniel remarked as he tacked her up with a bridle and a thick riding blanket. 'She will do fine and we shall take it easy.' He looked at Imma. 'You wanted a fine black stallion? You would not think so when he goes galloping off and we like two straw men bouncing along on his back.'

They were leading the horse out of the field. Imma patted her neck as they walked. There was a slight mist above the ground and a dawn chill in the air. The light had that special something of early morning when it seemed the gods were giving you another chance.

'Now we are *allowed*,' Daniel said, 'this trip is not so exciting.'

'It is better we are allowed,' Imma told him. 'I don't understand you.'

'Yet you trespassed on the island of your own goddess.'

'That was different.'

'How so?'

'I had good reason.'

They were leading the horse down the long slopes to the river. Ordinary people were already beginning to put shoulders to the plough. In the wide water-meadow they saw a group of maids driving cattle to the pasture. The Lady of the Sun was dipping herself in the river and sparks showered from her glistening body. The first flies were lifting from the grass and there were butterflies with pinched wings on the many colourful flowers. Imma took off his cloak and folded it over his arm.

'Daniel?' he enquired.

'Yes?'

'Are we going to walk the horse all the way home or are we going to get on it?'

'You are mocking me.'

'It seems silly to bring the horse along for her own pleasure.'

Daniel did not answer. He merely led the horse onward.

After a while Imma said to him: 'Have you ever ridden a horse before?'

'I have seen it done and I have seen how people attend to them.'

Imma sighed. 'Let us take her back then.'

'No we shall ride her.'

'When will we?'

'In a moment.'

They carried on this way until they had left the maids and the cattle far behind. 'Well,' Imma said, stroking the mare's neck, 'she is good company anyhow.'

'Here, hold her steady,' Daniel said, glancing about him.

Imma held the bridle while Daniel swung onto the horse's back using her neck as a pivot. He almost slipped off but by grabbing the leather belt of her blanket managed to stay on. 'Good horse, good horse,' he said, patting her and looking a bit wobbly. 'As I said she is a friendly beast. Now you …'

Imma swung himself up and Daniel helped pull him on. Soon they were settled with Daniel taking the reins and Imma in front holding onto the horse's mane. Daniel jogged the mare with his knees but she did not move. 'Let her have her breakfast,' he said. 'Then she will move.'

'Her breakfast is taking too long,' Imma complained. 'She is lazy.'

'Nonsense,' Daniel said, giving the mare a sharp kick with his heels. To his obvious surprise the horse moved forward and carried on going. 'We shall be there in no time.'

Imma laughed. 'Yes by Yuletide at least.'

He had to admit that once they got moving it didn't take Daniel long to get the hang of it and as they approached the crossing at Ufford the mare even broke into a canter.

They followed the line of the river from Gipeswic, sometimes losing the trail in the dense woodland but after a while always finding it again. Occasionally they were forced to dismount and lead the horse through a tangle of trees. Midmorning they stopped in a meadow for a snack of bread and cold bacon. They drank water from the river. The sun was leapfrogging over the earth. Imma told Daniel about some of the flowers. 'The juice of that one can make you sleep,' he said, pointing to a poppy. 'Very interesting,' Daniel said with a smile.

One moment they were in a forest Imma did not know and then all at once he recognised the Motherwood. They had come to the fork in the river. 'The Island of the Goddess,' Imma said, pointing upstream.

When they arrived in Wulfingstow it seemed everybody was about the chores. The men were in the fields or in the wood and most of the women in the weaving sheds. It was Edwin who saw them first. He had set his lathe outside in the sun and was turning a bowl. He was making quite a racket. With a great cry he ran over to them followed by his son Wulf. Then women and children began stepping from the houses and shouting. By the time they had walked the horse up the hill to Aldwulf's house most of the village, except those in the farther fields, had collected about them.

'Imma!' Eanfled cried, as he almost fell off the horse. He ran forward to hug her. 'What have you been doing you silly boy?' The tears streamed down her face.

'I am sorry Cousin Eanfled.' It was a shock to him that evidently he meant so much to her. She shook him by the shoulders and scolded him for running away and everybody laughed. Frida and Hilda came from the weaving house and Imma took turns to hug them too. He turned and saw his uncle puffing up the hill.

'A homecoming feast for Mother Sheaving's boy!' Aldwulf cried.

Somebody suggested they eat outside for it was fine weather. Imma and Daniel sat like honoured guests on the grassy bank and cold meat and ale was brought to them. Imma felt like an exiled king who had returned. He did notice though that some were not as pleased as others to see him. That was to be expected. The person whom he wanted to see most was not there and he felt funny asking about her. Neither was her father. Only her sisters and little Alfred, who was in the care of his aunt, sat there munching away happily with shining eyes. He patiently endured the endless questioning and answered all with a smile. It was good to have Daniel there because his charm worked wonders on all.

After folk had eaten their fill they began to drift back to what they had been doing. When the only people left were those closest to him he asked about her.

'She has gone a-wandering,' Eanfled said with a grin. 'The more she is cuffed for not attending her chores the more she goes off. Her father will never learn.'

'I will go look for her,' Imma said, standing up. 'It would be a pity to miss her.'

'A pity indeed,' Eanfled answered. His adoptive family smirked at him.

He didn't stay to say anything more because he knew they were making fun. Instead he ran down the hill toward the meadow without looking back. The meadow with its long uncropped grass was the most likely place she would be. The sun was hot and the field buzzed with armies of honey bees. He stopped and looked across the gently waving grass, shielding his eyes from the sun. He could not see her but he knew this was where she loved to be at midsummer. He walked through the meadow calling her name. The grass was as high as his waist. He kept straining for an answer but none came only the whisper of the soft breeze through the field and the hum of an occasional insect at his ear. He reached the edge of the Motherwood and wondered whether she had gone as far as the river. Sometimes they had gone together but he did not think that she would go as far alone. He turned away from the forest and walked back across the meadow. 'It is for the best,' he thought to himself. 'I was not meant to meet her. I have been thinking too much of her. I have a new life and maybe I will not even marry. A body does not need to wed to have a good life. Yes a fine life. When I am older I might do anything or go anywhere. Perhaps I shall. The Goddess meant for me to go to

Rendlesham. I do not want the life of a man of the land. I do not want any of it. Yes it is better that I have not seen her.'

He turned to glance a last time across the meadow and he saw her. She was standing a stone's throw from him with the high grass at her hips. She must have been lying down. Her hair was exactly as he remembered: the girlish mane of a white horse. 'Leda!' he cried, running over to her with some difficulty because the grass was so long. It was exactly as he had pictured. They would hug and then he would tell her about his plan to become a royal smith before returning to marry her. It was a surprise when instead of hugging him she pushed him over and stalked off.

'Leda!' he called. 'What's wrong?'

'What's *wrong?*' she answered, with a look of fury. 'What's *wrong*, you *idiot!*'

'But Leda,' he entreated, as she pushed away from him again. 'I have come from Rendlesham specially to see you.'

'How kingly of you,' she answered, folding her arms. 'You go merrily off to Rendlesham without even telling me. Leaving me here with all these pigs and sheepheads.'

'Sheepheads?' Imma said, grinning.

'Yes, sheepheads,' Leda repeated. Her face was set in a frown. He continued to stare at her and soon he saw what he was looking for: a slight wrinkling of her nose. 'Imma come over here,' she said with her arms still folded.

'Not if you are going to push me again.'

'Push you. I only *blew* on you and you fell over.' She pursed her lips and shook her head.

He went over to her. She looked into his eyes and then they were hugging. He didn't think he would ever let her go. Her hair smelt of meadowsweet. Then something happened that had not happened before. She kissed him full on the lips. In a moment all that he had been thinking before about his new life at Rendlesham left him. He wanted to stay with her forever. It was that simple. She was the most beautiful girl the Goddess had ever created and for some reason he could not fathom she had chosen him. 'I knew in the cradle we were supposed to be together,' she whispered into his ear, 'but you frightened me when you ran from me. If ever I say again that I hate you, don't run away, but hold me until I stop saying it, because then I shall say that I love you. At the end I will always say this and nothing can change it.'

'You have a bruise above your eye,' Imma said, gently pushing her hair away from it.

'Yes well,' she answered. 'You know my father.'

'Come back with me,' Imma pleaded. 'To Rendlesham I mean.'

'And do what?'

'You could put yourself in service to the Queen as I have.'

'I don't want to be anybody's servant. Not even the Queen's.'

Imma was hurt. 'I am to be a metalsmith.'

'That is good Imma,' Leda said. 'I will wait until you come back for me.'

'What about your father?'

'Mostly he is too drunk to see me or he sees me severally and swings at the wrong one.'

'Come away with me,' Imma insisted, taking her hands.

'I cannot,' she replied. 'My family needs me.'

They sat down together in the long grass and it was like when they were small. Except now they spoke of more serious things. Leda was wearing a pale yellow gown. She kicked off her shoes and lay back with her hands behind her head. She picked a stalk of grass which was the exact same colour as her shift and chewed on it. Imma lay beside her and they both watched the cloudless sky. 'I should be doing a zillion chores,' she said. 'Probably catch it when I go back.'

'Leda,' Imma began but then stopped.

'What?' the girl asked, turning her head to look at him.

'How much of a bridal gift do you think your father wants for you?'

Leda rolled over on her side and propped her head on her elbow.

'They say he is going to show you off around the hundred.'

'Who's they?'

'You know, *they*, folk.'

'What do *folk* know about anything?'

'Enough.'

They lay for a while in silence. Imma knew she was looking at him.

'Leda, if I could get a bridal gift would you wed me?'

The girl sat right up. 'I thought that's what we were talking about. Now I think on it I've changed my mind, I think I'll wed somebody else.'

'Leda,' he said and squeezed her hand. 'I was making things clear.'

'How much clearer do you want them?' Leda shouted. 'I told you I loved you didn't I? Which by the way you haven't returned to me.'

'You know I love you,' Imma said to her. 'Do I need say it?'

'Yes you need say it,' Leda said haughtily. 'To make things *clear*. Mother of Earth, if Lord Ing talks to the Goddess like this it's a wonder anything is alive.'

Imma stood up and brushed the seeds and loose grass from his tunic and trousers. The whole of the meadow was bathed in a yellow light the colour of rich butter. 'Let's go swimming Leda,' he said. 'Like we used to. It won't be dark for ages and maybe myself and Daniel will stay on for the night and go back tomorrow or maybe I won't go back at all.'

'Who's *Daniel?*' Leda enquired, getting to her feet and slipping on her shoes.

'Somebody I met. He's up at the village. You'll like him.'

'Will I?' Leda said warily. 'He's not stuck-up Rendlesham folk is he?'

'No, nothing like that. He's a foreigner and really funny.'

Imma set off toward the forest. A short while later he turned around and saw that Leda was not following. She was standing looking at him with her arms folded again.

'What is it *now?*' he called to her.

'You still haven't said it.'

'I did say it.'

'Not really.'

'I love you Leda,' he shouted at her. 'I *love* you. Can you hear me?'

She picked up her gown and ran to him. Imma had not been alive for many years but this was the loveliest thing he had seen and he doubted if it would ever be bettered.

'I want this day to last forever,' Leda cried, breathlessly. 'Feel my heart beating like a drum at festival. It is the day you came back to me as I knew always that you would.'

shipburialnovel.com

Lightning Source UK Ltd.
Milton Keynes UK
19 July 2010

157189UK00002B/1/P